HARRAGA

BY THE SAME AUTHOR

An Unfinished Business

HARRAGA

Boualem Sansal

Translated from the French by Frank Wynne

BLOOMSBURY
LONDON · NEW DELHI · NEW YORK · SYDNEY

First published in Great Britain 2014

First published in France in 2005 by Éditions Gallimard

This book has been selected to receive financial assistance from English PEN's
Writers in Translation programme supported by Bloomberg and Arts Council
England. English PEN exists to promote literature and its understanding,
uphold writers' freedoms around the world, campaign against the persecution
and imprisonment of writers for stating their views, and promote the friendly
co-operation of writers and free exchange of ideas. www.englishpen.org

Bloomsbury Publishing Plc
50 Bedford Square
London WC1B 3DP

www.bloomsbury.com

Bloomsbury is a trademark of Bloomsbury Publishing Plc

Bloomsbury Publishing, London, New Delhi, New York and Sydney

A CIP catalogue record for this book is available from the British Library

ISBN 978 1 4088 4398 7

10 9 8 7 6 5 4 3 2 1

Typeset by Hewer Text UK Ltd, Edinburgh

Printed and bound in Great Britain by CPI Group (UK) Ltd, Croydon CR0 4YY

To the memory of Daniel Bernard

To the Reader

How beautiful it would be if this story were purely the fruit of my imagination. It would read like a retelling of the parable of the grain of wheat, it would speak of love, of death and resurrection. And there are enchanting ghosts on every page, and characters so colourful you could wear them as a scarf.

But it is a true story, true from beginning to end, the characters, the names, the dates, the places are real and so it speaks only of the wretchedness of a world which no longer has faith, or values, which can only trumpet its transgression and its disgrace.

The reader is free to take it as either or indeed as both since even the people in this book are incapable of telling the real from the imaginary.

What follows is the story of Lamia. Driven to abject solitude by the vagaries of life, like the grain of wheat that falls on rocky ground, she is dying, until one miraculous day in summer, something within her blossoms, something as profoundly real as it is utterly fantastical: love.

The best thing to do is to listen as she tells her story which, like the seasons, unfolds over four acts with an epilogue that leaves open a window onto the future.

Act I
Bonjour, Oiseau!

Even as my life was leaching away
As sand was slipping through my fingers
As silence numbed my soul
For always
A bird landed on my shoulder.
'Cheep cheep, cheep cheep . . .!'
He chirruped in my ear
As he fluttered and frolicked.
I did not understand.
But when one is lonely
A single word brings joy
And so I threw away my rosary
And I danced.

A bird is a thing of beauty
But, alas, a bird has wings
Which, just as they serve to alight,
So too they serve to take flight.
That is the tragedy of birds.

1

M y door is making a worrying sound. It doesn't go knock knock, it goes *bang bang*. It's reinforced steel, which I suppose might explain the racket, but with things the way they are these days, I can't help but think of other reasons.

I open it, staying pressed against the doorjamb for protection. A reflex. '*Chkoun?* Who's there?' It's not the patrol, nor some sermoniser nor the Defenders of Truth, it's not my neighbour from the rue Marengo, a chubby-faced old gorgon of a woman who's forever popping round for a gossip and believes in a hundred clichéd theories, none of which are desperately interesting. Thankfully it's not old Moussa our postman, the fearless factotum of the Rampe Valée, an old warhorse who's constantly banging on about something and who, day after day – excepting riots and strikes – leaves a paper trail of panic and contagion in his wake. No, it's some funny-looking slip of a girl. 'It's me!' she says. I've no idea who 'me' is. Skinny, dressed in a get-up cobbled together from shreds and patches that looks like something off *X Factor*. Whether it's a fashion faux-pas or a flash of inspiration, all these flounces and frills make it look like a drag outfit for a family of screaming queens. She could probably pull it off, were it not for the clashing colours. Her hair is a mix-and-match of everything from historic styles to the latest fashions. Her face is plastered with make-up, her eyes – black, white and twinkling – are bobbing in a pool of eye-liner surrounded by a lush meadow of green eyeshadow. All she needs is a blade of wheat behind her ear to know she comes from the back end of nowhere. The acrid cloud of her perfume could rival the fallout from Chernobyl. She's a walking scandal who has somehow inexplicably escaped the wrath of Allah. A battered holdall lies at her feet like a recently shed snakeskin, completing the 'look' of this sixteen- or seventeen-year-old globetrotter. Her full, perfect lips are set in a blood-red pout pitched somewhere between impatience and bewilderment. It's clear that behind her regal smile, she's got some nerve. To cap it all, she's several months pregnant and her belly button is on display for all the world to see.

'Tata Lamia?' she says bravely, drawing herself up to her full five feet nothing.

'Well . . . that depends.'

'I'm Chérifa!'

'Good for you . . . and?'

'Sofiane sent me. I've come from Oran.'

'What?!!'

'He didn't phone you?'

'Er . . . no.'

'Can I come in?'

'Um . . . I suppose.'

'Thanks.'

'You're welcome.'

'It's weird, your place.'

'You said it.'

This is how a whirlwind sweeps into your life. Nothing, absolutely nothing in my past led me to suppose that one day I would open up my door, open up my life, to such mayhem. I opened the door because that's what you do when someone knocks, you answer. You might worry that it will be some hoodlum – and Lord knows the neighbour-hood has its fair share of thugs – or more likely a sermoniser, a rapist or the cops, and you're thinking 'these people, they've got no consideration, no manners', but to set your mind at rest, and perhaps even in some surge of hope, you open the door anyway, thinking maybe this is the promised miracle, maybe this is fate bringing the good things we're told come to those who wait, you think of all the happy things a gloomy life conjures in the mind.

There is also the premonition, the primal impulse, the subtle power of things unseen, the call of another world, the sudden longing to brave the mystery. All these things urge on more powerfully than fear holds back.

Truth be told, I just opened the door without thinking. What can I say? I'm an impulsive woman. Maybe not entirely without thinking: I have never given up hope that I might see my little brother again, might hear him knock at my door. Every sound rekindles that hope. It's a constant torment. I know that Sofiane is gone, I know that he is never coming back.

★

5

A good upbringing is a terrible handicap. You end up being a well-bred little chick in a nest filled with cuckoos. One polite gesture led to another: I offered this interloper a glass of lemonade, then some supper – an egg and an orange – and stoically I listened, all ears, to her endless chatter. Could I refuse her a bed for the night? The duty of hospitality does not stop at the bedroom door. As it turned out, she didn't wait to be asked; while I was clearing the table the cheeky little thing put on her nightie. What could I do? I gave her a pillow and some clean sheets, I favoured her with a sing-song *'goodnight'*, something she took as an invitation. She laughed so hard and talked so much about this and that, about everything and nothing, about Raï music and Les Chebs, about things that even Scheherazade, that incomparable insomniac, never told of in her tales. The moment she opened her mouth, I was completely lost.

In all honesty, I wasn't really listening, though, out of politeness, I feigned interest. Her shrill falsetto irritated me. I thought about Louiza, my gentle, sweet Louiza. God, how I miss her. About what had become of all our promises.

Three am and night drags on. The old clock that stands sentry in the hall hasn't chimed since its first owner died – something I can relate to – but it still clanks and grates at regular intervals out of habit. Three times, it struggled bravely to toll the passing hour. The endless witterings of the damsel grew fainter until it was just a vague cloud hovering above our heads, then it faded into the ether. In this silence, this true mineral silence, the house began to give voice to its aches and pains, to creaks and groans fit to rouse a poltergeist. We had reached that hour that does not truly belong to us, when only a silver thread connects soul to body. Finally, she fell asleep, sinking down into the sofa and the multicoloured cushions. She slumped back, her arms folded, her mouth wide open – to say nothing of her legs – leaving my head still spinning with her twaddle. Sprawled there as she was, she might have appeared indecent were she not so innocent. In sleep, she looked every bit as outlandish as she did awake and it was clear that inside her was a world very different from the one in which we live, a world of fairies and Prince Charmings in which everyone else – the supporting cast, the minor players, the evil witches and wicked stepmothers – exist only so they can be foiled by the good, by the dreamers.

I thought I knew all there was to know about long nights dedicated to silence and the endless game of introspection and now, suddenly, I no longer knew where I was, what I felt, I didn't know what to think, what to do, I had lost the measured tempo of those who are solitary by nature. I felt flustered, my natural rhythms thrown out of kilter. I felt restive. By which I mean consumed by curiosity. Such a strange feeling! This is the danger that stalks the misanthrope: the world encroaching on one's cocoon.

Never mind, I'll read for a bit, or turn on the TV and channel surf, I'm sure I'll find something to send me to sleep. At this hour, everything makes you want to kick the bucket. First thing tomorrow, as soon as she bounds out of bed, my little damsel will have to set me straight on three things:

First: Who is she?

Second: Where is she from?

Third: Where is she going?

I can't think of anything else to say, that's how it happened. To say more, to relate the details, the impressions, the misgivings, the repetitions, the hesitant silences, would add nothing. On the contrary, it would take away from the incident, which, in and of itself, was curiously moving: Sofiane has finally made contact and the means he has chosen is this strange little girl.

That day, a trite grey day like every other, a day of nagging doubts, I could not have guessed what upheavals lay in store for me. Worse still, I couldn't think how to get rid of the silly little goose. Did I really want to be rid of her? It hardly matters, the presence of this giddy girl is the bombshell that will shake my defences to the core. Already I sensed this, I knew it was inevitable, another life had grafted itself on to mine and would consume it from within, engulf it, twist it off course.

To what extent, my God, are our lives really our own?

I spent a long time watching the intruder. She slept the sleep of the fairies. A fine-looking girl with the face of a spoiled child. The colours of the cushions, the soft light, the deep silence, the familiar rumblings from the depths, the delicacy of the sheen, all these add to the aura of enchantment. The image of happiness, that serene happiness that makes us beautiful and gentle. If angels slumber, this surely is how they look, like Chérifa adrift in her dreams. And if demons surrender to sleep, surely they too look like this. There is no reason to think that the good and the wicked do not take equal pleasure in their natural urges.

I don't know how it happened. Hardly was she out of bed than my interloper had ploughed up the whole house and scattered her belongings like seeds. Some people don't need to move in to feel at home. The bathroom, *my* bathroom, had suffered a complete makeover. 'What's all this mess?' I shouted finally. Never in the depths of my depression had I wreaked such havoc on my old dwelling place. The silly goose never stopped but she started, I could see her slight frame rushing round, turning on lamps, torturing the radio, flicking through the television channels, rummaging through my chest of drawers, delving into nooks and crannies, then reappearing looking like a package tourist at the end of a tour realising they've missed out on everything. She batted it back to me when she said 'What mess?': I was a stranger in my own house. She was eyeing me up the way you might a greengrocer out of season. Following her lead, I ate a breakfast of biscuits standing up in front of the fridge and brushed crumbs from my clothes without worrying about ants coming in from the garden. Just yesterday, ants were my worst nightmare, I could keep them at bay on the other side of the kitchen door only by sheer force, cleanliness ... and a healthy dose of pesticide. The ancient scents and smells so deeply rooted in my memory yielded before the radioactive perfume of this little strumpet and the irritating odour of youth metamorphosing uncontrollably. I was absolutely furious, disgusted by my own passivity and, unless I'm very much mistaken, thrilled by her presence. I felt like a big sister reprimanding her naughty little sibling.

Novelty has its charms, but it also shocks in that it forces us to change. I was alarmed and, at the same time, I was spellbound. Our beliefs, our habits, after all, are what they have always been: a stopgap. To suddenly discover that she is an old maid is a terrible thing for a woman. Chérifa terrorised me by her dissoluteness and charmed me by her untidiness.

But while there is a time to be soft-hearted, there are many more when it is best to be hard-bitten.

'Listen, *little girl*, it's all very well letting yourself go, but it helps to know where you're headed! Who are you, where have you come from and where are you going in that condition? You can start by telling me how you know my idiot brother and what he has to do with that big belly of yours. And don't think your little Lolita act will save you!'

'But, Tata, why are you angry with me?'

'What's with this "Tata"? I'm not your auntie! And I'm not your mother!'

'What can I call you, then?'

'Well, really! You don't *call* me anything, you address me as *mademoiselle*.'

'Aren't you a bit old to be a mademoiselle?'
'Well, really!'

Anyway, I'm not about to give chapter and verse of such an inane conversation, especially one that hardly portrays me in a flattering light.

With simpletons, everything is simple, the trick is not to overcomplicate things. Seen in this light, the problem seems pitifully banal. Somehow, in Oran, Chérifa, one of so many lost girls, encountered my idiot brother who was also on the road to ruin. In their misery, they exchanged ideas, no doubt kisses, and all the calamities that this entails. The little damsel is not backward in coming forward, though she has clearly retained some sense of propriety, since she makes no mention of her belly. Did she conceive by the Holy Spirit? Well, all that matters is the result. At a guess, I'd say she's five months gone. Beware, there's trouble brewing, I wouldn't be at all surprised if this girl is the kind that attracts problems. Well, I'm telling you right now, she can go bake that bun in her oven somewhere else!

Knowing the silver tongue Sofiane has, and the gullibility of silly little geese, I assume that their goodbyes went something like this:

'Chérifa, my destiny is not to stay here in Oran but to continue on my way. I must find freedom and fulfilment. Those who went before us swear by Allah that such things are only to be found over there in the West.'

'All I want is to get as far as Algiers, the capital, a girl can live there like a queen. All my friends back in the village dream of going there. Look at my belly . . . I'm starting to show, aren't I?

If I go back to the douar *with a baby in tow, they'll cut my throat.'*

'Go to my sister Lamia. She has a big house, there'll be a room for you and a cot for the baby. She's a doctor, so you won't lack for medicine. She's old and she's prickly as a cactus, but that will be good for the child, it will keep him on the straight and narrow. I'm off to Tangier to look for a ship.'

This is how they talk, the children who have strayed from the path.

But, humbled by age and by wisdom, how are we supposed to talk to them – especially when life has long since taught us to bite our tongues and pretend we still believe?

Unable to talk to her, I tormented her. My questions came so thick and fast that she was paralysed, she did not understand what they meant nor why they were so urgent. There I was expecting the truth, the whole truth and nothing but the truth, but she started blubbering and hiccuping like a barking seal. Her eyeliner trickled miserably down her face. Then, *hup*, she leapt to her feet and rushed out, slamming the door behind her. For minutes afterwards, the walls of the house shuddered from the bang. When it finally finished sundering, my heart was left in pieces and I cried my eyes out.

She came back at midnight, on the twelfth stroke. Or thereabouts. This was the time limit I had set before hanging myself. I was guilty. Past midnight, only corpses and their killers roam the streets of this city. I had allowed her to go out, alone, after dark, in a neighbourhood where even murderers are scared of their own shadows. I rushed to open the door, expecting to meet with a violent death. Whew! It was her, with her holdall and her regal airs. She went straight into the living room – her bedroom – without so much as looking at me. I fought the urge to bump her off myself, right there in the hall. Next time, I'll kill her and I won't lose any sleep. A woman has a right to a little respect in her own home. As I closed the door, I thought I saw among the shifting shadows of the poplar trees that guard the neighbourhood, the figure of a man disappearing into the darkness.

One more worry. And a major one.

> *Day, night,*
> *Within, without,*
> *The rough beast*
> *Waits*
> *With dagger drawn.*
>
> *Against all faith*
> *Against all laws*
> *The rough beast*
> *Strikes*
> *With burning hook.*
>
> *Beware, woman*
> *Beware, child,*
> *The rough beast*
> *Runs*
> *With tail erect.*

Cowering
Contented
Man awaits
His beloved beast
HIS FEAR.

I'm not sure whether I miss my former solitude, those long, leisurely evenings, the weekends spent like a worker bee on strike, the wanton wildness and the associated absences, the curious habits of a confirmed spinster which, though unrewarding, are familiar, the delicious thrill of fear in the darkness and my heroic rebellions against the ghosts who share with me the mysteries of the past and the murmuring of walls steeped in forgotten stories. No, I have no regrets, only fond memories. I enjoyed my rootless solitude, enjoyed shutting myself away in this house which, for more than two centuries, has seen so many people come and go, taking on the wrinkles, the wilful habits and the curious odours of those who came before us, the janissaries, the hookah smokers, by their own intrigues or by some insidious illness; a high-ranking Turk – an officer in the Sultan's guard – built this house as a weekend retreat; after him came a viscount, a blue-blooded Frenchman, part soldier, part naturalist, who, in time, put down roots in the *medina*, embracing Islam and one of its daughters; next came a Jew whose ancestors it seems arrived on the Barbary Coast before the upheavals began; he was followed by a succession of *pieds-noirs* who arrived in wretched hordes from Navarre and Galilee and are now exiled to the north pole; then, shortly after independence, it was my parents' turn. They came down from the mountains of Greater Kabylia, and for a while they housed friends and allies and, during the 'Years of Lead' that followed when honour was at a low ebb, they took in furtive strangers who showed up with their secrets and left before we could discover what they were. How we tried to eavesdrop on those whispered conversations! But this house is big, we were small, inexperienced, and much went over our heads.

I enjoyed my forays into impenetrable silences, and all the questions that come to mind when time moves on without us; I would embellish them according to my whims, my moods. I would drift far away, reluctant to return. Reality is but a port of call on our journey, a succession of mindless chores, repetitive gestures, tedious stories, so we might as well be brief. And yet I enjoyed tackling domestic problems as antiquated as the house itself with cold determination and an almost perverse punctiliousness. In a way a simple life is very complicated. There are the unknowns and all the shifting imponderables in the background. The walls are crumbling, the pots are chipped, the iron cuts out during ironing, the pipes are leaking, everything creaks or groans and sometimes the house is plunged into darkness in broad daylight. Increasingly, it seems to me, whole sections are falling apart. Why, I don't know; sometimes these cave-ins took place inside my head. I was surrounded by antiquated things which gave up the ghost faster than I could fix them. You deal with it or you don't. Even the screws can come unscrewed, I thought, at the end of the day as I reached for a hammer. For a while, it was like a religion to me, a form of post-industrial asceticism made up of transcendental shrugs and sighs and bouts of blind rage, a type of OCD complete with the liberating rituals that entails. But at least it gave my arms some muscle tone and distracted my ears from the revolutionary claptrap fed like milk and honey to the masses. This was the era of diatribes and mass protests, of gobbledygook spouted all the working week and silent only on the Sabbath. There's not a single gadget in this house I didn't manage to dismantle only to have to replace it with a new, more complicated model which immediately sneered at me from its state-of-the-art technology. Not a single object was made within these walls, they all show up without warning, cash on delivery, and are promptly put in the right place, there to age safe from prying eyes. The real feat is not getting them to work – something that can be done with the press of a button – but in deciphering the instructions. It's astonishing the sheaves of booklets that spew from the cardboard boxes, you can picture yourself dying, stupid and useless. Finding your own language in an instruction booklet is a riddle in itself, so I would read the first page that came to hand, Chinese, Korean, Hindu, Russian, Turkish, Greek. I would stare and stare at the text. It's so complicated. It seems impossible that people can speak and understand these languages. I avoided the French booklets, churned out by polyglots who learn the language of Molière from fast-food menus. They infuriated me, I felt an irresistible urge to rewrite them before reading them point by point. I ignored the Arabic, which reminds me of the hateful slew of paperwork that our glorious government uses to manipulate us from January to December all the civic year. I shunned the manuals in English because, though I can muddle through, it gives me the creeps, it makes me feel ignorant and anxious. English is the language of those who travel, and I don't travel. Who but me would confess to turning on machines without reading the instructions? The phase was short-lived, I didn't have many gadgets, and since everything comes with time, it was something I was determined to work out for myself: technology is serious business, it's man's work, something women have no right to meddle with. I quickly worked out how best to proceed. Tonton Hocine, a friend of Papa's who lives on the Impasse des Alouettes, a veteran of some war or other – independence probably – would come round with his box of tricks whenever I asked and, with the air of an indignant expert, make it clear what a terrible mess I had made of things. I had the poor man wrapped round my little finger. Once you got him going, he was a powerhouse, he would immediately set about finding the leak. I found it fascinating to watch him sweat blood, blowtorch in hand, trying heroically to fix the pipe. Aside from the tiny garden, now parched as the savannah, the house was suffering from nothing more serious than mild arthritis, something an old man could do nothing about. The wind whistling through cracks in the windows and the doorframes grated on my nerves, but there was no through breeze. To thank him, I found nothing better than to stroke his hair over a cup of strong coffee. Having often seen his breath flame in his unkempt thatch of beard, I knew that Tonton Hocine was fuelled by rotgut, but how could a woman buy wine and how could I offer him alcohol without shocking him and losing his respect? Besides, I had my scruples, his limbs were plagued with gout, and it was bad enough that he was using what little strength he had to help me out. So I stuck with serving coffee thick as tar, which I pressed until it yielded rubbing alcohol. I listened to him, blissful to the point of brainlessness, chin resting on his hand, as he refought his battles with pen-pushers, relived old quarrels with a certain Corporal Abou Hitler and, towards the end, when the important things remain to be said, he would rail about Arabs whom he claimed power made particularly cruel. Old men have their pet subjects, there's nothing you can do to shut them up. Hocine was a sweet little man. He was a Kabyle and still very much a hill tribesman, a rough diamond with a bushy moustache that tickled his ears, a paunch that pulled him forward and down, rheumy eyes and a tuft of lank hair that fell over his warty nose making him look like an ageing walrus capable of hibernating for six months at a stretch. He talked the only way he knew how, in the Tamazight dialect of the distant, precipitous Djurdjura Mountains, so, for him, words probably exceeded the sheer, sad reality. These crafty old devils have a tendency to make categorical pronouncements, there's never any debate. I thought no differently to him, but I wasn't old enough to share my thoughts without consequences so I simply nodded meekly. All this was fascinating, but it was terribly expensive since the man could spend whole afternoons talking and tinkering and, being retired, I found it difficult to pay his hourly rate. Then one day, he dropped dead and I cried like a child.

I used to love saddling up some wild fantasy and slipping into the parallel lives that loomed out of the whispering darkness, away from the cold sheets of my bed, and see myself cantering off to that place where things end, where real life begins. At their most intense, these reveries could wake me with a savage jolt, like a demon dropped into a font of holy water, my throat choked with anguished cries. In our eagerness to dream, we living dead have a tendency to forget that a mere glimpse of life can be fatal to us. Afterwards, I tell myself that such affectations are unseemly, but then I remind myself that to dream only of the life we know is to darken our days. I was panting and dripping with sweat as I listened to the dying echo at the foot of the stairs as it descended into the cellar like a corpse suddenly conjured or ascended the attic to pass away in among things long forgotten and never to be exhumed. Then I would sink back into the silence, my ears still quivering, and fashion this spontaneous commotion into a skilfully orchestrated tragedy. Sometimes, when the silence was filled with strange noises, I was so terrified I would rush out of the house in my slippers. There, in the sullen shadows of the poplar trees, I would slowly get my bearing. I was alone, lost in the jungle with darkness my only guide. The aim was for my excitements to go hand in hand with reality, and so sometimes I would lay it on thick. I have some rather manly ways of exciting myself, not all of which succeed. A heroine in carpet slippers, a dressing gown and a headscarf is pathetic. I reminded myself of Miss Marple aggravating her arthritis running around spreading gossip. But pain has its own pathways, strange shortcuts that I discover from time to time when it pounces unexpectedly and makes me howl. Then there is the dread, the muffled dread that torments me the way needless fears torment a hypochondriac. Trapped within my hallucinations, I would curl up like an animal, everything inside me quivering and pulsing, and sometimes I could feel my eyes shine with the comforting resignation of death. My life is measured out in long prostrations on the terrace at the far end of my little garden, or in the bathroom where I would scrub myself like a dog to suppress the breathless panting of my soul. Eventually, overwhelmed by the absurd, I would wind up at the foot of my bed, at the end of the night with my dreams, my rebellions. Silence was my refuge and wandering my quest. My life was both rich and poor. And a little histrionic. I asked nothing of it, and it gave me nothing, it was a curious symbiosis, and it was enough. The days shambled past, I abandoned myself to abandonment, everything was fine. How reassuring a barren wilderness can be when the path is well trodden!

And yet it frightened me, that solitude. Jealous, vindictive, it wanted me all to itself, its walls closed in on me, scowling. Would it leave me an open window? I felt myself fade as the life-force guttered inside me. But still I longed to live, to live like a madwoman, to dance like a heretic, to scream exultantly, to get drunk on happiness, to embrace all the misfortunes, all the wild dreams in the world.

I was mad but did not realise it. Kind souls, in their own way, would tell me as much with a reticent look, a pitying smile on their lips like an offering. I would respond with a gale of laughter which merely paved the way for truly malicious gossip which would eventually get back to me, from other, more authoritative mouths, from great-aunts weighed down with victuals and wise maxims who were quick to show up with hot news and remonstrate, from visiting female cousins with hearts so placid I feared for their health, and even from perfect strangers who gaily appeared uninvited pretexting some family connection as tenuous as it was unverifiable, each of them blessed with husbands, legitimate progeny and the assurance that experience gives them the right to speak of good and evil. Behind their words was a vehement dislike, behind their eyes a warning. This was an Islamic country, not a holiday camp. I took it badly, censure calls down the Last Judgment. To be mad does not mean to be unnatural, to live alone is not a crime, it is not the indulgence of the depraved! Could Allah be afraid of a poor forsaken woman?

My work takes up eight, ten, twelve hours a day. I don't count, I work on cases triaged as urgent while other colleagues – guys with a string of high-flown titles after their name – lie around sunning themselves or stalk the hospital corridors. Sometimes, I feel like I'm a skivvy, it's humiliating. I arrive first thing in the morning and get home last thing at night or vice versa, constantly rushing. I button and unbutton my white coat on the go. But then again I'm not paid to stand around and daydream. Paediatrics is sheer slavery, by far the most taxing branch of medicine. Children are charlatans; if they're not crying out of pain, they cry out of sheer spite. And the Hôpital Parnet is hardly a shining example of medical care in Algiers. I spend half my time telling off snotty brats and the other half at loggerheads with the fools in administration. It wears you down. At thirty-five, I've got the wrinkles of a sixty-year-old. They call me 'The Old Woman', pretending it's an affectionate nickname to sugar the pill. I don't take it well. For a doctor, such signs of deterioration are the first steps on the road to ruin, and for a woman who is still young and beautiful it is like being thrown on the scrapheap.

My solitude consoles me for my spinsterhood, my prema-ture wrinkles, my pernicious habits, it consoles me for the pervasive atmosphere of violence, the constant Algerian bilge, the national navel-gazing, the moronic male chau-vinism that regulate society. But it cannot make up for the absence of my little brother which is as painful as on the day he disappeared. What has become of him, my God? He has been gone over a year. I haven't dared contact the police who would only have been annoyed that I had bothered them, who would have invented some trumped-up charge and put us on a blacklist. Sofiane is eighteen, old enough they'd probably think, they would hunt him down to tor-ture him. I've done my best to look for him without raising suspicion. Besides, my idiot brother left of his own free will. Legally, he can go anywhere he likes. Democracy has its good points, even in the eyes of the police. Truth be told, the more rights they have the less they worry about their responsibilities.

Bluebeard plays a role in my dreams and my nightmares. I don't know whether he really exists. He is a shadowy figure behind the Venetian blinds of the house across the street, a ramshackle hovel splintered to the bone that has lain empty since the mysterious disappearance of its owner, a Frenchman – a real one, so I'm told – sometime back in the 1960s. There's no way of knowing what happened to him. At that age, I did not notice neighbours, any more than in a corner of my childhood memory I registered the comings and goings of a shadow no different from that of any other man. The figure I see now could be the shadow from my childhood trying to resurface. How can I know? A lot of blood has flowed under the bridge since then, an ocean of bitterness through people's hearts. The population of the neighbourhood has changed several times, it's a wonder I can find myself. Change grew out of the barrel of a gun, the swift got out while they still could, the stragglers got it in the neck. There was no remission, no pity. The exodus from the land, which was the great success of the period, turned Algiers into a boundless sea of poverty, people come and go and are swallowed up by one of the many shantytowns whose numberless tentacles coil and uncoil from one horizon to the other. Wherever you go, you're held within its grip. In a sickly city, a breath of rumour sets all tongues wagging. Stop one and ten more scuttle out of the shadows laying claim to some scrap of truth. People began to say my house was haunted. Children got goosebumps, old ladies shuddered, scurrying past as fast as their withered legs would carry them. The fear was such that the street became deserted. Shopkeepers packed up and moved on and their customers followed. Haunted, my eye! Everyone said there had been some funny business, some underhand ploy to divest the Frenchman of his property, but no one was prepared to be a witness to anything, certainly not to a crime so cunningly contrived. Where there was conspiracy, there were threats, and where there were threats, most people quietly assumed the government were involved. Personally, I used to believe it was haunted and I had nightmares about it. Doubt crept in. Ghosts are fun, they get a kick out of scaring people. But the ghost I saw was different; rather than flitting about going *wooooo*, it lay in wait, watching intently, which meant the shadow was something real, something flesh and blood with a head full of ideas that were reactionary if not dangerous. Which broadens the scope of possibilities. Is he an assassin lying in wait, some killer in a turban; is he a cornered, desperate fugitive, or a suicide-bomber determined to set the neighbourhood ablaze? In my more paranoid moments, that is how I imagined him. In cheerier moments, I gave my imagination free rein, I pictured him as a lover racked by remorse, a Quasimodo dying on a dusty bed, a mystic fascinated by his own navel, a kind-hearted Elephant Man, a cantankerous old grouch abandoned by his family, a wild-haired scientist involved in some astounding research. Does he ever leave that window? Never when I am at home. How does he occupy his time when I'm out? I could not help but wonder. For the most part, I simply glanced in his direction and casually turned away.

I dubbed him Bluebeard. A memory from the past, from a childhood spent reading, but also a stupid, cruel reference to the present in which *les barbus* – the bearded men – oppress this country and its *banlieues* beyond the seas, beyond religion, leaving nature but a straw through which to breathe.

I finally decided that my particular *barbu* is harmless, if a little mysterious. If he has a beard, it's probably just because he doesn't shave. I can't believe that this ghost, this character out of Grimm's fairytales, cultivates his facial hair as part of a fanatical ideology consumed with hatred. He probably loves his beard, and those who love, suffer. On the other hand, the real Bluebeard cut women's throats, a fact that briefly gives me pause for thought. But there's nothing to say that my Bluebeard even has a beard, that's just how I picture him, what I named him, because these days the beard is the symbol of the evil that lurks all around, gnaws away at us, the evil that kills. In any case, whether or not he has a beard, Bluebeard is a part of my life. I share my solitude with him, as he perhaps shares his with me. There is no escape, we are caught in the same net, we breathe the same polluted air, separated only by a narrow street and two sets of shutters, mine and his, both crumbling with age. It's not as though I could go over there, knock on the door and ask him to move out. What if he turned out to be a ghost?

★

This house has known happier times, when the whole family was in residence. Papa, Maman, my big brother Yacine and little Sofiane, who was growing like a little devil, not to mention the puppies in the courtyard and the kittens under our feet and – how could I forget? – a beautiful pair of short-lived lovebirds in an intricately carved cage that hung in our living room like a chandelier in a palace. Everywhere, there were lush, green plants, hanging from macramé potholders we made ourselves. Out in the garden, silent and invisible, a tortoise lived out its life at its own pace, nibbling everything in its path. Sometimes, we would accidentally step on it but nothing happened, these tender creatures are so well armoured they've never needed to learn to scream. And there was me, Lamia, a pretty, bubbly daughter of the house, born midway between the two boys. Maman's women friends came and went as they pleased, they stayed, they talked, they helped themselves to endless cups of sugar, flour, couscous and so forth. One day, I'll demand every cupful back and bankrupt them. I should think about them more often. Thanks to them, we knew every secret, no one was better at nosing out a dead body, we would have been lost without their skills. Our afternoons were enlivened as we listened to the sins of our neighbours. The worst thing that could happen was for us to fall asleep after lunch, so we did everything we possibly could to stay awake. It was not that I felt we were listening to some terrible tragedy, but I sensed that, being girls, we needed to find out what life held in store for us in the future. Since the house was as riddled with holes as Swiss cheese, every local breeze arranged to meet there. On every corner there was some girl or boy asking after one of my brothers. There was no reason to panic, but all this commotion was contagious. Doors slammed and the crash-bang-wallop scampered along the walls to join in the collective hysteria. Music blared at ear-splitting volume, *yéyé* and 1960s pop were all the rage: Johnny Hallyday, Eddy Mitchell, Les Chats Sauvages, Les Algers, these were our idols. We were young, we lacked gravitas. The truth is, we made more noise than an army barracks on R & R. During the War of Independence, Papa had fought with the *maquis* and so earned the coveted title of veteran *moudjahid* entitling him to a pension, which, after long years of repeated applications, finally arrived like manna from heaven. Nationalism is a terrible thing. Cholera is easier to survive. But Papa had the good grace to keep his sickness to himself and never imposed his ailments on us. 'A country liberated by its own people, what could be more normal than that!' he'd mutter every night, listening as the TV recounted the litany of the dead and the maimed as a miracle. His pension was not enough to provide food for the lovebirds, so he went to work in a state factory that made – what was it? – I can't remember. Papa was constantly bending our ears, complaining about all the things that were wrong with the factory which, we were convinced, manufactured rusty widgets or churned out scraps and memos for the Head of State, known as the country's foreman. The constant harping about 'dead wood', which peppered his laments, sounded to my young ears like 'redwood' and I imagined some miraculous tree had sprouted in the middle of the factory, something which conferred a mysterious significance on his pronouncement, though I never dared to ask the question. But at home things were fine. The comings and goings, the shouting and screaming, the clattering footsteps, the whispered secrets, the squabbles, the fights, all made for stormy days and leisurely evenings. There is nothing better than the calm that comes after war. The kittens purred in utter bliss. They had a way of curling up into a ball that commanded respect, they looked as though they would be ready even if the sky should fall. We were as hypnotised as they were comatose, and before long our snores and their purrs began to resonate and the house retreated into a cocoon of cotton wool. My happiness would have been complete and I would have thanked God unreservedly if only I had had a little sister. 'You should thank Him anyway,' Louiza would say, 'having sisters is worse than having spots.' Louiza, my best friend from school, was plagued with freckles and devastated that she did not have a little brother to look after. With her permanently stunned expression and her big buck teeth, she might have looked like she was crazy but she was sweet as could be and I thought she was cute. She had freckles like raisins and a shock of red hair; she looked good enough to eat. So we nicknamed her Carrot Cake. We'd cup our hands and yell, 'Come here and give us a bite!' This warhead detonated in three stages: first she would pull a face, then force a laugh, then – *bam* – she'd burst into tears. We would cover her in kisses to staunch the flow, petrified in case the cavalry showed up. Her mother was more terrifying than the whole Mexican army. I was often teased myself, given that I was a collection of . . . well, we don't need to talk about that, it's ancient history. 'I wish I had a little brother,' Louiza would wail. 'I wish I had a little sister,' I'd sigh. Hand in hand, we would walk to school and hand in hand we returned home. I think I remember us swearing on our mothers' lives that nothing would ever part us. We couldn't have been closer if we'd been monozygotic and all alone in the world. Her whole family was female with the exception of her father, a former member of the *maquis* and an honest-to-God invalid besides who, never knowing which way to turn, kept himself to himself. Apart from stroking his moustache, he had no other distinguishing tics. It was his way of dreaming about his beloved *douar*, because though you can take a farmer from the land, he will forever be a ragbag of preoccupations: digging, ploughing, hailstorms, cattle rustlers, foxes, tax collectors. His true home was the Moorish café down the hill where the rootless men of the district gathered, that was where his daughters went to tell him it was time for bed. Being a believer of the old school, of the time before the upheavals when Muslims devoted themselves to tilling the land, he felt that being part of an increasingly secular family living in the city was a terrible waste aside from being the anteroom to hell.

People assume that little girls spend their whole time talking about boyfriends when in fact they also dream of the brother they long for or the brother they would turn into a toad without a second thought. That was true of us. We had boyfriends and we did talk about them, but only to say they were dumb and boring. Little girls also think about the sister they desperately miss or the one they would happily see burn in hell, but rarely talk about them. This too was true of us: we avoided the subject since Louiza was determined that none of the little witches should be spared and I was furious at the idea she would consign her adorable little sister to the flames.

At sixteen, the beautiful Louiza was married off to a pauper from some distant, utterly benighted suburb. He gave her a string of daughters and not a single son. In genetics, it's either one thing or the other. Poor darling Louiza always got the opposite of what she wished for. She was the youngest of the family and no one listened to her. The wedding was a leper's funeral. Beneath the tattered rags of an inoffensive city tramp, her husband turned out to be a dangerous fanatic hostile to joy and to fantasy. His lips flecked with spittle, he harangued us with verses ripped from the Qur'an and baleful threats from the terrorists' handbook. Since the situation called for spinelessness, the other men puffed out their chests and began spouting *suras* like suicide bombers. Ever since, I've been traumatised, I keep asking myself: does Islam produce true believers, craven cowards or just terrorists? There is no easy answer since all three are talented actors. And besides, it turns out that Islam these days is both a performance and a powerful weapon in the hands of grave-robbers. The girls suppressed their rebellious ways, gave up the fight and quietly stared at each other all night, huddled behind their grandmother's skirts. It would have been good to cry, but the philistines had all but forbidden us from breathing. In the distance, as night enfolded the city like a shroud, we could hear bitter rumblings and shameful silences. I never saw my beloved

Louiza again. What mortuary does she live in now? What little news I have of her seems to come from beyond the grave.

Time flew by and I found myself alone. As I stumbled on, I stockpiled sorrows: university, the dreariness of college work, the pettiness of fellow students, the endless betrayals and setbacks, the scrabble to find a job – any job – the self-seeking recommendations and those that led nowhere. All this takes time, takes years, and leaves its scars. Then, finally, a stroke of luck, a smile sent from heaven: I happened to be at the Parnet clinic when the consultant paediatrician tossed his white coat at the feet of the hospital administrator, a cousin of the Minister for Health and a nephew of the Pasha. He was exultant, brandishing a visa offering him refugee status in Canada; from seven thousand miles away Lady Luck had smiled on him. His luck was also mine. That same day, I donned my white coat. The hospital administrator thought it best to prove he was a man and act quickly before the rumour mill started. 'Go to hell, you little queer,' he spat, grabbing his crotch. 'The next person I come across gets your job!' I was there, I heard him. For better or worse, I signed up. The salary didn't exactly break the bank, but it pays enough to eat and I've learned to make the best of leftovers, potluck stews and ratatouille. That day I learned all there was to know about the Arab-Islamic economy: at work just like at home, the men chat and the women toil and there's no rest on Sunday for anyone. My married colleagues, mothers with children, daughters-in-law with mothers-in-law, work a forty-eight-hour day, with twelve hours in arrears that count double as soon as the grandchildren arrive, so I've got nothing to complain about, my time is my own. Allah's sun shines on some and not on others. How to deflect its orbit is a prickly question, one I no longer think about.

Time and again death visited this house and with it came the cortèges, the mourners, the funeral vigils, the steady string of solicitors, offers on the house, tongue-tied acquaintances, marriage proposals from men clutching a measuring tape in one hand, and, always in full view, the imam in his slippers pontificating. On the fortieth day of my last period of mourning, I drew a line under things and I shut the windows and the doors. Emptiness closed over me like a tombstone over the dead, but it was my emptiness and I could fill it as I pleased. On the blessed day, I accorded myself the minor privilege of dying as I chose. Better to be a prisoner who is free inside her head, I thought, than a jailer who is a prisoner of his keys and besides, it is good and necessary that there should be a wall between freedom and imprisonment. In doing so, I joined the most reviled mob in the Islamic world, the company of free, independent women. In such circumstances, it is best to grow old quickly, hence my premature wrinkles. For a woman living beneath the green flag of Algeria, growing old brings not devastation, but salvation.

In a few short months I had faced a lifetime of mourning. Death dogged my family, determined to wipe out everyone. It ignored me, though I pleaded on bended knee. I am the last of the Mohicans, I wonder who will wear mourning weeds for me. Papa was the first to go, he died of heart failure; three months later, my mother died of a broken heart and not long afterwards my brother Yacine died at the wheel of his car – the one great love of his life – a Renault 5, periwinkle blue fitted with a radio and a steering lock, a bargain imported from Marseilles by 'Scrap Iron Ali', the local racketeer. Paid for out of family money, as we reminded him every Sunday when, pristine as a bar of soap, he prepared to take French leave. He looked like a ladykiller from the 1930s, ready to fall for the first *femme fatale*. We pretended to be watching over the crockpot while he hugged the walls, knowing that he had to find himself a wife. It was high time, he was almost thirty, he was beginning to stoop, to cough at the slightest gust of wind, to sit in his slippers and snore. He had got a job in the administration, he was inured to it now. We lured the prettiest flowers in the neighbourhood to our house, we scoured the city for miles around like guardians of a harem. We looked for true virgins, no counterfeits. The matchmakers quickly got involved and poor Maman suddenly found herself busy going to cemeteries and funeral vigils – the key places where marriages are arranged – and visiting the shrines of *marabouts* where unthinkable things are done and undone. I was left to search the usual haunts: secondary schools, dressmakers' shops, weddings, *hammams*, bus stops. I brought home heaps of girls, beautiful and intelligent girls, fervent traditionalists and borderline crackpots, blondes, brunettes, eccentrics and teenagers, every one of them free, but every time the idiot turned up his nose, turned his back on the parade, he was determined to comb the streets like a big boy and find his

35

own Mata Hari. The poor bastard thought he could outwit the wily matchmakers. He was driving his little car slowly past the government buildings towards the Club des Pins, when a sports car ploughed into him, we were told, it was more an insinuation than an explanation. Fed up seeing him spend half his life waxing the car and the other half watching it like a hawk in case a bird shat on the paintwork, we used to mock him: 'Are you planning to marry that old wreck of yours?' He took it badly. It had been our way of warning him, since there was something animal about his passion for his car, about his need to show off. Our mourning was tinged with bitter guilt, as our jokes and jibes came back to haunt us. I've never been able to shake off the thought that we brought him bad luck. To refer to his car as a 'wreck' was like sounding a death knell. Forgive me, Yacine, forgive me, my brother. Lastly there was Sofiane. With his first cigarette, he got it into his head that, come weal or woe, he would leave the country and get as far away as possible. 'Better to die elsewhere than to live here!' he would scream whenever I tried to reason with him. 'If you can't live at home, what's the point of dying next door?' I would shout back. This was my argument, the only one I could think of. What I was trying to say is that dying is not difficult; the trick is learning how to live, the locale is of secondary importance. But he could think of nothing else, could focus on nothing but finding an escape route, getting his papers, studying the stratagems of those who had made the great leap, poring over their glorious failures. He barely spoke, barely ate and came home only to brood over his rage. Then, one morning at dawn – *bam!* – he left. He headed west, taking the most dangerous route: to Oran and via the border to Morocco, Spain and from there to France, to England, to anywhere, that was his plan. I only found out later that day, after I had trawled the neighbourhood and finally flushed out one of his friends – another candidate for suicide – at a secret, mystical meeting. There was a crowd of them, a veritable congregation, drunk on their own tears, dreaming aloud, telling each other how the great wide world was waiting for them with flowers, and how fleeing this country would deal a fatal blow to the reign of the dictator. Long story short, they were all touched by the same fever. They gathered round me like a big sister ennobled by great sorrow and informed me that Sofiane had gone the way of the *harragas* – the 'path-burners'. I was familiar with the expression, this was how everyone in the country referred to those who burned their bridges, who fled the country on makeshift rafts and destroyed their papers when caught. But this was the first time I had heard the word from the lips of a true zealot, and it sent a chill down my spine. He said it nonchalantly; to him, 'burning a path' was something only they knew how to do. I was lumbered with 'honour' and they with the responsibility of covering Sofiane's still-warm tracks. What can you say about such morons? I stared at them the way you might at a lost prophet and shook their dust from my sandals. I would happily have denounced them to the police but for the fact that the police – who constantly interrogated them, frisked them, manipulated them, spat in their faces – were at the root of their delirium. On the road the *harragas* take there is no turning back, every fall leads to another, one harder and more painful, until the final, fatal plunge. We've all witnessed it: satellite TV beams back the pictures of corpses lying broken on the rocks, or tossed by the waves, frozen or suffocated in the cargo hold of a boat, a plane, in the back of a refrigerated van. As though we did not already have enough, the *harragas* have invented new ways of dying. Even those who succeeded in making the crossing lost their souls in the terrible kingdom of the undocumented immigrant. What kind of life is it, to be forever condemned to a clandestine existence?

And what kind of life is it that I am leading, entombed here in my ancient house?

I spent a whole month going round in circles, I shed every tear in my body. I scarcely looked up: Maman, my little brother is lost; Papa, my little brother is lost . . . I was racked with guilt at the thought of having let them down. I slept in Sofiane's room so I would feel better.

Then one night he phoned. From Oran. From that god-forsaken hole where nothing – not the language, nor the religion, not even the taste of the bread – is the same as it is in Algiers.

'Where in Oran?'

'At a friend's place.'

'Who are you trying to kid? Your friends are here, in their own homes or in conclave electing a new pope.'

'Don't worry about it.'

'This has gone far enough, come home.'

'Later.'

'When?'

'I dunno.'

'Give me your address so I can send you some money.'

'I ain't got no address.'

'This friend of yours, is he homeless?'

'. . .'

'Hello? Hello? *Helloooo?*'

The little shit had already picked up an Oran accent, he said *yeah* for *yes*, he even clicked his tongue. Otherwise he was just the same: impulsive, mule-headed, thick as two short planks . . . and sweet as an angel when it suited him. He never phoned again. Was it something I said? Maybe, but it doesn't matter; they're all the same: stupid, easily offended, quick to pick a fight. Even now the question haunts me. It's hard to be the sister of a man who's still a boy. How many men realise that?

Suddenly, the house seemed terrifying. The emptiness swelled, the silence became oppressive. I had no answers, I had no more questions. Nothing mattered any more, the daily tedium could come and sweep everything away. Dying did not seem like an agonising inevitability but a consummation devoutly to be wished. I won't deny, there were times when I contemplated suicide. I even made my decision; all that remained was to work out when and how. I couldn't make up my mind; premeditation made it difficult to think straight. After a while, I bounced back. That's what I'm like, I lose hope and I bounce back.

And then Chérifa showed up. 'Invaded' might be a better word. What on earth am I going to do with her? She gets on my nerves, I can't be dealing with her vanishing acts. Or her tantrums. Or her mess. Or her being here. And I can't abide that high-pitched little-girl voice of hers. I need peace and quiet, I need things in my life to be straightforward. At any moment, I need to be able to tell myself: this is my freedom, that is my will.

Just how much, dear Lord, do our lives truly belong to us?

The first disappearing act came soon enough. It came the morning after her arrival. We were finishing our breakfast. To apologise for my torture session the night before, I brought out Maman's best tablemats and the secret stash of Turkish delight I'd been hoarding since Eid al-Fitr. We were in slippers and dressing gowns, our eyes still thick with sleep. It was nice enough, pleasant, domestic, I still feel moved at the memory. She popped a sugar cube into her mouth and went upstairs to get dressed. What she said, what I said, I don't remember. It was short-lived. And I was spiteful. To be completely frank, I gave the little madam her marching orders. I regretted it straightaway.

'I'm just going out for a walk, Tata Lamia,' she announced from the lofty height of her elephantine heels.

'Go wherever you like, go with my blessing, but I don't want to clap eyes on you again.'

'Could you give me some money?'

'You've got some nerve! You've had a good night's sleep, you've had food, you've had a laugh ... look, here's 100 dinars ... no need to thank me.'

'A hundred dinars? Is that it? What am I supposed to do with that?'

'It's enough to phone your parents ... Are you listening to me? What was I saying again? Look, I don't know the first thing about you, I have my own life, and just because my idiot brother gave you my address doesn't mean I have to take you in. All right, here's another hundred ... which, I'll have you know, leaves me without a *santeem*. Salaries are paid once a month, not that you'd know ...'

'...'

While I was rambling on like a half-wit, she pocketed the money, grabbed her bundle, popped a piece of Turkish delight in her mouth, shrugged her shoulders and stormed out. If I was waiting for a goodbye or a thank you, I'd be waiting still.

Good riddance!

The return to the void was brutal. I hadn't been expecting it, I'd assumed I would calmly go back to my solitary bliss. It was a wrenching pain, that emptiness that comes with separation. Then a sense of loss takes hold, saps the will. I had suffered it before, now here it was again. Shit! That crazy girl is no concern of mine. Only yesterday, I treated her like an extraterrestrial who had brazenly materialised in my garden and made itself at home. I wondered whether her swollen belly had something to do with Mars or Jupiter. The fact that she comes from Oran, a one-horse town in Algeria, and that my brother sent her doesn't change a thing. What little I know about her – homeless, destitute and pregnant by person or persons unknown – is hardly likely to endear her to me. If everyone minded their own

42

business, we'd all be better off. Now, suddenly all is silence and sorrow. Bluebeard's shadow is still standing guard. Does the man never sleep? I don't mind him being mysterious, but not all the time. A hieratic statue, he is watching me from above. Then, suddenly, the shadow turned and vanished. What the … ? Are my eyes playing tricks? Did Bluebeard just turn his back on me contemptuously? Damn it, what the devil has any of this got to do with him?

At the Hôpital Parnet, I glared at my male co-workers as though each one harboured murderous thoughts. I looked again. But, no, they bore the usual scars, nothing more. God, they're vile, and they dress like a symposium of scarecrows. I don't like the way they puff out their chests, the way they cut a swathe through the air before them. I'd hear their delusional prating: 'Hum, hum, we're the friends of the Sultan, get out of our way.' They come and they go with the same couldn't-give-a-shit attitude that has not only destroyed this country but, by the miracle of globalisation, fobbed off any responsibility on others. They talk in loud, bellowing voices, leaving the rest of the populace half-deaf. Whether singing or whistling, moaning or snivelling, whether bickering, backslapping or brown-nosing, they do it with the same gusto; there's never anything new or different. Their lives are pitted with a thousand and one crimes, routine mistakes, petty slip-ups, but they don't care. I can't help thinking that they smile too much. Can there be a reason – any reason – to rejoice in failure? Can there be any excuse – however slim – to justify why they strut about like peacocks when their work is only half done and that badly?

I wonder what true crimes they have committed to have such an air of inane innocence.

Shame is a funny thing. The world seems to whirl endlessly, it makes me dizzy. I'm ashamed that other people are not as ashamed of their flaws as I am of mine. On their supercilious faces their faults stick out so much you could forget they had a nose. Maybe I should see a shrink and talk to him about it.

I can tell it's going to be a long day. I'll visit the children's ward, kids understand comedy, to them it's not a synonym for hypocrisy.

My head is spinning, I'm sweating; worse still I have the terrible feeling of something wriggling in my belly. Could I be pregnant? By what? By whom? The Holy Spirit? An extraterrestrial? A film noir is running through my head, I feel like I'm about to kill somebody.

I'm tense and overwrought.

Where can the little vixen have got to? She hasn't the first idea what she's letting herself in for. Algiers will sweep her up in its madness. This crumbling city is pitiless, constantly reviling and condemning girls, and every day the outcry grows a little louder. The first passing taxi will whisk her away to some seedy den of iniquity. The way the old rattletraps prowl the streets makes you sick. 'Get in or I'll run you over!' She's a child, a stranger, a tourist, she has no idea, she's too trusting. What does a girl from Oran know about the pitfalls of Algiers? In Oran, they take their misery and turn it into mournful melodies they call Raï, here in Algiers we play double or quits. That way Chérifa struts about, that hair of hers, that smile like a precocious nymph, that perfume, that ridiculous scarf – are these the signs of a good Muslim? Damn it, you don't go around playing the starlet during a religious epidemic!

I spent the day pretending to work, tormenting myself, fearing the worst – which is usually the most likely. I just hope I didn't accidentally poison some child on my ward, they're so distracted they'll swallow anything you give them. I was beside myself, in my mind I was running through the streets of Algiers, trying to imagine where I would go if I was wearing the sort of grotesque Chérifa favours. It was useless thinking about the places that marked my childhood, they're all ancient history. What attractions are there left? The area around La Grande Poste, with its feverish crowds and its cosy tearooms, is a trap for any girl. Then there's *Maqam Echahid* – the Martyrs' Memorial – with its fancy boutiques and its hanging gardens where gilded youth parade, trailing the wannabes and the work-shy from the suburbs in their wake. In such situations it's the followers rather than the leaders who are the real problem. There's the famous Club des Pins – formerly the *hacienda* of Lucien Borgeaud, the greatest colonist of all time – now a state residence where the overlords of the regime live corralled in close quarters guarded by four watchtowers. The stories you hear about the place would have police around the world on alert, but to giddy little girls, it's like the *Big Brother* house, they flock there in droves. Disaster dogs their every step but all they can think of are the dances, the parties, the surprises. The grand hotels are run by pros, placed there by the Organisation, but with her supercilious air, Chérifa could pass for a first-class vestal virgin. The old men scouting for prey from their comfortable armchairs would pay a lot of money just to nibble her earlobe. The hypnotic way they smile at cute girls and pretty boys would put a rattlesnake to sleep. A childlike Lolita sets the old pigs grunting. I despise them.

'Hey, Lamia! Hey, wait up!'
    I recognise that voice. It's Mourad, a colleague from the hospital, the crackpot on our wing. Working with cancer patients drove him round the bend. He's probably the only man I know who doesn't dream of emigrating. Not that he lacks the capability or the courage, he just hasn't got the energy any more. I'm very fond of Mourad. There was a time when he would try to chat me up, but he's come to terms with it now. His liver is shot, he's overweight, he drinks like a fish – a real Romeo. But he's a sensitive soul, he's philosophical when he's in his cups and he wouldn't kill a fly. I'm guessing no woman has ever looked twice at the poor man and now his liver is about to explode. At first, I thought he drank to reinforce his air of blithe indifference. Time was, he constantly undermined the young interns and laughed at the brown-noses. But he has evolved, these days he subverts authority by encouraging the go-getting doctors to work like dogs. On the day the director hired me on a whim and set me to work, Mourad sidled up and, having looked me up and down and found my belly button, he said: 'Listen, kid, you're cute and all, but I'll save that for later, right now I just want to let you know what you're letting yourself in for. This place is like the *maquis*,

there are mines and booby traps everywhere. If you need any advice, come find me, but be discreet. In the meantime, think about this: less diligence makes for fewer problems.'

And he sauntered off, his hands in his pockets. A comedian. Men are contemptible, they see a woman wanting to do things properly as a problem.

That day, I opened up to him, about Chérifa, her whims, her disappearing acts, my helplessness, my shame. He immediately understood. There are facts, which can be viewed as a logical progression, but there are also feelings and what lies, repressed, in the deepest depths of the human heart. To put it bluntly, I feared the worst. He spent a long moment biting his lip and then finally he said:

'You're obviously fond of the girl! Why on earth did you throw her out? Oh well, I suppose women are never straightforward, or if they are something is up. You're not going to find her by searching around the Martyrs' Memorial or the palaces or the Club des Pins, that's where the high-class girls hang out, it requires special dispensation from the Organisation. I'm not sure about La Grande Poste, the girls there work for crooks and gangsters and the takings are pretty slim. But this girl is pregnant, and that's bound to influence how she thinks. A fish swims towards the sea, not towards the gutter. You'd be better off checking the bus stations or the women's halls of residence at the university. If she headed for a station, then she's planning to move to another city, so you might as well give up hope because rural Algeria is the arse-end of the universe. If she went to the university, then obviously she's looking for help, she's assuming that in situations like hers women

47

support each other ... well, you know what I mean, she'll be looking for a place to stay and a little female sympathy.'

'I can easily do the bus stations, there aren't many, but I don't see how I can check the halls of residence. How many are there? I can hardly knock on the door of every room and say: is Chérifa here?'

'You don't need to, you just get a message to one girl and you wait. Talk to any of the female students and you'll have your answer within twenty-four hours. At university, girls are cut off from the outside world, they're a closed network. Surely you remember what it was like when you were at college – though in our day, the segregation was more of a revolutionary nature, you could hold your meeting, propose your motions. These days, that's all over, everyone is insane and no one messes with religion. Try not to terrify the poor things, they all have something to hide, some idea, some dream, some secret crush, some little foible, sometimes even a plan to commit suicide ...'

'The easiest thing would be to wait. I'm sure she'll come back, she's got nowhere to go.'

'That's up to you, but you know as well as I do where hope leads around here.'

These words struck a chord. I don't know a single Algerian who doesn't blithely talk about hope a hundred times a day. Not a single one. I can't help but wonder what the word means.

I stopped by Hussein-Dey station before I went home. Have to start somewhere, I thought, and at least it's on the way. The place was teeming. The world and his wife were there. The suburban commuters, the season-ticket holders who travel in battalions, silent, grey-black, half-dead, rucksacks slung over their shoulders, staring at the ground. Every morning they are swallowed up by crumbling factories from the socialist era and every evening they are spewed out after eight hours of being pointlessly ground down. They look like they've wandered out of a gulag and are just waiting for the siren to call them back.

The whole thing is preposterous, the economic war is taking place elsewhere; it is waged by computers and satellites in utter silence. These people would be better off going home and comforting their families, it's impossible to escape both poverty and the IMF. A mother would be hard pressed to spot her child in a crowd like this. And, even in high heels, Chérifa is knee high to a grasshopper; how would I spot her? While I was trying to work out how long it would take to search the premises, the train arrived, surging out of the mists of time. A thunderous rumble shook the ground and half the sky was blotted out with smoke. How had such a crowd managed to pile on to the train so quickly, cramming into carriages like sardines and perching on the running boards? Damned if I know. This whole scene, the calmness, the patience, the hands stuffed in pockets, the rucksacks on the ground, it was pure cinema. The poor – all paid-up members of the school of hard knocks – have an ability to pretend that beggars belief. They surged forward en masse and, in a split second, dozens of them manage to slip through a crack a gloved hand could barely squeeze into. In the time it took to catch my breath, I was standing on the platform alone, with the bitter feeling that I had missed the last train of the year. An old soldier in a peaked cap and with a wooden leg calmly walked over to me and said: 'Don't worry, madame, there's another train at 6.37 pm, but you'll have to elbow your way on, this is rush hour.' He was the station master, I could take his word for it. Thank you. I rushed off. If Chérifa had gone to a station I would never see her again, she would move from one crowd to another.

What about university students? Girls at university were ferried between the halls of residence and lecture halls by bus. How many such buses weave through the streets of Algiers? I don't know, in this ossified city things grow like mushrooms. They're everywhere, those buses, each one full to bursting. What are they really ferrying around? I asked myself. Boys with beards and girls in *chadors*, the boys dare not talk, the girls dare not move and the drivers careen through the city as though obeying secret signals. There's nothing very educational about it. In my young day, buses did not go unnoticed, or were clapped-out Russian wrecks, half-eaten with rust and smoky as a damp cigar. We would sing 'Qassaman', 'The Internationale', 'Le Déserteur', we would spit on the bourgeoisie and their lackeys, make drivers nearly crash by flashing them a glimpse of breast, or by pretending to take down their registration number so we could denounce them to the KGB. Times have changed.

The journey home was painful. I dragged my feet, my heart in my mouth. The neighbourhood seemed seedy and unpleasant and the house – my house – gave me a cold welcome. I needed that. And yet I loved this grey dusk, caught between sun and moon, between waning day and emerging night. Relief comes, hope is reborn, we dither on the doorstep, fumbling with keys, eager to cross the threshold. We are done with the world, we retreat to our refuge, we shed our coats. Somewhere deep within us, an internal clock or a guardian angel activates a switch and we settle down to dream like children. For the poor, this is the true meaning of happiness. We relax, we move to a gentler rhythm, we do housework and minor repairs, potter around brooding over our uncertainties, we take a bath if the water has been reconnected, make a call if the phone lines are working, settle in front of the TV if the power cut is over, laze around, read a book, do a little cooking, water the plants, sprinkle insecticide to keep ants at bay, do some knitting. Then there are the evenings when the only thing we can think to do is prop our elbows on our knees and bury our face in our hands. Life is blank, it is useless to fuss.

What was it Mourad said . . . a little female sympathy? How dare he say that to me! What am I, a bear, a rock, a machine? What does he really know about me? What does he really know about women? He's a man, he knows nothing. He probably thinks there is such a thing as male sympathy. What a romantic.

Am I seeing things? There . . . hanging on a coat peg in the hall? It is! It's a panther-pink pullover with flowers in blue fabric crudely sewn on the front. If it's not mine – and I know it's not – then it must belong to Chérifa. *Snff . . . snff.* The house smells of weapons-grade plutonium perfume. A quick tour reveals a G-string in the bath, a bead necklace on the cooker, a handkerchief under the phone, a powder compact next to the TV, a pencil in the vase, a pair of ballet pumps hanging from a nail in the corridor, a beanie hat dangling from the handle of a dresser. The girl strews her possessions in her wake, she'd have a job going under-cover in a detective movie. Where can she be at this hour? If she doesn't come back to collect her belongings, it means she's lost. No, the little minx would do anything to reclaim her treasure, it's all she has.

Later, under a sofa cushion, I found a little handbag, the kind of preposterous clutch bag a bride might carry, so tiny that just trying to get your keys inside could result in losing a finger. It reminded me of the story of a chimpanzee in a laboratory, putting his hand into a jar, grabbing a piece of fruit and discovering to his consternation that the narrow neck would not allow him to withdraw his fist. I'm not sure which is sadder, mocking the chimp or thinking that we're smarter. I dared not open the clutch bag, but I opened it anyway; my house, my rules. Inventory: a pencil stub, a brush, a pin, a coin, another pin, a full-length photo of someone. Well, well, would you credit it . . . ? A man. Thir-ty-five? He looks ordinary . . . or rather conventional, his every feature conforms to the new biology of exceptional Algerians: chubby-cheeked, pot-bellied, fat-arsed, he sports a hirsute adornment around his mouth which, depending on circumstances, is intended as a sign of moderate piety, an aid to seduction or a proof of intelligence, he is dressed like a mobster at a mafia cocktail party. It's all so tacky, the minute these people have money in their pockets, they're all over the place. There is a self-consciousness to the way he holds his head and a twitchy nervousness deep in his eyes. It's an expression I know only too well, in every photo I look as though I've been startled by a one-eyed badger. He's a little young to be her grandfather but too old to be a brother or a schoolfriend, although all families are dysfunctional. Obviously, the possibilities do not end there: an uncle, a cousin, a neighbour's husband. Then again he could be a drug trafficker or a bar owner, professions that are all the rage in the new biometry. The Chérifas of this world are their preferred prey. Or he could be ... as I racked my brain, I realised I knew this reprobate, I'd seen his ugly mug somewhere. A celebrity? Yes, that was it. What was he? A sportsman, a politician, a captain of industry, an artist with connections to the ministry? Whatever he was, he was some sort of bigwig.

What was the connection between the man in the photo and Chérifa's swollen belly? It was a question I could not help but ask myself. And now I have.

It had been three days since I saw that old trout from the rue Marengo and now, bang on time – *knock, knock* – she shows up, all hot and flustered. And – unusually for her – she didn't beat around the bush.

'Oh, my dear, young people today, you simply can't depend on them! They're here one minute and gone the next! They're only too happy to have us worrying and fretting over them, when all we want at our time of life is a little comfort, a little peace, but you might as well ask the town council for running water. How is it that I've never met this girl? The clothes she wears! What's her name? Where's her husband? What was she thinking, going out last night and coming home after midnight? Where did she go? And what was she doing, storming out again at dawn in such a terrible temper?'

'Ah, Tante Zohra, what a coincidence! I was just going to pop round to see you. I hadn't heard from you and I was starting to worry!'

I know how Tante Zohra's mind works, I've heard it all before and I've learned the best thing to do is bombard her with information and bamboozle her.

'Were you talking about Chérifa? Pretty little thing, don't you think? She's my cousin's youngest, you know – the cousin who moved to Oran just after the War, back when the Americans were bombing the mountain villages because they thought we were hiding Nazis. Then, when they realised that we were only hiding ourselves, they came back and showered us with chocolate bars. The kids stuck to them like leeches, the Yanks adopted them as mascots and we never saw hide nor hair of them again. Up in Kabylia, we had nothing to eat but acorn flour, green olives and goat's cheese. Oh, I nearly forgot, up in the mountains our favourite fruit was figs, we used to pick them off the trees. You can't till the soil up in Kabylia, it's all rocks. So, anyway, this cousin of mine is on his deathbed and, sensing that the end is near, he's asked his youngest daughter to visit the family on his behalf. Our family is scattered to the four winds, Allah alone knows us by our lamentations. You know better than I how widely scattered the Kabyle people were, hounded from town to town when we weren't hounded out of existence. Well, anyway, little Chérifa, she comes, she goes, and likely will for some time, because, like I said, there are cousins everywhere, furtive exiles weighed down by sorrow and homesickness. And being an insomniac, she keeps odd hours. But what's to be done, Tante Zohra? *C'est la vie!*'

'And how is Sofiane? Did he go to Oran, surely he must have gone to say his goodbyes to this cousin of yours?'

The way she just came out with it! She's a cunning shrew, trying to trip me up.

'No, no, my dear, you know Sofiane, he always did have his head in the clouds! Remember how whenever he passed your house he pretended not to see you?'

My little performance earned me a week of peace and happiness. The old bat didn't believe a word of my rigmarole, but it hardly mattered since all she needs to do her scandalmongering is her tongue and a little spit.

That night, I didn't sleep a wink. I scrubbed the house from top to bottom, I might even have cleaned it twice. While I was about it, I did the laundry, then I pottered around. I felt like I was in Kubrick's *The Shining* just before all hell is unleashed. On my wanderings I discovered a makeshift corridor on the second floor running from the back of an old wardrobe to a sort of box-room – it was beyond me how I had never noticed it before. The door to the box-room creaked like it was a thousand years old. Slave quarters? A place to hide when things were tough? It was probably something constructed by the Turk, those people have a lot going on under their fezzes. Inside, I expected to find a skeleton or see a ghost surge forward and slip between my legs, but nothing. The room smelled of mildew. No gold doubloons, no pirate map, no clue what to do next. Some day I'll leave a sheet of mysterious drawings here that will help my successor live, secure in the knowledge that his life will be rich and carefree. A pinch of gold dust, and the results would be better. This rickety old house evolved over time, there's always something left to explore.

Then, suddenly, my knees gave out. I'd overexerted myself. I went back to the living room and lay down, I read a book. I went into the kitchen and made some herbal tea and sipped it as I watched the cockroaches gorging on scraps of food. It's been a long time since I've waged war against them. The future belongs to cockroaches. In some old scientific magazine I read that the more you persecute them the stronger they get, so I leave them be in the hopes that indolence and overeating will kill them off. Then, sadly, I listened to the radio babble on about this and that, a phone-in for parish-pump problems from far-flung, probably fictional listeners convinced their nightly ramblings are advancing some great cause. Tonight's topic: civic-mindedness and household refuse. To a man (and woman), they put the blame on everyone else, not one of them was prepared to take any responsibility. The pathetic fools. When you're this deluded, better to keep your mouth shut and not spout such drivel! When you've made your bed, you have to lie in it.

Then I wept and wept and wept.

I can't help but wonder what times they are I'm living through. Things fell apart so quickly. Was there ever a before? Did I ever really live? Did I ever have anything other than my beloved parents who died too soon, my idiot little brother who disappeared into himself or is in the process of doing so? And Yacine, my big brother, who died by the roadside having known no greater love than his rickety old banger. It is easy to be overwhelmed by such emptiness. What century is it out there? The din and the dust that reach me in brutal waves have nothing of interest to say to me. The world has taken a wrong turning, ominous Islam and garish consumerism are battling it out with mantras and slogans. Their conflicting cacophony makes my ears hurt. Here in Algeria, even time itself – humanity's world heritage – is torn between rabid reactionism and a ghastly futurism; its energy, its drive, its clarity have all been sapped. To embrace such twisted logic is to embrace the void. To say one thing is also to believe the contrary, it is to plunge furiously, hobbled and blinkered, into the fray. Why the blindfold? I don't know. Time to these mutants is what dark glasses are to the blind man, it speaks to their inability to see and their inability to do. Through their fault or Voltaire's, my life has gradually shrunk to nothing, to less than nothing, to a series of fits and starts between waking and sleeping before it stops altogether just as the clock in the hall fell silent when its master died. Time, where I am concerned, is a hodgepodge, a thing of shreds and patches, it blends scraps of my – happy but unfinished – childhood, a little of what I read, a lot of what I watch on television, fragments of dreams, a goodly helping of what fury proclaims to the four winds and, on a day-by-day basis, dictates my course of action. I have fashioned a life for myself that does not depend on money or on incense, I have no truck with religion, with clutter or procrastination. Or perhaps this is simply the way things are when you retreat to a desert island, when you sit rusting in a traffic jam. You make do with what you have. To be perfectly honest, I've never understood where wishes come from nor how disappointments are made, all I know is that I don't care a tinker's curse for the rantings of the truth-mongers. Like Penelope, I am deaf to suitors, committed to my work. My loneliness is my shield.

In this life, you have to hold your own if you hope to emerge unscathed.

The house – my house – has left me no choice. There are mornings, those gloomy mornings that seem like a painful prolongation of the night, when I feel as though I am a prisoner, albeit a willing one since I have no place else to hide. The house is over two hundred years old, I keep a weather eye on it, but I know, I can sense, that one day it will crumble with me inside. The house dates back to the seventeenth century, to the Regency of Algiers. The rooms are poky, the windows Lilliputian, the doors low and the stairs, which are treacherous, were clearly made by carpenters who had one leg shorter than the other and very narrow minds. This perhaps explains – if explanation be needed – why everyone in my family grew up to have one calf muscle thicker than the other, a pronounced stoop, a waddle like a duck and very narrow minds. It has nothing to do with genetics; the house made us that way. Back then, the perpendicular was a mystery, since in this house lines never marry at right-angles, because they were never introduced by the mason's trowel. It is a shock to the eyes. The nose, too, since a musty smell impregnates the walls. Sometimes I feel like an ant in a maze, sometimes like Alice in Wonderland.

The house was built by an officer of the Ottoman court – an *Effendi* – a certain Mustafa Al Malik, whose name and coat of arms can still be seen to the left of the entrance, carved into an ornate marble plaque worn away by the years. Which is why people in the neighbourhood refer to us as *the House of Mustafa*. It's a little unfortunate, since the man had a terrible reputation for being a paedophile – though back in those days, such crimes were tolerated in polite society.

The house's charm comes from the primitive mosaics, the nooks like the holes in Gruyère cheese into which are set old brasses, narrow corridors and the steep staircases which meander this way and that. Mystery pervades this house, around every corner is a ghost in a *djellaba*, a goateed genie rubbing his lamp, an overweight courtesan chained to a wizened old crone, a pot-bellied vizier plotting against the Caliph. Of course there is nothing really there, and yet you feel as though you might encounter anything.

I grew up shrouded in this atmosphere, so it is hardly surprising that it has distorted my sense of time. Things would be different if I had grown up in an overcrowded tower block in some blighted suburb, on a marshy plain buffeted by the fumes from factories. Here I have space to dream to my heart's content, all I lack are the funds. My salary is more conducive to sleepless nights than idle days.

After the death of the Turk, the house embarked upon a new career. Whether by a twist of fate, or because it was built on the highest point of what would later be called the Rampe Valée – named after the Maréchal de France and Governor-General of Algeria whose contemporaries said he ruled with an iron fist in a velvet glove – but whatever the reason, the Turkish officer was succeeded by a French officer, a certain Colonel Louis-Joseph de la Buissière, who was a viscount besides. His name and coat of arms are carved on the right-hand side of the pediment on a garlanded marble plaque eaten away by time. Nothing is known about his military career. I assume he earned his rank by proving himself on the battlefield, unless it was his by virtue of his ancestry. The fall of Charles X in 1830 brought about his own fall since, being a legitimist and a romantic, the colonel refused to allow the tricolour to replace the white cockade on his regimental pennant. He resigned his commission before he could be dismissed by Republican *arrivistes* and melted into the crowd of nobodies in Algiers. He was also a respected naturalist whose name features in the prestigious gazettes that paper the attic. He criss-crossed the wilds of Algeria on foot, by caleche, under the blazing sun, pencil in hand, making notes and sketches of everything the desert could offer up to his insatiable curiosity. He filled several volumes with extraordinarily meticulous drawings. It's funny how beautiful a bitter, stunted, sprig of goat's-foot can become beneath the scientist's pencil. But little minds have little respect so the gazettes ended up in the attic where they have fed generations of mice hungry for knowledge. The world is as it is, made up of scholars and simpletons; what the former create the latter destroy. Somewhat belatedly, in the grip of who knows what passion, the colonel embraced Islam and married one of its daughters, a certain Mériem, the youngest child of a respectable apothecary in the Kasbah and took the name Youssef, which is simply the Arabic spelling of Joseph, favoured son of Jacob and Rachel. It was generally accepted that the colonel was a devout believer and he is often cited whenever someone feels the need to demonstrate how Islam is superior to all other religions. It has to be said that when famous Christians convert, it's a bonus, which is why there's so much media hype about Western celebrities who suddenly go over to Islam. I don't really understand why these people embrace Islam with the sort of bluster usually reserved for defecting to the enemy. There's a lot of *nah, nah, nah-nah, nah!* in their neurons. Now, a Muslim who converted to Christianity wouldn't admit to it under torture, he wouldn't tell his confessor, he would continue showing up to the mosque, fervent and fearless as a Taliban. It doesn't matter, let people believe whatever they want as long as they don't use it as an excuse to go around bumping people off. As it says in the Book: '*I have sent to you the Qur'an and Muhammad to close the prophetic cycle of revelations.*' Thus it is permitted to grow and to improve, which is precisely what the viscount serenely did. The good Youssef died in the odour of sanctity at the ripe old age of ninety-something, he passed away in bed surrounded by relatives and friends, but there were those in Paris who were puzzled by his curious end. Being so far from civilisation, they expected him to die a violent death, to kick the bucket in some unseemly fashion, or at the very least to expire from some fever obscure enough to be considered exotic. And perhaps in the end he did, though in those days people were more likely to die of old age, starvation, an excess of sun or a kick from a horse though I'll admit one could also die of a malaria epidemic, a plague of locusts or a dagger between the shoulder blades. The colonel left an estate that was enough to tempt the most disinterested observer, since he had substantial properties in Barbary as in his native Sologne. There ensued a confabulation between solicitors and much coming and going between Algiers and Paris. With consummate skill, the shysters quickly scoured the law books to see what portion they could reserve for the rich and what pittance might be left to the poor and order was thereby restored. They evicted old Madame Mériem with only her memories while the French branch of the de la Buissière family succeeded in clinging to their inheritance.

The house was entrusted to a certain Daoud Ben Chekroun, a Jew from Bab Azoun who made a living brokering property deals between the retreating Turks and the advancing French and would end his life as rich as Croesus. At least that's what it says on the daguerreotype we have which depicts him hunkered, leaning against a tumbledown hovel, one hand flicking a bull's tail flyswatter, as hairy and dishevelled as an old gorilla. But I suppose it's possible for a man to be rich and underhand. And we can't rule out the possibility that he hoodwinked the photographer who in all good faith immortalised him in his poverty. The local elders of Rampe Valée, who convene their meetings in a *café maure* at the bottom of the valley, could think of no better names for the Turk's citadel than *the Frenchman's palace*, *the Convert's fortress*, *the Jew's lair*, *the crow's nest*, *the fox's den*. The names stuck and did us considerable harm. Applied to us, devout Muslims since birth, in a free, independent, overzealous country imbued with Arabo-Islamic contempt, 'convert' meant '*kafir*', 'Frenchman' was synonymous with *harki* – the name given to the traitorous Algerians who fought with the French during the War of Independence – and what could the word 'Jew' mean but 'thief'? The fact that we earned our living as indefatigable shopkeepers only served to fuel the rumours.

It is to Monsieur Louis-Joseph that we owe the magnificent fireplace in the parlour, the passageway that leads into the garden, the conversion of the *hammam* into a bathroom and of the baker's oven into a modern kitchen. He cleverly solved the water problem by sinking a well in the garden and installing a labyrinthine network of pipes. Being warmhearted and compassionate, he erected a public drinking fountain on the street which, in the short term, bankrupted the local trader who peddled this precious commodity and in the long term sparked a bitter war between those who voted to keep the fountain and the free water, and those who maintained the water was poisoned and brought forward as many snivelling witnesses as there were beggars in the medina. While he was about it, Monsieur Louis-Joseph installed a splendid grandfather clock in the hall whose golden pendulum was later substituted for a lead weight by some light-fingered person. Ever since, weighed down with lead, it has groaned as though being tortured. Having converted to become Youssef, he had his study-cum-oratory decorated with beautiful tiles bearing *suras* from the Qur'an calligraphed by great poets, he divided the ground-floor living room in two, placing a stunning *mashrabiya* down the middle to create one side for the men, the other for women. On the first floor, he had a gynaeceum – a harem – built, sealed on four sides, and fitted with all the modern conveniences so beloved of subjugated females: a coal-fired stove, a pitcher and a washbowl. He raised the walls surrounding the house and topped them with shards of glass to reinforce the prison atmosphere I find so painful now that there is fighting in the streets, now that I have reinforced the doors and windows and no longer go out. Finally, he installed a charming ablutions area where the faithful could perform *wudu*.

After Ben Chekroun had finished his labours, the house fell into the hands of an immigrant newly arrived from far-off Transylvania. We never quite knew what that meant, but we suspected that he was Romanian by day, Hungarian by night and a ferryman in times of trouble. It was as he took his last step down the steamship's gangplank that the rogue and the stranger met by sheer chance. It is possible that, as has been attested, the deal was struck quickly and quietly in the best interests of all concerned. But that is simply legalistic jargon, a magical incantation; I am more inclined to believe that two deaf-mutes could not have made more noise in trying to make themselves heard. Ben Chekroun was, after all, a man of some importance and the newcomer was not just anyone. He is remembered as a character who might have stepped straight out of the silver screen. Perhaps it is possible to be born in the Carpathians and retain one's humanity, but our character believed only in the supernatural. Vampires were his friends, he spoke of them as of some eternal truth. When he arrived, he bore the unpronounceable name Tartem-something-or-other; his first name, a real tongue-twister, was Crzhyk-I-forget-what. A simple greeting was a real mouthful. Back in the snow-capped mountains of Transylvania, he had served a *Voivode* – a warlord – descended from the race of Phanariotes about whom the literature of the region has nothing good to say. In short, he had learned from a master the gentle art of treachery. I suspect the negotiations were dramatic and long-drawn-out and attracted a vast crowd. A quick trip to the town hall and suddenly our friend Tartem-thingumabob declares himself ready to die for the country of Rousseau. Immediately, the insults hurled at him by first-generation immigrants ceased. Overnight, he became just another *pied noir* like everyone else. Back then, integration simply meant shucking your shoes and donning a beret. Once you'd done that, you could run around proclaiming that you had truly arrived. '*Ze suis frantuzească!*' he roared, as the Negroes on the docks waiting for corvettes might have yelled '*Bwana, bwana!*' I assume people said such things, it was in the spirit of the times, part of the local colour of the period, like gas streetlamps. From that day forth, he styled himself François Carpatus. He cannily established a reputation as an excellent repairman, which brought customers to his ironmongery-cum-seed-merchants-cum-grocery-cum-haberdashery-cum-gunsmiths-cum-perfumery, a chaotic Aladdin's cave of the kind that existed long ago. A terror of vampires, hitherto unknown in our part of the world, mysteriously spread through the *medina* and with it the remedies to be rid of it, from garlic braids to consecrated wooden stakes. It was François Carpatus who converted our barn into a shop, something that proved extremely profitable for those who came after him – all except for Doctor Montaldo, the last occupant of the house before we arrived. Nor was it particularly profitable for us, since by then the Algerian government had decided to adopt the Soviet model of feeding a starving populace, and we were not granted a licence to run a shop (Papa dreamed of owning a delicatessen stocked with everything that anyone could want).

Towards the end of his life, at the turn of the twentieth century, M. Carpatus suffered a mysterious ailment, a sort of delirium tremens brought on by an overdose of garlic. After a number of fruitless treatments, he emigrated to the United States and was never heard of again. American vampires clearly did not recognise him as one of their own.

It's difficult to know exactly what happened next, the machinations and the manoeuvres, the whole business was shrouded in secrecy, but the house was bought by . . . a certain Daoud Ben Chekroun! By this time, Carpatus was no longer in his right mind and may rashly have sold his assets at a knock-down price; then again, pretending to be mad can be a great advantage in negotiations.

All sorts of ridiculous rumours have been circulated by wagging tongues about the aforementioned Mustafa, Louis-Joseph-Youssef, Ben Chekroun, Carpatus. A crooked Turk, a Frenchman who stumbled into the melting pot of Islam, a wandering Jew, an abominable snowman from the Carpathians, a Doctor Schweitzer who died on the job. What better tales to inspire a wandering storyteller? As children we lapped it up, we delighted in these far-fetched stories which also enhanced the prestige of our house. Genies, vampires, hidden treasures, apparitions by prophets, paranormal phenomena, Jewish fables, we had stories enough to while away many a pleasant evening. Other people might have envied us.

These tales still run through my head, they fuse, they feed on one another, speaking in their different tongues, garbed in their different costumes. I shift from one century to another, one foot here and my head on some distant continent. This explains why I seem to be from everywhere and nowhere, a stranger in this country and yet firmly entrenched within these walls. Nothing is more relative than the origin of things.

Fantasies have always been the means of killing time in

Rampe Valée. People who live by old stories do not notice the passing of time, if I can put it like that.

Throughout the first half of the twentieth century – a dismal period – the house was occupied by various nonentities, pen-pushers, newcomers, large families. They all knew Daoud Ben Chekroun through his kids, Jacob, Zadok, Elijah and his great-nephews Ephraim and Mordecai (though they knew them by their Muslim names). Sceptics might suspect some posthumous ploy on the part of the old curmudgeon, but in fact the subterfuge was dictated by events. The turbulent period was marked by successive waves of Jewish immigrants to Algeria which, with a contemptuous click of their tongue, people back then brazenly referred to as the Yid Invasions. Such prejudices were fuelled by the Socialist anti-Jewish leagues, the Crémieux Decree, the Dreyfus Affair and Musette's tales of the vagabond Cagayous. This is history, it is convoluted and calamitous. The newcomers, as I said, stayed just long enough to put together a case file and lodge it with the town hall. Meanwhile, an ideal habitat for the Town Mouse had just been devised: the tower block. As wealth trickled down to the colonies, tower blocks sprang up in Algiers and its suburbs. A vast procession of people cheerfully rushed to live there, transporting their belongings in vans, in handcarts, on pack mules, in convoys led by children singing at the tops of their voices as little old ladies trailed behind devoutly muttering *suras*. No sooner had they climbed the stairs and set up camp than pennants – and laundry – were hoisted on the balconies. The war between neighbours could now begin. As I set down the story of my misfortunes, that war is beginning to seem like a massacre, one covertly fuelled by those who work as government officials by day and estate agents by night. At the foot of the stairwells, the children finish off the wounded and race to see the imam for their reward. All these fleeting comings and goings did much damage to the house. The series of 'renovations' proved in time to be mutilations: veneer, formica, linoleum and leatherette gradually invaded the venerable old house driving out the terracotta floor-tiles, the stucco, the mosaics and the coppers, even the lingering smell of old leather. It was a terrible shame.

The neighbourhood changed radically. It became a warren. Buildings sprang up here and there, this way and that, aslant and askew, seedy hovels and lavish residences, a maze of narrow streets and blind alleys appeared out of nowhere and with them crooked flights of steps, rubbish tips, open sewers, filthy gutters, cowsheds, cheap restaurants, a synagogue, seven mosques, some sort of temple that vanished into the crowd, three cemeteries, cramped shops, brothels, overflow pipes, smithies and, later, two or three schools built of corrugated iron on the children's playgrounds and a complaints office that was burned to the ground on the precise day and time it was inaugurated by the mayor and his entourage of estate agents. Out of the misery of the mid-twentieth century, a *favela* was born, one that may endure for centuries.

And yet, for the longest time I found it impossibly

romantic to be living here in Rampe Valée, this tangled world where mystery and misery battled it out in a hell of noise and dust and mud. It was a particular phase in my life when I subscribed to a certain idea of utopia, I was discovering Gandhi and Mother Teresa, Rimbaud and his cohorts, I felt a kinship with Calcutta, with Mogadishu, with the ghettos of Pretoria and the *favelas* of Bahia. I was electrified by tragedies in far-flung places. These days I've had enough, now I dream only of palaces, of carriages, of high society, of passionate fleeting affairs.

Opposite our lavish mansion was a drab little house, a sand-castle crowned with a peaked cap built by a man about whom we never really knew anything. Some said he worked on the streetcars, others that he worked for the National Tobacco and Safety Match Corporation, that he was a fitter for the gas company, a sales rep for Orangina, a tax inspector, a cement packer with Lafarge, a teacher of some unknown subject, and various other things. Too much information is no information. In short, everyone had their own view of him. During the war he was rarely spotted. After Independence, he disappeared or at least he kept a low profile. Some insisted that he was a traitor who had secretly supported French rule as an active member of the OAS and that sinister meetings had taken place within these walls, while others maintained it had been used as a safe house by one of the leaders of the FLN during the Battle of Algiers. Gradually, people began to forget, they left behind those stories of good guys and bad guys. Life after Independence was no bed of roses, the good ship Algeria was being skippered by

70

incompetents and crooks, everyone aboard was panicking. With time memories fade, but they emerge again and so the thread of history remains unbroken. We told each other strange stories, about how our enigmatic neighbour had abandoned the house across the road because it was hunted – I mean *haunted*. It was a sorry sight, shrouded in cobwebs, creepers and weeds and encased like an ancient mummy in desiccated bird droppings. Only a single pair of shuttered windows is still visible; the windows that face my house. A ghost was the only logical explanation for such a baleful building and so that was what we decided, and ever after- wards we called it *the ghost's house*. This is the ghost I now call Bluebeard. The neighbours give him other names, each related to their deepest fears: Bouloulou, Barbapoux, Azrael, Frankenstein, Dracula, Fantômas.

Only the old-timers still remember the period the good Doctor Montaldo spent living here. They refer to it as *the poor man's house*, as though God himself had sojourned here and they resent me for not carrying on the tradition. I pull a few strings for them at the hospital when I have a chance, it's my way of applying a little arnica to their memory, of earning their respect. The good doctor spent too much of his time tending to the poor and needy, he gave little thought to repairs, to comfort, to cosiness. His legacy includes a basin and a tap in the room he once used as his surgery, a collection of surgical instruments and medical books – which proved very useful to me in my studies. It's astonishing how, in the past half a century, medical knowl- edge has changed without really changing. There is some indefinable difference between the textbooks of then and now, but I'm too dim to spot it. I would say it was context, but where does that get us? Mourad talks about governance, in fact it's all he talks about, but I don't know what the word means. I'm not ashamed to admit that medicine is just a job to me, there is nothing profound or poetic about it. How the hell can anyone practise genuine, sincere, caring, holistic medicine when everything – people, ethics, cities, hospitals – is going to hell in a handcart? If proof were needed, the good doctor died penniless and exhausted while many of his patients ended up rich and powerful. Many went on to rule us with an iron hand and their successors – military and religious – still do so today.

The memory of Doctor Montaldo brings a human face to my relationship with time even though I disapprove of treating villains as effectively as honest folk. In choosing paediatrics, I opted for the innocent; with children there can be no qualms of conscience, nice or not you treat them just the same and – *hup!* – off to bed.

Finally my family arrived here on a September day in the year of our Lord 1962. It was a Sunday, the sun was at its height, we stepped into the house as into a temple, heads bowed, awe-stricken. At least that's how I imagine the scene, since I came into the world somewhat later. We had come from Kabylia – from the mountains, the poverty, the cold – and we were little more than troglodytes, stubborn to the marrow and in permanent revolt against the Caïd and the capital. Now we found ourselves perched high above the capital, living in this magnificent mansion – vast, labyrinthine, mysterious, Olympian. And antiquated, with deep wrinkles and a look about it as though it had forgotten how to weather time. How Papa came to own this house I have no idea; he had his secrets and he took them to his grave. I was born ten years after my older brother Yacine on an October day in 1966. For seven long years, war had kept my parents apart, and it took them three more years to learn to rekindle the passion of lovebirds. Papa needed to forget the harsh realities of the *maquis* while Maman needed to remember what, over time, she had forgotten. We were the first native-born Algerians to own this extraordinary house. We felt as though, since the dawn of time, it had been waiting for us to arrive when in fact we hadn't had the first idea where we were going. Uprooted from our mountain lair, we looked out at the sky as though it were boundless. The house had known so many people, had travelled far and wide. It taught us much about ourselves and about its former occupants. Scarcely credible stories of lives as hazy as mirages, true tales filled with spice and suspense. The lightest ones always float to the surface, but vast, unfathomed depths lie beneath, throbbing like a pulsar. How would we ever have known of the existence of vampires if the mysterious Carpatus had stayed in his native Transylvania? The *djinns* that populated our oldest memories suddenly seemed less powerful, but they were more sympathetic since they fed, not on hot blood sucked from the carotid artery of another human being, but upon the same misery we did. Would I have chosen to study medicine had I not stumbled upon Doctor Montaldo's textbooks as a girl? Where else would we have come upon the stories, the sayings, the jokes from distant lands that enlivened our evenings? Not to mention the humdrum things we gradually discovered about life, the world, the customs and habits of different peoples, the way their stories intertwined with ours, and the interminable questions that clutter the mind from dawn till dusk – the why of one thing, the how of another – and all that this entails, the obsessive fears, the wounded silences, the constant migraines. An ancient house is a succession of stories laid down in strata, thick or thin, with evil sprites flitting along seams and veins. And this is how we experienced it – in exaltation, striving and doubt.

Everything about this place speaks of ancient mysteries.

This house, my house, has also taught me sorrow, fear and loneliness.

That is the story of my family. The house is the centre, time is Ariadne's thread which must be uncoiled without being broken. I am the last to live here. When I am gone, it will crumble and the story will be over.

While brooding about all this and cursing Sofiane's recklessness, I had a sort of epiphany: yesterday, today and doubtless tomorrow and on until the end of time, more people have fled this country than have arrived. There is no logic to it, it is not in the nature of the earth to bring forth a vacuum, no mother dreams of driving her children away and no man has the right to uproot another from his birthplace. It is a curse that has survived from century to century from Roman times when we were wild-eyed Circumcellions razing farms all the way to the present day when, since we cannot all burn our bridges and flee, we live with our bags permanently packed. This is a huge country, vast enough to accommodate whole peoples; if necessary we could have taken more from our neighbours who don't need so much space, but no, at some point or other the curse returns and the vacuum brutally swells. Since the beginning of time we have always been *harragas*, those who burn a path, such is the course of our history.

Could it be that my time to leave was coming?

Algiers never ceases to amaze. Though it is a master of the low blow, it knows how to take care of its own and, when one of them is in the depths of despair, it never fails to throw her a lifeline. Today was one of those auspicious days for which Algiers is famous. The heatwave unexpectedly abated, the southerly wind shifted and now blew from the north, singing through the leaves. The air was filled with the whispers of the Mediterranean, its subtle scents, its piquant charms, its musky pleasures, its sun-dappled dreams. And the natives of Algiers, the worst city dwellers of the century, suddenly, eagerly, surrender to peace. They are amazed, they look at each other in shock, but still they forge ahead, curious to discover the extent of this illusion. One thing leads to another, there is a surge of optimism, a ripple of friendliness and before they know it people begin to think that this, too, is life. Suddenly, there is an outpouring of joy and a glorious torrent of heedless happiness sweeps across the city like a *wadi* bursting its banks. Hearts stirring, the women feel themselves come alive, they dare to raise their heads, to steal a glance through their *hijabs*. It is perfect bliss to see them taking part in life, to witness their strange and fascinating radiance dispel the darkness and the pain. God Himself is moved by such a sight, you can see it in the faces of the children which glow with good intentions. People dazzle so brightly it puts their drab Islamic rags to shame and they risk being publicly excommunicated. This just goes to prove that people should never give up their instinctive irreverence; some day the Islamists will dig their own graves and people will mock their shrivelled poisonous humps. On a day like today the Islamists feel ill at ease, swept up by the tide of joy, hemmed in on all sides, they scrabble away desperately, run to their caves there to dream of the glorious crimes against humanity yet to be committed. The exultant atmosphere of celebration begins to course through the streets, to scale the buildings, to flash from one person to the next. This is a critical moment: the devil himself, tail whipping high above his horns, might suddenly appear and ruin everything. When Algiers is beautiful, it happens of a sudden. She wrong-foots her citizens. It is love at first sight. We think of her as a wizened old crone who died in misery and is buried beneath the dust, but still sometimes she steps into the light, she dazzles, bewitches, steals, ravishes, enchants. After a little prenuptial perplexity, the city grows more civilised in leaps and bounds, great discoveries are anticipated. We would dearly love to make the most of our good fortune, to pause this moment, to bask in this hopefulness, build castles in the air; but we know Algiers all too well, she is a pantomime villain, playing the innocent is her favourite trick. Because we know this, whenever she strikes a pose we simply shrug. We simply dare to wish that a crowd of tourists would arrive in one of these magical moments so that we might surprise them, might strip away the precon- ceptions they have about our nonsensical stories, our dirty wars, our conspiracies against reason, our crimes against the heart, our medieval customs, our insufferable weather, our tortuous geography. Algiers is a trollop who gives of herself the better to take. Her going rate is five minutes of pleasure for one month of bitterness.

A straw mattress in the hand is worth a four-poster glimpsed on the silver screen. Maman had her little maxims, she served them up for dinner with endless split-pea soup: *If you don't eat it, you'll be sorry in an hour.* Now, I mutter them to myself to help me endure the grinding poverty, but I don't make a business of it like the people who run around with their hands out, going from pillar to post, from bank to bank, shamelessly pleading and prattling. In Algeria, the poor – like the rich – are ruthless, they're constantly running, tackling, dribbling, scheming, gradually gaining ground. Nowhere in the world have people better mastered the trick of distracting someone's attention in order to steal their place in a queue. But what is wealth when people don't know the value of things? And what is poverty when people scorn knowledge? Those who would overcome misery must first accept it! It's time for the poor to decide whether they want to stay in a hole or climb out, and for the rich to learn how to behave. The way they behave drives me mad.

All this to say that Algiers is no picnic.

There I was, slowly trudging home, dog-tired but deliriously happy to be leaving the hospital, looking left and right, thinking to myself how wonderful life would be if everyone would stop lying. I made the usual detours to avoid the women who lurk on their doorsteps, waiting for news. For as long as I can remember they have stood there, waiting, in fruitless, uncertain expectation. They no longer remember why they're waiting; time has forgotten them, only the ritual remains, carved into their daily routine. Each woman brings a personal touch to her vigil: tears, prayers, tremulous dirges, pitiful pleas to the men who stop and stare, and crude obscenities at those who pompously look straight ahead. I always pretend to be preoccupied with things I need to buy on the way home – milk, bread, water, vegetables, candles, salt, insecticide – so that I can give the impression of an absent-minded woman innocently remembering something she has forgotten. It's best to pretend to be deaf to the calls from behind you. I'm tired of having to bring news of the outside world to these women who have cut themselves off. In fact, they are the crux of the problem, I can understand that they need to know their fate, but for pity's sake, why can't they just read the State newspapers!

I have to admit I can be a hateful bitch sometimes.

Parked outside my door I discovered a sinister contraption like a bus that had been spared the wrecking yard, a heap of twisted metal designed to ferry the dead. I've never seen anything like it in the neighbourhood. The streets here are so narrow that cars scrape their bodywork as they pass. A stone's throw away, in the Kasbah, it's like driving through the eye of a needle. The streets of the Kasbah are so narrow that when two pedestrians try to pass each other, one has to reverse or abandon her family. After a flicker of hesitation born of fear – *hup!* – I dashed inside my house and double-locked the door behind me. I just had time to see a figure in the bus waving and gesticulating.

Routine makes us deaf and blind. I never notice buses in the city, never hear their horns honking. There are so many and they make such an infernal racket, they're like bulls in a *corrida*, hooves thundering across the sand, herding together at bus stops, muzzles steaming, bellowing like rutting bulls, jostling each other for space, only to belch black smoke then roar away in a cloud of dust. Want to know what a bullfight at a *feria* sounds like? There's one outside my house right now, plain as the nose on my face, covered with a moth-eaten caparison, bellowing fit to burst. Then *bang, bang,* someone pounds on my door. Of course, I brush aside my fears, I open the door and who is standing there, looking more like Lolita than ever … Chérifa! And, as always, at her feet is her magic holdall.

My heart soared heavenwards.

And my eyes rolled heavenwards. Behind the shutters, Bluebeard's shadow shifted this way and that like a hunchback dancing a jig. I remembered an image from Perrault's fairytale, a devoted sister watching from the battlements, hoping for deliverance. *Oh, Bluebeard, Sister Anne was right, Chérifa has come home to us!*

Behind her comes the bus driver, teeth clenched into a smile like a boy scout who's done the good deed of the century. Did I invite this guy?

The rules of hospitality are what they are, but I really feel they could do with a little clarification. The matter of preconditions isn't addressed, for example, or the problem of consequences. Before offering hospitality, it would be nice to know whether it's compulsory, what the conditions are and whether – when it's over and done with – you'll have the strength to stomach the sense of indignation. We wouldn't find ourselves so frequently put upon, upset, humiliated and disgraced if we took the necessary measures and sent people packing.

In this case, the bus driver – whose name, like the number on his vehicle – was 235, proved to be a crude but charming individual. I have fond memories of him.

This, then, was how things had played out, not in the way Mourad had suggested. Mourad obviously doesn't understand the first thing about girls. No bus stations, no university halls of residence.

Whenever I come through a crisis, I tend to become a little crazy. I threw myself at Chérifa, prepared to tear her to pieces on the spot.

'You could at least have let me know you were alive …' I spat in her face. 'You had me worried half to death!'

'But, Tata, you said not to come back!'

'I said, I said … that doesn't mean you had to believe me!'

'Well, as it happens, I didn't believe you … that's why I'm back.'

'That's still no reason!'

The bus driver was staring at us, his headlights on full. The day men finally learn to listen to women without standing around looking pathetic is still a long way off.

'So tell me, my dear Monsieur 235, what were you doing when you crossed paths with Chérifa and what exactly have you done to her since?'

The guy was obviously not one of nature's storytellers. He seemed to think that our actions are entirely decided by *mektoub* – fate. Which didn't get me very far. A storyteller who doesn't give his characters room to develop has no business in a *souk*. The whole reason people tell stories is because they're sick to the back teeth of *mektoub*, we want our characters to act, to take decisions, hatch plots, screw up, land on their feet like a cat, win the game, make the sultan look ridiculous, we don't want pathetic creatures like ourselves who wait pointlessly for heaven to send us a sign.

'What could I do, sister? Three days ago, this girl got on my bus first thing in the morning while the engine was still cold and coughing like it had tuberculosis, I couldn't even change gears. I've told the supervisor a thousand times that imported engine oil is better than domestic, but he'd rather foul up the engines – it makes no sense, I mean, we're talking thoroughbred Magirus Deutz motors, they only speak German!'

'Why can't they be converted into Arabic?'

'You're not allowed, it invalidates the warranty. Anyway, like I was saying, I work route 12, from Chevalley to La Grande Poste via Rampe Valée. That's a lot of steep hills, as you know yourself. So anyway, she takes a ticket and she sits behind me. Even looking at her in the rear-view mirror I could tell she was . . . well . . . a lost soul. Her *mektoub* . . .'

'Yes, let's leave her *mektoub* out of this . . .'

'She spent the whole day sitting in the same seat,

shuttling back and forth from Chevalley to La Poste, La Poste to Chevalley. Well in the end she fell asleep, as you can imagine . . .'

'I can easily imagine, I feel myself nodding off right now, but I'd like to hear the end of the story . . . So, where were we?'

'What's the matter, Tata? He's telling it just like it happened, I swear.'

'I'll believe you, I'll believe anything, I realise disbelief is not an option . . . So, monsieur, you were saying?'

'At 8 pm, when I finished my shift, I said to her, I said: Last stop! All change, please!"

'And did she change?'

'No, she asked if she could sleep on the bus. I've never heard the like. I told her it was impossible, that it was against regulations, I have to take the bus back to the garage and you're not allowed in there.'

'The plot thickens.'

'Absolutely not, we're devout Muslims, we know all about hospitality. I said to her if you've nowhere to sleep, you can come back to our house, my mother would be happy to have the company. The poor thing, she . . .'

'OK, so you get to the house and . . .?'

'My mother looked after her like she was her own daughter. You have to understand, I'm an only child, and I'm a man and *amah* needs someone she can talk to about cooking and cleaning, someone who'll listen to her problems . . .'

'I can well understand her. And then what?'

'So, anyway, three days later, this morning to be precise, the girl says to me, I'm coming with you.'

'Would you credit it! And?'

'So she came with me. And after a little while, when I was inspecting the bus before taking it back to the garage in case anyone had left their papers or their lunchbox under a seat, she says to me: I'm going back to Tata Lamia.'

'That's me!'

'So, well, anyway, I brought her back to you. Now, I must dash, the depot closes at 8.30 pm sharp.'

'Not before you have a glass of lemonade, dear Monsieur 235. I know a little about hospitality myself, and it doesn't only work one way; besides, the garage is hardly likely to vanish because it's missing a bus.'

'A minute late is a minute too late!'

'Only in Switzerland, my friend, only in Switzerland. Here in Algeria, it's more like: where there's life there's leeway. We'll tell the depot that the bus broke down, it probably happens six times a week and if they can put up with six, they'll put up with seven.'

And then the gallant bus driver told me his life story. This is it in a nutshell: at the age of sixteen, he was hired by the Greater Algiers Urban Transport Authority – GAUTA – where, by dint of perseverance and engine oil, he worked his way from cleaner to grease monkey to bus conductor right up to the dizzy heights of bus driver in less than twenty years. And from here? Ticket inspector, if God wills it. And why should God not will it, isn't it what He has always wanted, to punish fare-dodgers and nit-pickers? Maybe, but his bosses operate on a different policy: they give jobs to their friends. Things had taken a philosophical turn, so I put on the brakes. Was there life after work? Truth to tell, he had never had time to dawdle, he spent his leisure hours looking after his saintly mother and his great dream was for her to make the pilgrimage to Mecca. Married? No, unfortunately, *mektoub* had dictated otherwise. His problem is he's an awkward so-and-so who wants everything to be perfect for him and his elderly mother. Any sporting activities? Pétanque with his co-workers sometimes during lunch break, but otherwise ... Hey, wait a minute, do you shoot or do you point, I've heard that in pétanque it makes all the difference? Um ... it depends. So, what else? Fishing, during holidays. And? Dominoes with friends in the neighbourhood and um ... going to the mosque on Fridays. And I'll bet you watch TV? Oh yes, every night.

Good old 235 clearly lived a life almost as thrilling and hectic as my own, all that was missing was the essential, those little extras that make the heart skip a beat. I was sad to see him drive away in his thirteen-wheeled, four-eyed dragon.

The Greater Algiers Urban Transport Authority is very fortunate to have a man of such calibre. As is his sainted mother. There aren't many like him these days. Though she might loosen the aprons strings a bit, the poor guy needs to let his hair down.

Chérifa left me in a foul mood and has returned to find me in a foul mood. The little baggage is completely brazen, she sulks, she does a bunk, she shows up whenever it suits her, she brings bus drivers to my door. People behave better in hotels – you let the hotel know when you'll be arriving, when you'll be leaving, you leave your taxi driver at the door, you're polite to the staff, you put your things away, you flush the toilet and turn off the tap when the water is running low. A few rules and a little common decency are essential in any family. She should tell me everything, whether there are people looking for her, whether she's in danger, whether . . . Well, the possibilities are endless.

'Now listen to me, *mademoiselle*, since my idiot brother has cleverly finagled things, I'm prepared to put you up, but let me tell you right now that my home is not a hotel, and it's not a crèche where you can drop off your little problems. Now it's not an army barracks, either, but I do expect a little discipline – assuming you know what the word means – and you'll need a permit if you're going out!'

'But, Tata, I can't stay cooped up in here!'

'You go out when I go out . . . is that clear?'

'Hmm.'

'I said is that clear?'

'Hmmmm!'

'Now, here's the deal. Tomorrow, I'll take you for a check-up, we need to know what's in that belly of yours. Then we're going to get rid of these frills and fripperies you're wearing and get you a wardrobe more appropriate for an expectant mother. And we need to think about the baby too, whether it's a boy or a girl, it's going to need a cot and some baby clothes.'

'And a bottle, a bonnet, nappies, a rattle, some . . .'

'We'll make a list. Thirdly, and this will be the hard part, you'll have to lead a healthy lifestyle: wholesome food, lots of exercise, lots of rest. And a little reliability.'

Over dinner, we drew up a list of baby things. The longer we sat at the table, the longer the list grew. We talked about colours. Unable to choose between pink and blue, we decided white would fit the bill. Before it's even born, this baby is costing the earth and creating problems. But, well, you treat people according to their merits and this child had already tugged at my purse strings and my heart strings, there was no going back now. Never forget that children are the oldest and most expensive joy in the world.

Today was truly one of those auspicious days for which Algiers is famous.

What a wonderful moment, I could already see myself going gaga!

Suddenly I felt a flash of pain. An association of ideas, a call to order, a warning to be cautious? I was besieged by memories of Louiza, my foster sister, my beloved little Carrot. What morgue does she live in now?

> *We were no older than our dolls*
> *We dreamed our dreams of wonders*
> *Eternity cupped us in its hands*
> *In a world filled with enchantment*
>
> *Little noticing*
> *Little realising*
> *We died*
> *Walled up alive*
>
> *Such is the law*
> *Allah be praised*
> *And may they rot in hell*
> *The Defenders of Truth!*

I scrawled this in my splenetic notebook, one day when loneliness had the acrid taste of poison.

That night we laughed until we cried. I was liberal with the jokes, with the Turkish delight, thinking this was a good way to coax the little runaway's secrets from her. By midnight, she was doubled up in stitches, her cheeks streaked with tears she was too tired to wipe away. Mustafa, Louis-Joseph-Youssef, Carpatus, Daoud Ben Chekroun excelled themselves – I could see them sniggering in their graves. I tore Mourad off a strip, the silly man, him and his tales of proletarian bus stations and university halls of residence. Ending with a flourish, I put Bluebeard in the dock and accused him of comical crimes of my own invention.

All that remained was to steer the conversation to get her to open up. The trick is to begin with 'I've never told anyone this, but ...' to bait the hook and then pass the baton, 'What about you, what did you do and with whom?' It's essential to recognise the perfect moment, to create an expansive mood, nurture the urge to talk freely – that is the real trick.

Being a well-brought-up woman of a certain age, I had little to confess beyond a small scar and a bruise that had long since healed. I was evasive, I was not about to invent trials and tribulations simply to cajole her, after all I'm not the one who's pregnant and isolated from everyone I know. I told her about the secret boyfriend I had back when I was eight and Papa had already begun to stand guard at the school gates. An only daughter is a father's worst nightmare.

As it turned out, I was right: the man in the photograph was indeed the culprit responsible for her swollen belly.

There was a moment when I both feared and hoped that it might turn out to be that idiot Sofiane. If my horoscope decreed I was to raise a child, I thought, it might as well be my own flesh and blood.

The man's name, she told me, was Hachemi and he was thirty-eight. In the photo, he could pass for ten years younger. It was this discrepancy that had dazzled the little ninny. 'He's so handsome,' she told me, squirming in her seat, 'he's so intelligent, and kind, and strong . . .' I cut short her litany, this man was not the good Lord, he was a swine, he was a complete and utter bastard. You can find a baker's dozen of them in the nearest alleyway.

'Where and how did you meet him?'

'In Oran. I was walking along the Corniche with my new best friends, Lila and Biba . . .'

'Lila and Biba, did you ever hear of such a thing!? So then what happened?'

'He came up to us and said: I'd like to buy you girls some ice cream.'

'So you went with him.'

'Yeah. Afterwards, he took me for a drive in his car.'

'Don't tell me, I can guess what happens next. He offered to show you his etchings, or his collection of human scalps.'

'Huh?'

'Never mind. What were you doing in Oran, I mean it's not your *douar*, is it?'

'I ran away, I couldn't stand it. My parents were getting on my nerves, they wanted me to stay at home, to wear the *hijab*, to hide away. There were Emirs prowling around slitting young girls' throats. The imam said the girls deserved it, but he's a moron. He expects us to be Muslims 24/7, that's no life for anyone.'

'That's obvious – calm down.'

'Oran is cool, we spent all day hanging out.'

'I never had the chance. Algiers is not like Oran, the government doesn't tolerate joyous outbursts, it's best you know that right now. So, you fell head over heels and before you knew it you were pregnant. So what did he do then, your brave and gallant friend Hachemi?'

'He went back to Algiers. He's a big shot, a manager or something. He promised he'd come back for me.'

'Don't tell me, let me guess: it slipped his mind.'

'No, he used to visit two or three times a month, he brought me presents, clothes, jewellery . . .'

'The get-up you're wearing now?'

'Yeah.'

'I see . . .'

'What?'

'Never mind. What else did he give you?'

'Money, and he took me to cafés and to restaurants.'

'Well, well, so you were a kept woman?'

'I already told you he was generous.'

'But then, one morning, he was struck by amnesia.'

'Struck by what?'

'By some pressing business.'

'How did you know? Biba came by and showed me a photograph of him in the paper, he'd just been appointed Minister or *Wazīr* or something like that. I don't know how to read, but she told me what it said, only I don't remember.'

'OK, I'm with you now, I knew I'd seen his ugly mug somewhere. Now I remember! I saw him on the television once, he was so wooden you could have sawn him in half.'

'What are you talking about? He's not a magician!'

'On that point we agree. Does he know about the baby?'

'I told him.'

'And that's when he forgot all about you.'

'He promised . . .'

'You silly girl, a government minister can't afford for people to find out he's got fleas.'

'Why are you talking like that? He's very clean!'

'Did you come down with the last shower? People like that are dangerous lunatics.'

'But he wasn't a minister when I told him.'

'You told him before the amnesia, that's good, and then the baby was thrown out with the bathwater.'

'What?'

'Never mind. So, given your choices were coming to Algiers to beard him in his ministerial den, committing suicide or going back to your *douar* where your father would likely cut your throat, what did you decide?'

'To go to Morocco, to Spain.'

'And that's how you met my idiot brother, there you both were down on the shore looking for a likely boat. And *viva España*!'

'Now where am I supposed to give birth? I don't have anyone to sign for me.'

'Sign what?'

'Everything . . . the paperwork . . . and what about money?'

'And you think that in Europe no one has to sign anything?'

'Sofiane said it was dangerous to be a *harraga* in my condition. At the Moroccan border, they shoot at people and you have to dive into the ditch. He told me to come to you.'

'And now that you're here, we'll make the best of a bad job.'

'. . .'

It's three o'clock in the morning and still the night drags on. Three times the hall clock has tried to make its presence felt but these are troubled waters, even a ghost would struggle to make itself heard. This is no country for rational people. Not that I have been rational recently, things have been moving too fast.

Chérifa passed out, arms folded, mouth agape, legs likewise, drunk on laughter and Turkish delight. I know, it's her way of dealing with things and now that I know her secret I find her a lot less indecent.

Secret is a bit of an overstatement . . . the whole story is a cliché! Older man seduces girl, refashions her to his taste, keeps her as a little indulgence for his business outings, then tosses her overboard with a bun in the oven. A well-worn tale that just keeps repeating itself.

It's a cliché I experienced myself – minus the bun in the oven – so I can hardly cast the first stone. I was the same age she is now, I'd just arrived at university, my hair still in schoolgirl pigtails. Like her, I was swept off my feet, like her I got to go to the ball, like her I waited patiently for my Prince Charming to call and like her I was tossed aside once I'd been used. I had my studies to take my mind off things, all she has is her carefree madness to keep her sane. Later, just as the brainwashing sessions were beginning, I found out that my Romeo was the Party bigwig assigned to keep the university under surveillance. This was his hunting ground, his personal fiefdom, the university chancellor licked his boots, the professors kissed his hand, those students who already had one foot on the Party ladder organised a guard of honour for him. He was handsome, his patter was slick, he only had to click his fingers and they would have hurled themselves from the highest tower. I felt privileged, all my girlfriends were infatuated. He and I talked of a bright future together, promised to help each other out, to marry our fortunes. Then, when the new academic year began, my mentor took his pick of the new students. It was his routine, he was exercising his *droit du seigneur*. This was the year of the blonde. The lucky girl had a shock of flaxen hair and about as much common sense as I had had in the year of the redhead.

Thinking about it nearly twenty years later, it sounds stupid, but at the time, it felt like the end of the world. At seventeen, coming straight from the bosom of a family, you never do anything by halves; you fall head over heels and it feels like dying.

It was not so much this incident that led me to this solitary life. There are the things that, day by day, slowly blacken and decay, sucking us into their quagmire logic, turning our stomachs and our hearts. The things that howl, that violate and slaughter. The things that smack of duplicity, the stifling atmosphere, the maddening charade. And above all, there are the unshakeable truths, the fearsome certainties, those dank prisons that engulf, demean, stultify, annihilate and vomit up fanatical mobs bent on nightmare. Then there is everything else, everything that is lacking, disappearing, crumbling, futile, mind-numbing. The monstrous show-down between those who exploit with a jerk of the chin and those who suffer with heads bowed.

Why would I want to be on such a ship? I am better off on my raft, I drink water, I watch the sky, I listen to the wind – everything is perfect. If sometimes I gnash my teeth, and if sometimes my flesh grates on my bones, it is simply a reminder of my failings.

The clock has just whirred four times. How time flies.

At this point, I am tormented by indecision, not knowing whether to sleep or wake.

Dear God, what a week! Like a marathon crossed with an assault course. The maternity clinic, the blood tests, the chemist and then straight on to the shops, the flea markets, the bazaars, the *souks*. The usual unpleasant encounters. Everywhere and elsewhere, restless hordes thronged the streets while droves of snorting old bangers charged the crowds and mounted the pavements. We were caught up in an end-of-the-world scare which turned out to be a dummy run organised by people with too much time on their hands. It's enough to give anyone a migraine. A race against the clock in the morning, a race against the clock at night. Taxis, buses, stairs, more taxis, more buses, more stairs. And in between, the endless standing around in the sweltering heat. We were offered free travel and person-alised stops on the route 12 bus, which was a relief. Intimately acquainted with every nook and cranny of Algiers, our friend from GAUTA, the master of the good deed, supplied us with useful addresses and even went so far as to drive us everywhere. There was panic aboard the 235, people accusing him of hijacking, of blue murder, of favour-itism, but the passengers all heartily approved when the gallant admiral, hand on his heart, explained his plan: 'Hey, they're my family, I'm taking them home, are you people Muslims or what?' A quick stop at midday to grab a bite, delicious morsels dripping with grease, coated in sugar, teeming with bacteria. Algiers seems to have one food stall for every inhabitant, but no one to sweep the streets. Dying of starvation here would take some doing, but it's not enough to eat, people need dignity. It's beyond me: the more dire the poverty, the more cheap eateries there are, and the more people snack! The haggling alone is enough to make you abandon all hope. This, I realised, was the much-trumpeted free-market economy in action. All the albatrosses, the white elephants, the turkeys and the shiny gadgets manufactured around the world are offloaded here where people scrabble to buy them, despite the fact that the people here have no jobs and don't know where their next pay packet is coming from. I wish some armchair economist would leave his comfortable sitting room and explain it to me. And spare me the nonsense about oil revenues and all that malarkey! The prices here read like science fiction. The swindlers make them up as they go along. And, God, their beady eyes! They specialise in exploiting people who are down on their luck, so my well-groomed appearance didn't help. Stallholders quoted us the sort of prices they reserve for the wealthy and the well-heeled. We moved on to the next stall double-quick only to be greeted by the same nightmare. It was Catch-22. Chérifa is impulsive, she wants everything and she wants it now! If I hesitate, she sulks and stamps her feet. She doesn't care about my purse or my health.

And, dear God, her taste! The colours, the patterns, the fabrics, it's enough to make you throw up. The girl is a disgrace. And she has a terrible temper. Even though she's an expectant mother, she's still determined to be *quirky*. Luckily for me, I have an old feudal law to deal with such eventualities: she who pays, decides.

But the evenings, what bliss: hot baths, fresh scents, beds so soft you dream of dying in your sleep! Not to mention the pleasures of tearing wrapping paper, opening buttons, trying clothes on, taking a step back, a step forward, twirling in high heels, laughing all the while. What can I say? Pretending to be a fashion model is the greatest pastime in the world. How glorious it feels to play at being middle class when you're penniless. And how dangerous. Chérifa is no princess, and everything I inherited, I got from my old prole of a father. I couldn't help thinking that for poor anaemic creatures like us, doomed to fretfulness and mumbling, every step forward brings fresh pain. When faced with such ethical dilemmas, we are tempted to retreat into our shell and watch the economy die on its feet, because we know only too well that, for the poor, the worst is always yet to come. OK, you killjoys, get out of my dreams, it'll be time enough to weep on Sunday. There is no abyss deep enough to wake the blissful dreamer.

In the end, I acquitted myself pretty well, I bought practically everything for next to nothing. Whenever my smile didn't work, I bared my teeth and went for the conman's jugular. Scam artists don't know how to deal with outraged women, panic sets in and suddenly they find their shop flooded by people attracted by the scent of blood and ransacked by every urchin off the streets. That's life, we all have our problems. Chérifa and her kid are now ready for the battle to come. I even got each of them a piece of jewellery worth a small fortune. We'll go on a diet to replenish the coffers.

Finding a room that was to her taste and decorating it the way she wanted took time – God, but that girl is a handful! My house has eight bedrooms, three reception rooms, four box-rooms, twenty alcoves and three terraces, one with a sea view, a vast cellar riddled with unexplored passageways that is a world unto itself and feels like a medieval crypt, an attic with three separate levels, hundreds of metres of winding corridors and tortuous stairways, and still Chérifa turned her nose up at everything. In the end, she settled on a room no more spacious than the others. It is right next to mine, and the rooms are connected by a grand, vaulted vestibule; it was the acoustics that decided her. 'We can chat all night without having to get out of bed or even raise our voices,' she decided. A pity Uncle Hocine is no longer with us, he would have made the room into a cosy little nest. I'm not sure how happy he would have been to do so for my little Lolita, he held attitudes from a bygone age when girls were girls to be seen and not heard – exactly the opposite of our Chérifa. But between the two of us, we did what we could. We managed to cover up the worst and refurbish the remainder. When I dimmed the glare from the bedside lamp by covering it with a veil of rarest crimson, we thought we were in paradise. Chérifa had tears in her eyes, and for the first time, I took her in my arms and kissed her ear. I felt an electric jolt of happiness. Dear God, she's all skin and bone, I thought, and suddenly I felt a pang of guilt. My poor Louiza was another one who didn't have much flesh on her bones, but there was something plump about the way she moved, it was a joy to behold. I miss her so much. And I worry about my little refugee.

I immediately put Chérifa on the UNICEF African baby diet: all the sugar, fat and carbohydrates she could eat. I gave her vitamins, too, I measured every spoonful. After a week on this diet, she was a little heavier and my conscience a little lighter. She had some colour in her cheeks and her new clothes made her look almost human. The baby began to kick and squirm. We joyfully followed its progress. At six months, the little tadpole was beating all records. All was for the best in the best of all possible worlds.

We argued over baby names and colours. Chérifa is a pain in the neck, she's so stubborn I have to scream to make myself heard. I realise that this is her baby, but this is my house so I'm entitled to my say. If I couldn't persuade her to choose a beautiful Amazigh or Phoenician name, at least I might dissuade her from plumbing the depths of Oran where they give kids names that make me wonder what planet they're from. She had two names in mind, the first would have made a dead man's skin crawl, the second would have had him biting a dog.

'Are you completely out of your mind? What on earth is Seif El Islam – a declaration of war? Believe me, giving your child a name that translates as "The Sword of Islam" would make him a sitting target for terrorism, not to mention counter-terrorism. Is that really what you want for your son?'

'In Oran, people think it's cool.'

'Well, it's not, it's repellent! And what was the other one again?'

'Benchiha ... you know, like Cheb Benchiha, the Raï singer from Canastel.'

'You really are out of your mind! What on earth is Benchiha, an order to kill? Believe me, a singer called Benchiha has a one in a million chance of ever making the Top 40. Is that really what you want for your son?'

'In Oran, people think it's cool.'

'Well, it's not, it's hideous! When it comes to names, you have to think about things carefully. You can't imagine the handicap a name can be. You need to choose something short, musical ...'

'And besides, it's going to be a girl, and I'll call her ... um ...'

'You see. Now you're thinking. If it's a girl, we'll call her Louiza, it's beautiful, it's charming, it's elegant.'

'Hmm.'

'OK, that's settled. And if it's a boy, you'll call him ... um ...'

'Hachemi?'

'Don't even think about it!'

'Sofiane?'

'Oh, no! One *harraga* in the family is more than enough! Now Yacine is a fine name, a very fine name. It's all the rage in Algiers.'

'Hmm.'

So, that's one thing settled. Now I need to come up with a system for tackling the rest. Teaching her to read is the most pressing problem, I can't possibly live with an illiterate under my roof, I'd end up killing her. Once I've taught her to cook, to sew, to mend, at least she can make herself useful. But first I need to get the golden rule for living in Algiers through her thick skull: be suspicious of everyone: passers-by, neighbours, sermonisers, hooligans, policemen, judges, and especially well-dressed men who use their refined manners to seduce young girls.

Then there are the basic virtues she needs to get into her head once and for all: order, discipline, kindness, cleanliness and whatnot. I set great store by the inspirational properties of self-control, cleanliness and a dulcet speaking voice. She'll feel my fists before long, believe me.

Good God, you can't help but wonder sometimes what it is that parents teach their children.

My first plan of action is to re-read *Robinson Crusoe* which is full of pointers on how to teach savages. I feel a certain affinity with the congenial castaway. I already have my desert island, my house is out of time and far from any thoroughfare, and if memory serves, my own little savage showed up on a Friday or some other day. As for me, even in these straitened times, I have no shortage of pugnacity and good manners. All of which is good news for her. Providence has brought the sickness to the cure. And another thing, I'm beginning to enjoy my role as the kind-hearted lady of the manor. All I need is a sedan chair or a Rolls-Royce to bear my solitude, I already have a pallid complexion, a deportment that is aloof without being excessive while the house itself is pervaded by an end-of-era atmosphere, while outside, in Algeria, life is strange: the proletariat are disoriented, the patricians exhausted by their vices, the Emirs sated on blood and the poor President has no opponents left to assassinate. What news of the outside world trickles through to us arrives centuries late, drowned out by the whine of machines and the sighs of the mourners. All of which seamlessly becomes my image as the benevolent lady of the manor holed up in the ancestral home.

Chérifa falls asleep earlier and earlier. By midnight, she has drifted far away. She's sleeping for two. I've started giving her herbal tea enriched with baby sedative. I continue on my own, as I've always done. I potter around the house, tidy up, have a nibble, I read, I think and when my legs or my eyes start to tingle, I curl up in a corner and doze off. I listen to the silent darkness, to the creaking of the house and, high above it all, the ineffable pulse of time. It is a beautiful music, it enfolds me, seeps into my skin, into every molecule, every atom and deep inside me it blossoms as a giant corolla. It comes from so far, and extends so far, that everything becomes hazy, everything stops, and little by little the moment becomes eternity. I don't move, I don't breathe, a gentle, preternatural warmth radiates through me. I feel at peace with everything. I am about to sink . . . I am sinking . . .

As I teeter on the brink of sleep, a cry goes through my head: I have to contact Chérifa's parents, to let them know she is all right. How could I not have thought of it before? I spent more than a year with no news of Sofiane and all the while every fibre of my being was waiting: I know their pain, I can feel it. I'll talk to Chérifa, we'll do what we have to do.

Another thought occurs to me: we should contact the man in the photo, the minister-for-whatever, make him face up to his responsibilities. I immediately dismiss this thought, the bastard has power, he could have us thrown in jail, have the baby adopted by a tattooed harpy like some *chador*-wearing Madame Thénardier who would force the child to fetch and carry water and later introduce her to a life of crime. He could have the child taken from its mother, taken from me, he could set the State against us. Dear God, he could mould the babe in his own likeness to become a wheeler-dealer, a crook, a profiteer! There's no point even considering it, the man doesn't deserve to live.

And while I'm thinking about such weighty matters, tomorrow afternoon I'll go and find out what's happening down at the Association. It's been a while, maybe they will have news for me.

I don't hold out much hope, but still I go. When your whole life is measured out by nagging heartache and the same haunting questions, you need some sort of ritual. Where are you, Sofiane? What has become of you? When are you coming home?

The Association offices occupy the ground floor of a city-centre building that in some former life must have been palatial. Half ruined, it still has a certain magnificence, surrounded as it is by buildings wholly ruined. The plaque next to the entrance is inscribed with a name as long as a gibbon's splayed arm: 'Algerian Family Crisis Centre for the Location and Rehabilitation of Youth Missing as a result of Clandestine Emigration' – the AFCCLRYMCE. There is a lot to be said about this splayed gibbon and his murderous missions but I prefer to keep things short and simple: I call it the Disappeared Association. At the bottom of the plaque on the aforementioned sanctuary, it stipulates that the Association is authorised by the Ministry of the Interior. I don't know whether this stipulation is a requirement or whether in this case it expresses a sort of voluntary allegiance. I'm not about to cast stones, I know that in a criminal State such things are easily confused and if you don't like it, well, too bad. I found out about the Association through Mourad, who gave me the address. The man's brain is cluttered with information. I wonder about him sometimes – does he come to the hospital out of the goodness of his heart, or is he working there as a sort of unpaid spy? I can't help but admire my colleagues, they know everything, always, before anyone else. I don't know one of them who retreats in the face of complexity. Not a single one. Where do they get such self-confidence? Sometimes I feel like killing one of them, putting a bullet through his forehead just to see that flicker of disbelief, that glint of fear as he faces the unknown; to hear him fall silent as he confronts something beyond his comprehension. Mourad is one of those people who knows everything, I thanked him profusely, I hope he remembers that.

The first time I met the President of the Association, she informed me I was asking all the wrong questions. I was helpless, I was desperate for information, I was bombarding her with queries. What she meant, she explained, was that wittering and whining were useless, I needed to stay calm, to let the experts do their job. As she said this she flashed me the sort of smile reserved for polite little girls and cheerfully strode off, briefcase in hand, phone pressed to her ear, with a sardonic swagger. A modern superwoman in pursuit of glory – even TV commercials don't feature such airheads any more. I never saw her again, thank God. She's a show-off, a charlatan, the sort of person who frequents salons, fraternises with the lumpenproletariat who monopolise the upper echelons of government and chairs pointless meet-ings. Her assistant, a sea lion wallowing in an ocean of files, simultaneously advised me not to give up hope and to pre-pare myself for the worst. This, she took great pleasure in emphasising, showed dignity and responsibility. She show-ered me with statistics, with grisly photos and press clippings, she bamboozled me with statements intended to reflect the seriousness of the tragedy. The country is being drained of its young and no one is doing anything about it – this was the gist of what she managed to say.

'I'm not looking for advice on how to behave,' I snapped back, 'I want you to tell me what you plan to do to find my idiot brother!'

'We have our ways,' she whispered as though discussing assembling a neutron bomb in front of an audience of illiterates.

How dare she! I swear, I'll rip the bitch's heart out!

'And what precisely are these "ways"?'

She glibly began to reel off the protocol, stabbing the air with her finger.

'We draw up missing persons' files . . . we liaise with the authorities who in turn liaise with the relevant overseas organisations . . . um . . . we regularly chase up queries . . . we have meetings . . . we draw up a confidential annual report which we submit to the government . . .'

'Why the secrecy? A missing person is a missing person, everyone knows that.'

'Um . . . actually I said confidential, there's a difference.'

'I realise that, but that doesn't change the fact that a missing person is a missing person.'

'We ... um ... we are planning to set up a newsletter to be sent out to family members.'

'Now that's a stroke of genius. A newsletter is a brilliant way of keeping patients warm.'

'I suppose you can think of something better?' she snapped back, lips pursed.

'I can actually. Toss a message in a bottle into the sea and go home to bed.'

This outburst calmed me a little. Maybe I should have told her that the only way to truly extricate this country from hell itself would be to toss the government into the sea and the wagging tail of the civil service with it. Then young people wouldn't dream of taking to the sea any more for fear of meeting them bobbing on the waves. But that's politics and politics is dangerous, I'm rather attached to my life and to my little job at the Hôpital Parnet. You have to understand that in this Mickey Mouse country, people have every right to complain, but they have no right to complain to the pen-pushers who work for the government. They're understandably nervous, given that they are constantly plagued by international organisations who want to know why they are cruel, scheming parasites and how so many poor wretches manage to disappear right under the noses of their families, their friends and the powers that be. It's a valid question, but it's not the only one that deserves an answer. No one can convince me that the Association aren't complicit in the whole thing. They act as a screen, they exist so that the administration can sidestep the issue. Who better than a delegation of shrewd women to blindside the bigwigs at the international organisations and force them to admit they were mistaken? These women have a trick or two up their sleeves, they can explain away anything – right down to a concierge's lumbago – and lay the blame on colonialism, imperialism, Zionism, the IMF and the machinations of *You Know Who*. What they can't tell you is how to comfort a decent, upstanding woman.

'If you take into account the fact that those who resort to clandestine emigration do so in secret via underground networks often linked to multinational terrorist groups – which, by the way, are not necessarily the groups our friends in the West are quick to blame – and furthermore that as often as not they die in secret, then perhaps you might begin to understand just how difficult our work here is,' she said, suddenly pedantic.

I don't know whether she's planning to bore me for the whole evening or masturbate in front of me until cock crow. I need to wake her up.

'What I understand is that young people are leaving because everything in this country, right down to the taps, is closed to them. Do you know many young people who enjoy captivity? And another thing, why do you refer to it as "clandestine emigration", when a better phrase might be "mass exodus" … though "collective suicide" also has a ring to it.'

'And what about you?' she squawks, twin harpoons darting from the eyes of this foul-mouthed goose. 'What did you ever do to stop your brother from leaving the country?'

'So you're saying that it's up to us, the prisoners, to free the young, to provide schools to emancipate them, work to give them some self-esteem, some goal in life beyond reciting poems for the hard of hearing, some hobbies other than the vicious, bloody pastime of enlisting with the army, the Islamic Salvation Front or – God forbid! – the Defenders of Truth?'

'What are . . . you're talking gibberish!'

'Well, I know what I mean.'

'. . .'

This, then, was my first visit to the Association. Later visits were not what you might call a success. Whenever they saw me coming, they all ran away screaming, they all suddenly remembered some urgent meeting. My attitude was absurd, it was counterproductive. These minions don't need much excuse to bury a case file and yet there I was naively thinking that I simply had to motivate them efficiently. I took a different tack. To best a hypocrite, become a hypocrite. I tried to reinvent myself as the arch-defender of dignity and responsibility, as a woman proud of her new-found friends.

But to no avail: my mind refuses to play along, I still can't stand the sight of them. I thought about Chérifa. It drives me insane to think that she too might end up abandoned in this accursed country or wandering the streets of some port out in the wide world. The mere sight of these stout matrons sitting on their arses, these government lackeys licking their lips in the sunshine, this bloody farce plain for all to see, has me choking with rage. All in all, this was likely to be a grim encounter. I arrived with a solemn smile on my face and Chérifa on my arm looking every inch a queen.

'So nice to see you again, my dears. How are you all? I feel confident that today you will be able to reassure me, to finally give me some news of my idiot brother.'

'Sadly not, my dear friend.'

'Excuse me?'

'We have been a little behind schedule lately, you understand ... We're expecting a delegation from the European Union ... We're counting on their financial support ... we're working on the files ...'

'What files?'

'You know, the budget, the development plan, the meeting schedule, the press releases ...'

'And where does Sofiane come into all this?'

'Set your mind at rest, he's in the database.'

'The database?'

'Yes, the database.'

'The database. Well, you learn something new every day.'

'Absolutely, the database of our dear disappeared. We will give a copy to the EU delegation who will integrate it into their own database. It's networking ... you understand?'

'Absolutely, people can disappear with a clear conscience as long as they are entered into the Great Database.'

'Are you mocking me?'

'I'll go one better, if someone doesn't stop me, I'll slap you.'

'. . .'

I was beside myself. I honestly believe that some crimes are to be encouraged. If every petty king and princeling in this country was broken on the wheel together with all their miserable jesters, our young people might finally see the light. This is what I was thinking as I stomped back, eager to get home and smash some crockery. Crowds parted as I passed, frightened or shocked. Wimps and weaklings who feel women have no right to be angry, to be out of control, pitiful excuses for men. I tugged Chérifa by the sleeve, jostling her along. The poor thing's whimpers were heartbreaking.

I've decided that I'm done with the Association. I'll do my own search. I don't know how but I'll find a way. I'll hire some neighbourhood kid, some other harraga, encourage him to 'burn a path' and find that idiot Sofiane and then . . . no, that's a stupid idea, I might as well pay for his trip, maybe he'll send me a postcard from Tangiers, from Marbella, from the great beyond. No, there's a better solution, I'll hire a retired cop, they're wily as foxes and some of them are honest. Late in life, they tend to recover some scraps of their lost humanity. I'd need to find one with a son who disappeared on the *harragas'* road, that way we can make common cause. I'll talk to Mourad, see if he knows anyone who might fit the bill. I . . . No, forget that, Mourad is no help, he gets me all muddled, with him it's always one dead end to another. I'm not about to forget that thing about bus stations in a hurry. I could put a classified ad in various newspapers, here, in Morocco, in Spain, wherever. 'Missing Persons', I wonder whether the category still exists? I remember Papa used to read it avidly, he had a lot of old friends he hadn't heard from in ages. It's strange how, even in more peaceful times, people could easily disappear. Back then, it was a routine matter: Missing Persons were classified as casualties of colonialism, *harkis* who died in an ambush somewhere, case closed. What was even stranger was that some reappeared, alive, roaming the streets, badly injured and unable to explain why, only to find themselves arrested for petit-bourgeois vagrancy, thrown into the back of a truck and tossed out again three villages farther down the road. These days, you have to work hard just to keep track of your own whereabouts. And missing relatives are a dangerous business; you find yourself being interrogated about the shady dealings they were involved in, who was financing it, who was pulling strings, whether the International Organisations are aware of it. It turns into a huge rigmarole. You go to the police station to complain about the police or another branch of the civil service and come away charged with some cold case pulled at random from the Criminal Records Office.

'You see what will happen if you don't keep a careful eye on the company your baby keeps?' I said, twisting Chérifa's arm.

'Ow! Why would you wish something like that on us?'

'What about you? You abandoned your parents, just like that idiot Sofiane, like all those morons who disappear, who run away instead of . . . of . . .'

Damn it! Suddenly I'm blubbing like a baby.

'Instead of what?' asked Chérifa, overcome.

'Instead of dying here, at home, with their families!'

'Why do you always refer to him as "that idiot Sofiane"?'

'Because to die far from your grave is pathetic, you stupid girl!'

The cold closed around me like the grave around a dead man. There is nothing to be said, nothing to be done, nothing to hope for. Evil goes about its business. In a hundred years, a thousand years, ten thousand years, when we are all dead and forgotten, life will reassert itself. Inexorably. Women and children will have their part. Right now, there are too many sermonisers, as many more Defenders of Truth, and so many cowards we haven't room enough to put them. Why do they have beards and warts on their heads when their heads serve no purpose? The question haunts me.

Chérifa and I huddled in a corner and wept buckets.

And then she told me everything. She was four years old when her mother died. She has no memory of her mother and doesn't know what she died of. I know how she feels, we get a lot of women at the Hôpital Parnet so damaged that it's pointless to try and work out what they are suffering from, we make a wild guess and we get it wrong. We write *Generalised Infirmity* and close the file. Chérifa's eight brothers, all older than her, worked in nearby farms and mills which meant she never saw more than three or four of them at a time. The road was their home. Then, one morning, the father married a she-devil sent back from hell who bore him a litter of sons and daughters. 'How many of each?' 'A bunch, I don't know, their mother spent all day coddling them and Papa left her to it.' He was obviously scared of her. When the Islamists showed up and started cutting the throats of local girls, the she-devil fawned on them, made couscous for them, tattled to them about the sins of others hoping to deflect their wrath from her own house. Chérifa posed a problem – being wayward, independent, a moaner, a truant and devilishly pretty, she was an irresistible delicacy for the bearded fundamentalists. One morning, she packed a bag and got the hell out. It is a story that is played out a hundred times, a thousand times all over the country and before long over the world. The green plague of Islamofascism knows no borders. One day, girls will be burned in towns across California, I can just see it, and it won't be the work of the Ku Klux Klan.

'. . . my stepmother hated me, I swear, it's like I was trying to replace her! I loathe her, she's ugly, she's evil, she's a thief. She called me the devil's daughter, she'd claim she'd seen me when I hadn't even done anything.'

'Seen you where . . . doing what?'

'With boys!'

'I suspected as much.'

'Papa is a coward, whenever he got me on my own, he'd plead with me, beg me to hide myself behind the *hijab* to avoid the wrath of his bloodsucking wife and the cut-throat religious bastards. So I packed a bag and left. It serves them right!'

'Now listen to me, around here I don't want you saying you're not religious. I swear, you're soft in the head. This is Islam we're talking about, they'll burn you alive and me with you!'

'I don't care.'

'Oh, but you do care! You've got a baby on the way, and I don't fancy being burned at the stake.'

114

'Then I'll go away and you won't have to worry.'

'Go where? These people are out there, it's like *The X Files*. And don't say you'll go to Europe, because let me tell you they've got their feet under the table there too, and things are getting to be pretty tough for girls!'

'Then I'll go somewhere else.'

'You little fool. It's the same everywhere.'

'I'll . . . um . . .'

'You see? You can learn when you make an effort.'

'Um . . .'

'But you're right – why should we give a damn about religion? Why should we go around weeping and wailing? If Allah doesn't love us, too bad! We'll go with Satan. Come on, let's go into town, we'll show them, we'll have a ball, we'll eat ice cream, we'll have a laugh, we'll walk in the sunshine, we'll squander my money on fripperies and while we're at it, we'll buy some shameless clothes! And if they burn us, so what? We'll shoot straight to hell like dazzling fireworks!'

Dear God, the tailspin! When your heart is in it, it's hard not to love Algiers. It was a revelation, the city opened wide its slick arms to welcome us. The shops, the bazaars, the *salons de thé*, we were all smiles as we strolled along the boulevards and stopped off in the parks. Chérifa swayed her belly and her hips as to the manner born while I – not having the figure of a skinny nymphet – was humble and unassuming. Hard on our heels, moving to the same rhythm, the freaks and fanatics followed behind, waiting for any excuse to pounce. Just before the trouble broke out, I turned into a scandalous woman and suddenly they scuttled into the alleyways like cockroaches. More cowards working towards their shame. To our delight, we did not see it coming. We did not even realise night had drawn in until we saw people heading home, heads bowed, walking quickly. Decent folk ran for cover. It was a stampede. Let them run, the cowards! The curfew in Algiers was lifted donkey's years ago, someday the siege will be over, the torture centres will disappear; these days the TV broadcasts nothing but popular music and idle chatter, the newspapers are full of tittle-tattle, the President spends his time taking pleasure cruises, life is perfect, but the old reflexes remain, the people of Algiers still live in fear. Lies terrify them as much as truth. Cars raced along suddenly deserted streets. Silence and the stench of death descended upon Algiers, rolling out towards the city ramparts.

We got back to the neighbourhood at about nine o'clock. There was no reason in the world that could justify two women being out on the street at such an hour. Rampe Valée is the middle of nowhere, a steep hill that scrabbles past the Kasbah to vanish into the suburbs, it is the far side of the moon. There were no taxis, no buses, and not a single streetlamp to light our way. It's stupid, this habit we have of seeking out the light, it would simply make us visible to men waiting in the shadows. It reminds me of the parable of the streetlamp ... the man who loses his wallet in the middle of a dark street but searches for it in the nearest pool of light. This is the absurdity of treating everything as black and white, you stop just where the sequel starts. Where did we come by the idea that light is always a blessing? Chérifa and I took our courage in both hands and plunged into the darkness of the labyrinth. I walked ahead, guided by memory. Everything is mapped out in my head, distances, bends, potholes, hillocks, walls. We were scared witless. There was not a cat, not a dog, not a rat to be seen, nothing was stirring, the neighbourhood looked as though it had been playing dead for centuries. Aside from our breathless panting, the click-clack of our heels and, always, ceaseless and mysterious, the hushed, distant pulse of the heavens, there was nothing: silence, stillness, emptiness.

Dear God, is every night like this in our blessed city?

Chérifa was no longer strutting brazenly, she was clinging to my arm with both hands, trembling from head to foot. Our little escapade had served its purpose. Rather than using words to persuade, it's better to demonstrate and devastate. Robinson Crusoe would have been hard pressed to come up with a better solution.

As I was closing the door, I saw among the wavering shadows of the poplar trees the figure of a man disappearing into the darkness. Could it be the same man I thought I saw when Chérifa first vanished? What can it mean other than that we are being watched? By whom? And why?

Nonchalance has its flipside, things are beginning to look grim.

As I always say: bring on the fear.

The days passed, we went out only to do the shopping. One morning, I took Chérifa to the Hôpital Parnet for a routine check-up and, ten days later, we dashed to the post office to queue for something or other, to fill out answers to questions I didn't understand. I don't remember which particular law required that I present myself at Counter No. 6 to deal with some legal dispute. What legal dispute? Where? When? As it turned out, the writ was intended for a third party, some oddball who had dared to complain to the management about the service at the aforementioned Counter No. 6 and had been summoned to suffer the consequences. By some unfortunate twist of fate, the summons had ended up in my letterbox. Legal documents will be the death of me, try as I might, I can never cure myself. They seem to be drawn up in Cyrillic from the time of the pharaohs or the Arabic of the international Islamist. I don't even take the time to check, I head for the hills. It's hard to believe, but legal documents throw me into such a panic I don't even recognise my own name. This is not the first time that Moussa, postman and general factotum of Rampe Valée, has made a mistake. There are days when he delivers his letters more or less at random. Now, I know precisely what his problem is, but he could make a little effort! Moussa was a postman of the old school, he used the Latin alphabet, he was proud of his peaked cap and his cape, he loved his thick clodhopping boots. As children, Louiza and I were in awe of him because he was always wrapped up warm and invariably punctual regardless of the state of the weather. I seem to remember that one bitterly cold day, we dreamed that someday we might marry him. He did well for himself, he got Christmas bonuses, his little calendars sold like hot cakes, and when he showed up we'd call 'Hi, Moussa!' and '*Bravo, la poste!*' as he left. Then, when the seismic shift came in 1976, when every street sign, every road sign was replaced in the space of a single night, he did his best to Arabise in the few short hours allotted, but the edict caught him off guard, as it did all of us. Here I'm prepared to reveal a secret jealously guarded by the administration: he lied to his boss, who was also of the old school; between the two of them they could barely decipher half the new Arabic script; Moussa admitted as much one day when I caught him red-handed pleading with some scruffy schoolboy to translate an address for him. In the course of a single night, the streets had changed their names, their language, their alphabet. It cannot be easy, and sometimes he is overcome by blind panic, he feels as though he is in some foreign land, his guardian angel replaced by a fearsome *djinn*, and, terrified of being hunted down for treason, he pushes envelopes into the nearest letterboxes, all the while doing his best to look like he knows what he's doing. He explained his dilemma to me one day when,

119

finding him in a terrible state, I gave him a full jug of coffee to buck him up. I hope that the old codger will escape the hornets' nest alive, I feel an intimate connection with the insane.

This was the only kind of outing I could come up with so that Chérifa could stretch her legs and get a breath of fresh air.

The third time I mentioned it, she shrugged and went back to painting her toenails. I had suggested she come with me to the town hall where I needed to pick up some form or other that my bosses at the hospital urgently required. At the time, I was annoyed, but when I got back I congratulated her, having just extricated myself, dazed and exhausted, from another preposterous situation.

Solitude can be brutal to those not armed against it. I have learned to make the best of it, I know how to fill my days with nothing, with silence, dreams, trips into the fourth dimension, empty soliloquys, outlandish outbursts and painstaking household tasks. I have active and passive moods and switch between the two as the whim takes me. I have my work, my books, my records, my TV, my illicit satellite dish, my little forays into the hustle and bustle of the capital, and my house which still holds its secrets. I have a window on to time, I know how to navigate its most secret places and drop anchor by its uncertain shores.

Chérifa has nothing; to her, solitude is an emptiness, it is suffering, pain, an incomprehensible abandonment.

What can I do?

She scarcely thanks me when I pamper her, barely

notices when I devote my time to her, as far as she is concerned it is completely normal that I should drop everything to attend to her every infantile desire. She is so self-centred!

What to do? I talk to her as much as I can, tell her about my day at the hospital, enliven things with the sort of juicy gossip beloved of housewives. I watch the Egyptian soap operas through her eyes at the risk of my own sanity. I'm attentive to her needs, I allow her to interrupt me, to change the subject – something I loathe – I hang on her every word, I always maintain eye contact. Every time she sulks or throws a tantrum, I offer abject apologies that whittle away at my self-esteem. But still she sees nothing, she's blind, I am no more than a shadow on the wall, something so familiar it goes unnoticed, a big sister who's not much to look at, an aunt who's a little soft in the head, a mother who is a bit embarrassing. I don't know, perhaps I mean nothing to her, perhaps I'm just an overbearing landlady, an infuriating neighbour. The way she cuts me dead sometimes, the way she says 'Get off my back!' would drive even a clapped-out old car round the bend.

When she starts a conversation, I'm so desperately eager to play along it puts her off. Too much fawning unsettles her. She gets angry. I try to patch things up. It ends in tears. Example:

'It's raining,' she says out of the blue.

'Is it?'

'Can't you see it is?' She's angry now.

'I was just wondering if you had noticed.'

'I'm not blind!' she screams.

'Sometimes people don't really pay attention, we listen without hearing.'

'I'm not deaf!'

'I was just saying.'

At this point, she throws whatever she's holding on the floor and stomps out of the room.

Does she even realise that I love her?

How do you raise a child? The question popped into my head as I was going through a bunch of old recipes I'd collected here and there. Papa and Maman left me a basketful and I accumulated quite a few while I was growing up. Evolution being what it is, and the Muslim world being what it is, I had struggled to understand why girls were put upon while boys were fawned upon and wondered whether the hand of God or the hand of the Devil was at work. I quickly realised that our society does not have ears capable of hearing girls.

What about me, how will I bring up this child? This girl!

With other people's children, it's simple: we ignore them, give them a clip round the ear or smile at them as if to say: 'Carry on like that and you'll turn out just like your ignoramus of a father or your cack-handed mother.' Or we find them unbearably cute and let them get away with murder. With other people's children, we don't have to worry about feeding them, clothing them, knocking some sense into them. They can be offhandedly loved, affectionately castigated, shamelessly forgotten.

★

The problem is that Chérifa is neither a child nor a woman. Between the two, it's difficult to know how to behave – we casually refer to girls of that age as Lolitas, but it brings us no closer to understanding them. Nature is fairly straightforward in its workings, it transforms us from larva to adult after briefly keeping us in a pupa stage there to eliminate our childhood dreams and fashion new ones. Sometimes, the machine unspooling time grinds to a halt and we hesitate as we wait for it to start up again; but I've noticed that some people, the foolish ones, cling to old dreams like rotten acorns, while others, the more enlightened, determinedly follow their star even in the blinding glare of noon.

I know I didn't much enjoy leaving childhood behind, nor do I much like what I see looming on the horizon. The future looks to me too much like ancient history, while the childhood innocence I trail behind me is a terrible handicap in this jungle. In the end, the problem is to decide whether it is better to die at our appointed hour or to live on through our ancestors. At first glance there would seem to be no connection, but I can imagine an explorer finding himself face to face with a sign reading: *turn right and you will be eaten alive, turn left and you will be roasted on a spit, straight ahead a boiling cauldron awaits you. Turn back and you will die of starvation.*

Enough of these riddles, I have a practical problem I need to resolve. I need to make Chérifa love me, I need to make her understand that I love her, as my own daughter, with all my strength, with all my weakness.

Where is the path?
From one door to the next
Hushed is the silence
The wind has nothing worthwhile to report
The crowd is running on empty
The nightmare draws out its shadow
My heart aches.
To say I love you to the walls
And hearken for an answer
Beggars reason.
Where can it be, the path
Which from the unknown
Will fashion my native soil
My love, my life
And my death?

Suddenly, I have begun to dread coming back to this house. This is new only yesterday I would be halfway home before I'd even left the Hôpital Parnet. In my haste, I would rip my white coat. This house is my haven, my personal history, my life. One question nags at me, unsettles me, slows my pace. It worries me. The answer, I know, will be there when I get home, Chérifa will be slumped in front of the TV, flicking through the channels or counting her toes, or she'll have taken off without so much as a note – she can't write, cannot even formulate thought, so alien is writing to her – and yet still I come back here, one moment fretting and fearing the worst and the next hoping for the best, I cling to that thought though it does not seem to put an end to the agonising uncertainty. At times, I walk more slowly, at times more quickly, and here and there in the twisting alleyways that irrigate this city I allow myself to be buttonholed by the women who wait on their doorsteps, I stop and take the time to give them the latest news about their case. They listen to me, beating their breasts or covering their faces with their hands, stammering *oh* and *ah*. There are times when I find this gesture infuriating, when

125

I see it as an abdication of responsibility, a thoroughly masculine cowardice; sometimes I browbeat them to the point where I fear for their lives and sometimes my heart bleeds and so I give them news that will have them singing and dancing all night. Dear God, how tenuous their life is, it hangs by a thread, a word, a glimmer, a law. And how absurd my own life.

Chérifa is bored. I've noticed that she's become less voluble, less frivolous; she is brooding, preoccupied, serious. I scarcely recognise her. She is like a caged bird that has forgotten how to sing, to splash in its bath, to hop and skip for joy – a joy it can scarcely remember, one too distant and too fleeting to gladden the heart. Chérifa is like a living doll, in her glassy eyes there is a faraway look; are they staring at the bars or past them to a distant something that glimmers in the sky, rustles in the wind, sings in the trees? I'm reminded of the story of the man who was born blind and who, one day, for a fraction of a second, recovers his sight – a miracle – and in that second he sees a sleek, handsome rat scurry along the wall. And ever after, when something is being described to him, he asks, awestruck and anxious: 'Does it look like the rat?'

The honeymoon period is over: our chats, our games, our rambles through the winding passageways of the house in search of some forgotten ghost no longer leave Chérifa spellbound, open-mouthed, eyes shining. I'm almost tempted to tell her the story of M. Seguin's goat being eaten by the big bad wolf, but that might reawaken the nomad in her and if I opened the door, would she even be able to resist the call of the sea long enough to say goodbye? The thing is, I've grown attached to her; the only solitude I can imagine now is in her company. Dear Lord, how much do our lives truly belong to us?

Something has changed in her, I can feel it, I can sense it. What did I do? What has happened to her?

Pregnancy – of course! – and all the upheaval that entails. The swollen body, the leaden legs, the hot flushes, the swirl of hormones, the mood swings, the sudden cravings that affect the very core of one's being. I've seen some odd cases at the Hôpital Parnet, women who chew their fingers, gnawing the bone down to the marrow, others who tear their hair, there are even women who stare at the ceiling like saints, oblivious to the hustle and bustle, to the midwives, to the cheeping of the chicks and the silences of the angels; there are the women who hit out at the nurses, lash out at their husbands, their brothers. There are the stately, old-fashioned princesses who come to us by chance or out of the goodness of their hearts; we crowd around to admire them, cajole and flatter them, but there is nothing to be done about their delusions, they are not of this world; with an imperious wave they brush us away like insignificant germs. They are difficult to deal with, the very fact that they are carrying the family heir means they are constantly in a state. There are the mother hens, feathery as eider-downs, who amble between the cubicles pecking at each other; life does not bother them, they love the chaos, they love the crowing, they are always in good spirits. No sooner have they laid this baby in a manger than they are back to bustling about the house, clucking all the while. Every

127

woman who comes to us has her own story, none of them banal. Then there are other problems, and God knows Chérifa has her share: youth, inexperience, vain hopes, bad dreams and I don't know what else, her mood swings, her wilfulness, those things she has inherited. She is volatile, fierce and aggressive one minute, dazed and sullen the next. Love and sex and all the bother and the upset that goes with them, they destroy, they damage, they scar. Chérifa is young, she's wild, she can't resist the lure of the sensual. I have long since left behind the agonies of desire but there was a time when I too rolled around on the floor like an addict in withdrawal.

What can I do?

It's a fact, I take her out less and less. Not at all, if truth be told. Where can we go? Algiers is no place for a quiet stroll, it's exhausting; women find themselves constantly followed, pointed at, harassed. The old men spout shrill scathing proverbs, the old crones make disparaging remarks as we pass, the cops wolf-whistle and stroke their truncheons suggestively. The little boys are the worst. They shout, they make obscene gestures, they walk behind us, egging on the crowds. It says a lot about their upbringing that hardly are they out of the womb than they're waging war on womankind. The more I think about them, the more they remind me of the film *Gremlins*. What a story: in the dim recesses of ancient China (an antique shop somewhere in the heart of Chinatown run by a venerable old man more ancient than his antiques), an American explorer – half crackpot, half bumbling inventor but wholly charming – discovers a curious creature, a strange furry animal with eyes like a lemur and ears like a panda, a creature so adorable anyone would want to take it home. The man offers to buy it: it would make an ideal birthday present for his son. The ancient Chinaman demurs. The American lays down another $100 bill. Still the old man refuses: *With Mogwai, comes much responsibility. I cannot sell him at any price.* But the old man's grandson rushes after the American and secretly agrees to sell the creature, warning the man: *keep him out of the light, especially sunlight, it'll kill him. Second, don't give him any water, not even to drink. But the most important rule, the rule you can never forget, no matter how much he cries, no matter how much he begs, never feed him after midnight.* These are the three commandments for anyone who would have a Mogwai under their roof. Our explorer agrees to these conditions and returns to present-day America – about three blocks away. Everything happens as it was foretold. The man's son is delighted, as is his mother since she doesn't need to feed or wash the new pet. And then one night, the boy feeds the creature after midnight, then spills a glass of water on his head in broad daylight. What follows is horrendous: the adorable Mogwai spawns a vicious creature, a Gremlin, which immediately begins to multiply. By the end of the film, America the indomitable is on its knees, besieged by these mischievous scamps who scream and laugh and pillage, eating and multiplying until they can overrun the planet and destroy it. This is a long-winded way of saying that I, too, felt under siege. It's impossible to face down everyone and so you bow your head, you cross the street, you put a compress on the wound. Typically, the few decent men, the genuine believers, the humble fathers – those lifeless men – express their compassion by not lifting a finger, by giving the impression that there is much they would say if only life were not so short. Afterwards, they resent us, they are embarrassed by our misfortune which serves only to emphasise their own. This country may lack many things, but we have no shortage of would-be sermonisers, of lazy bastards happy to leave you to sweat, of pathetic cowards quick to fade into the background. What with me trying to look like a fashionable mother and Chérifa's hip and glamorous clothes, we were an affront to the prevailing air of sanctity. We reeked of brimstone, of bitches on heat, of shameless heresy, our insolence knew no bounds. 'Like mother, like daughter' people whispered as we passed, squinting at us, pursing their lips. One day, I'll tell them exactly what I think of their 'absolute perfection'. Because they think they believe in Allah, they think that means they can do what they please, throw bombs and worse, sermonise from dawn to dusk, Monday to Friday. Is it my fault that Chérifa has the beauty of a fallen angel and I look like a Madonna? The streets of Algiers are dismal, dirty, choked with seething crowds, what is there to do but stare longingly through grimy shop windows and fend off rogues? It's true I scold Chérifa more than I realise. She's petulant by nature and I'm turning into a cantankerous old crone, I'm starting to lose the plot, I'm sick to the back teeth of the *bled*, I'm eaten up by worry, I'm missing Sofiane, I'm worn out working at the hospital. The compromises and cuddles of traditional family life are not

Chérifa's thing. And the best that can be said about house-work is that she loathes it.

If only she could read! My library is filled with treasures, the viscount and the saintly doctor left behind books enough to last us till the end of time. The others also left books by the basketful, but they're potboilers, I keep them out of pity. Aside from a respect for the old, Papa instilled in us a love of the printed word that I have never outgrown. Everything else, I could live without. Over time, I've made my own additions, a handful of pearls and dozens of third-rate novels bought by the kilo and mottled with aphids and fly specks. I had to buy them in order to ride out my grief, to survive my time in the wilderness. I think I've probably read more books than a monkey eats peanuts in its life. The whole house is stuffed with them and I could get more if she needed them. But Chérifa doesn't realise what she's missing. For every single person on this planet, there is a book that speaks directly to them, that is a revelation, that tells them everything they need to know. To read that book – your book – without being forever changed is impossible. The problem with people who know nothing is that you have to explain everything, and the more you explain, the more they shut themselves off. They cling to their igno-rance, it keeps them warm.

I decided it was time for a spring-clean. It was all I could come up with to keep us busy. Chérifa shrugged. I was about to suggest a tactical retreat but it was too late, the young hate it when their elders go back on their word. We put on our battle dress, tucked our skirts into our knickers, tied our hair back with bandanas and then set off, full steam ahead. This was spring-cleaning Algerian style – slopping water everywhere until it seeps under the rugs, making a racket loud enough to wake the dead, whipping up such a commotion a person could lose her marbles. It is a continuation of domestic housework by military means, a complete clear-out; it is the tradition of the harem.

This is how I learned to do it, this is how I do it, full stop!

By eight o'clock that night, we had made little progress and the house was a disaster area. We laughed, we larked, we vied to see who was faster, we set each other challenges, we slogged heroically, we mopped, we swabbed, we dusted, but it was joyless and half-hearted. In the thick of spring-cleaning, it occurred to me that playing the skivvy in order to ward off disaster was the worst thing to inflict upon a girl in love. I imagined how terrified Chérifa must feel, now that she glimpsed the yawning chasm between the dreams she had cherished and the reality I was offering. But when you have nothing, what can you offer? Sadness leached into our deepest thoughts and by a process of cross-contamination we polluted the atmosphere. Our laughter was too loud, too forced, our conversation filled with too many things unsaid.

Sometimes the defeat precedes the attempt, as it did in this case. When you're waiting for the end of the world, all bets are off.

★

The evening was pleasant, but it left a bitter aftertaste. It started out well enough, we were intoxicated by the whiff of disinfectant mingling with the soothing aromas of tea and Turkish delight. Lolling in our slippers, we began to drift off, exhausted from the big clear-out. I acted just in time, I put on a CD of Rachmaninov in his heyday to open our hearts, awaken us to the beauties of the world. A vast, sweeping, subtle music echoed through the house, happiness, rapture, golden dreams and carefully crafted mysteries. In this old place which broods upon its secrets, beauty produces ghostly harmonics. When I opened my eyes again, I saw Chérifa's face, she was deathly pale, she was about to throw up on the rug. Great music is not really her thing, she didn't know it existed, that it existed long before she was born. I put on some classic Aznavour, then Paradès singing *fado* that could level a granite mountain, then something by Malek, the Franco-Moroccan singer, then Idir, the Franco-Algerian singer, and seeing that even this was new to her ears, I slipped an old, scratched vinyl disc on to my battered old record player. Something recorded during *Am Charr*, the Year of the Great Famine, in 1929 or 1936. On the record sleeve, an old, tattooed woman sits cross-legged at the door of her tent staring out at the desert and written on the luminescent sky in a florid, cursive font is the title of a spaghetti western: *The Whore and the Flautist*. From the speakers came a threnody channelled from the bowels of the earth, one that would have put a herd of elephants to flight. The old woman, a famous *cheikha* from before the war with a rasping drawl, was lamenting the misfortunes of a young girl of noble birth abducted by slave traders and sold for thirty *douros* to an evil madam who immediately put her to work on her back. Straightaway we are plunged into pathos and misery. The girl's apprenticeship was swift and brutal; the once beautiful, joyous maiden sank into a deep depression. Then the harvest ended and so began the orgiastic season for the peasants. Amid the fantasies and feasts, libations and copulations, black magic and honour killings and heaven knows what. The summer sun is sweltering. As news of the girl's beauty and her doe eyes reached even the blind and the deaf in the desert, men came from fields in far-flung places to straddle the newest arrival. A brave troubadour who visited the bordello between society balls fell madly in love with her the moment he slipped into her bed. It is at this point in the story that the words of the chorus become clear: 'Enter my friend, enter, higher still you'll find my heart, it belongs to he who claims it!' Thirty times the *cheikha* sings the words, heartrending whimpers from the depths of her being. She would not be more convincing if she were in the throes of death. The minstrel carried off the girl on a thoroughbred stolen from the village *cheikh* and so our lovebirds are caught up in a gruelling adventure, pursued by the guards of the monstrous madam and the henchmen of the notorious *caïd*. The tale might have ended there on a hopeful note, since to flee is in a sense a synonym for salvation, but no, the poet decided to follow heartbreak to its logical conclusion: the couple are caught, the flautist's throat is cut and his body dismembered on the public square while his young lover is shackled and dragged back to the hovel where she will live out her days in untold pain. Since the dawn of time, the struggle to be free has led to tragedy.

I had discovered this ballad among Sofiane's belongings, it was just one of the curiosities he liked to collect. The young are only superficially modern, the slightest thing drags them back into the shadows of the past. And then I realised that the ballad was a bastardised version of the famous 'Ode to Hiziya', which brought our grandmothers to tears. At the first note, Chérifa fell into a trance, I mean a dance, listening to this cyclical rise and fall like a sultry summer that refuses to end, this violent, shuddering telluric rite from before the Gospels that abruptly segues into a bourrée of roughneck soldiers returning from war. I joined in as best I could, writhing wantonly, then passionately, in my chair, I even ventured one or two wails which went down like a lead balloon. Chérifa looked at me scornfully, I was ruining her rapturous trance. She looked at me the way someone might look at a Scandinavian tourist in Papua New Guinea who gets up in the middle of a ritual to ask the witch doctor how he does his tricks. 'You don't get it!' she said disdainfully. That irritated me, so I put on music from my region, Kabylie music and rock from the mountains, and showed her how we shake our hips down Fort National way. Music so powerful, a person would have to be born deaf, mute, blind and cold to resist it. The battle had begun, between the old country and the majestic mountains, provincial honour was at stake and Chérifa and I both gave as good as we got. The finale was pitiful, we collapsed, exhausted, just before daybreak.

I don't know where I slept or by what miracle I came to wake up in my own bed. I thought I knew all the ghosts in this house, but this one had clearly been a stretcher-bearer in life, he had done his duty and immediately set off for other theatres of war. I shall call him Mabrouk. I saw myself somewhere, I don't know where, in a dream, in some distant land, an island fringed with palm trees, washed up after some devastating shipwreck. With me were Chérifa, Louiza, Sofiane, Yacine and other beautiful, youthful innocents. There were recent friends, the flautist and his virginal maid, the girls from the university halls of residence, and there were others, acquaintances made long ago upon the journey of life. We were all naked as the day we were born or wearing fig leaves. We were dancing around a huge bonfire. Sweating blood and water, Tonton Hocine stoked the flames, operating a huge bellows with both hands while Monsieur 235 wielded a poker as long as the propeller shaft of an ocean liner. In the distance, a volcano was playing the tuba and smoking cheerfully. The earth was trembling just enough to heighten the rumba. Joyous minstrels perched high in the mangrove trees were strumming mandolins as though we were kings of the carnival. In the vast bonfire, people and strange beasts were burning. Whenever one of them tried to escape, we kicked it back into the blaze. I recognised the President and her sea lion, two or three skewers of gibbons wearing helmets, goats in *djellabas*, a single moray eel, the *Wazier* of who knows where, the evil madam, the infamous *caïd* and others, the mute parrots who roll their eyes at parades when they see the Supreme Leader of all Tribes strut past in his billowing *bubu* or talk about his days spent dealing with obsequious plenipotentiaries who come to show him some new model of tea glass. From a tumbril, the fire was fuelled with preachers and Defenders of Truth, bound and gagged. The inferno gave off a terrible stench which we breathed in in deep lungfuls, delirious with joy.

It was a glorious celebration. That night I slept the sleep of a queen, though tinged with panic as I waited for the sky to fall, or for the ground to open up beneath my feet.

The Moonlight Soliloquy

When images of children came to haunt my nights
It was always with two great silent eyes
In an unflinching forehead
And in those eyes that gaze upon the mischief of the world
The mayhem of its godless revelries
And the cold tremors of its mass graves
I saw their souls floating high above the maelstrom.
And their faces, radiant with a lingering light
Announced the Divine Judgment.

And always, in my darkest nights, those wide eyes
That dauntless silence
That deep-rooted pain
Spoke to me of life
Of its miracles, its mercies, endlessly reiterated
Its unquenchable euphoria and the promises
It makes in spite of all

Our rancour and our wild excess
Our hopelessness, our suffering
Our heartless crimes, our treacheries
Our baseness and our cowardice
And the impossible loftiness of man.

And, knowing that our punishment
Is not grim death but dearth of life,
I dared to dream I might embrace
The universe within my gaze.

S alvation lies in education. I have no intention of repli-
cating the Algerian régime in my house and keeping
this girl ignorant and dependent. In the long run, I would
be tempted to shamelessly take advantage of her or I worry
I might end up killing her. Teach her to read, open her eyes
to the four great windows on to the world: science, history,
art and philosophy – that's my plan.

My first task is to get her to accept this as a starting
point. It's not easy, the uneducated are self-satisfied,
thin-skinned and terribly suspicious. And Chérifa is contemptuous to boot. She needs to recognise the extent of
her ignorance, needs to be scared by it if she is to decide
to learn, for her own good and that of others. This is what
I need to do.

I spent all week thinking about the problem, made some
notes and came to the conclusion that it's best to be thrown
in at the deep end in order to learn to swim. I mean to
teach. Dynamics will do the rest. Probably best to start with
a guided tour of the capital. Algiers is not exactly a treasure
trove of culture, but, well, Rome wasn't built in a day. And

it's often an encounter with a monument, a painting, a curious object, a sudden insight, a system of signs that triggers the desire to learn. I thought back to the scene in *2001: A Space Odyssey* where an ape suddenly discovers all the possible uses of a mammoth's jawbone and his descendant, six hundred million years later, discovers space travel. I thought about Newton's apple and all the other hackneyed tales we tell schoolkids to awaken their sense of curiosity. My awakening was something similar: it was discovering Doctor Montaldo's medical books and his strange surgical instruments that first gave me a taste for medicine and for repairs; why should Chérifa be any different? Something will take her fancy and begin the incredible process that is the getting of wisdom.

The various outings I've planned will require about a week. I'll arrange to take some of the leave I'm owed, I'll get Mourad involved – we'll need his car. The presence of a casually cultivated man like Mourad will add just the right touch of jaded sophistication to my plan. Studying is a pleasure only for those who are truly initiates, I won't be expecting great things of Chérifa on our first day of lessons. More haste, less speed.

And so it came to pass. Unfortunately for me, and even more so for the little airhead, the result was the opposite of what I had intended. If there was a *click*, it was the sound of a door closing. Chérifa is totally, utterly resistant to all things intellectual. The magic of knowledge does not stir her in the least. My explanations, Mourad's comments rolled off her like water off a duck's back without eliciting so much as a shiver. She was more bored than ever. And this was only day one . . .

Dear God, what did they do to her at school?

I had decided it was best to start at the famous Jardin d'Essai. A lot of people don't realise it, but the botanical gardens there are as much a symbol of Algiers as the Bois de Boulogne is of Paris or Hyde Park of London. Algiers spends so much time bragging about its glories that these days no one visits the gardens any more. Jingoistic as they are, the citizens of Algiers don't like it when their leaders gild the lily. Television fills in the blanks in our collective unconscious with archive footage, something that is obvious to anyone watching since the visitors to the gardens are too obviously wearing their Sunday best for this to be a Friday. The footage comes from the Algiers section of the archives of the long since defunct *Office de radiodiffusion-télévision française*. The gentlemen in these film clips all wear bell-bottoms and have a cigarette dangling from the corner of their mouths *à la* Humphrey Bogart, while the ladies in their crinoline wear their handbags dangling from the crooks of their elbows mimicking starlets they've seen in the movies. And the poor children look so well-behaved in their smart berets your heart goes out to them. This, then, was why I put the Jardin d'Essai at the top of my list – we would be the only ones there to admire this ancient wonder.

It was a mistake, a fiasco; this little corner of paradise, like all the others, has been spoiled. Chérifa was not likely to catch the botany bug here. Papa used to take us to the gardens when I was a little girl. It was a ritual: the Algerian families at the time, fresh from the war of liberation, still clung to this colonial tradition of a Sunday in the park. Louiza and I would come back, our brains teeming with extraordinary images, magical perfumes, with burgeoning dreams, and immediately set to work on whatever composition we had to write for school. 'This is all very well, Lamia,' the teacher said when we had taught her everything there was to know about the gardens, 'it's all very poetic and so forth, but you are allowed to write about something else. And that goes for you, too, Louiza.' On our first visit, we felt dwarfed by the majesty of the place which conveyed such a powerful sense of abundance, of wonderment, of uniqueness, of strangeness, of otherworldly purity that it blew our minds, our eyes darted around like malfunctioning lasers. My God, how could anyone read, let alone remember, all the names attached to the trees, the shrubs, the flowers? Back in Rampe Valée, this glut of information left our heads spinning for a week. Our euphoria attained frenzied proportions when we visited the little zoo nestled in the heart of the gardens. Oh, the shock, the indescribable sense of discovery! Oh, those roars, the growls, the trumpets, the cackles, the howls, the strange rustlings that seemed both distant and so close, the barbaric chants, the harrowing cries, the endless echoes rippling out, jarring, merging, overlapping, falling eerily silent only to suddenly erupt again in a different register. And that feverishness, those piercing eyes, the colours and the smells that made up the wild savage harmonies of the world, a melody unchanged since the dawn of time when we first filled it with our fears. I remember feeling my hair stand on end. All this was very different from the cats and dogs, the canaries and the other pets we were accustomed to. To my dying day, I will remember the magnificent lion from the Atlas Mountains who lay dozing in his cage like a king in his palace. Immediately we were reminded of biblical tales so dear to Maman: I thought about Samson, the great strangler of lions, about Delilah, the repentant sinner – who, before she repented, had been an incomparable sinner. Watching the lion yawn, I could easily imagine that Louiza and I would fit inside that huge, gaping maw, even standing up with arms outstretched. I remembered us faithfully swearing not to leave each other's side. A brass plaque informed us: *A gift from His Royal Highness Muhammad V, Sultan of Morocco and Commander of the Faithful, to his brother Ahmed Ben Bella, on the occasion of his triumphant election to the highest office of the People's Democratic Republic of Algeria.*

The inscription infuriated Papa. 'An ass is an ass, even if he is a distant cousin of the king of the jungle!' he said. He was thinking about politics. Papa liked to make vague pronouncements: 'The worm is already in the apple,' he would mutter sententiously when Maman reminded him that the 'ass' had been toppled years before and the man who toppled him was no more likely to prevail in heaven. Louiza and I were young at the time, we found adult conversations boring, at that age other people don't matter. The only yoke we knew was that of our parents, the only ingratitude that of the neighbourhood trollops.

No one visits the gardens, I said, but we arrived to find milling crowds on every path and trail and even the once sacrosanct parterres and conservatories were swarming with

144

hordes of people so anonymous we passed without registering them, terrified pensioners plodding along in faltering groups, children and beggars dashing past, legions of wily street hawkers selling snacks, single cigarettes, digital watches, Islamic textbooks, aromatic incense (and other types of resin), posters of Bin Laden, Bouteflika, Zarqawi, Saddam, the Terminator, Zinedine Zidane, John Wayne, Madonna, Lara Croft, Mickey Mouse, Jean-Paul Belmondo, Bruce Lee, Benflis, Umm Kulthum and I don't know who all, it was a *souk*, there was something for everyone. The trees in the garden are afflicted by leprosy or maybe just by old age. The same goes for the shrubs and the crumbling arbours. Perhaps it's the drought, Algiers is in the anhydrous phase of its climatic cycles, there is no water, the air is fetid. One by one the zoo animals died off. Some burrowed deep trying to find water, the carnivores devoured each other before they expired, those few that remain are afflicted by the blind staggers. I remembered a newspaper publishing a letter from a man so outraged by the park authorities' neglect he had taken to watering the poor dying creatures himself. The joker called it a crime against humanity. It's not exactly how I would have put it, since there is a danger of contamination between that idea and an underlying one. Every morning, he would make his rounds with his jerry can, going from cage to cage, giving water to each according to its needs. Exhausted by the task, the man appealed to people through the pages of his favourite newspaper. I don't know how many responded to his plea, but chronic neglect has certainly contributed to the carnage: the place has an air of decline that is noxious to sensitive souls. Nothing saddens the eye like rust and decay and I have

145

to admit the garden bears its mark, as does Algeria, a Third World country chasing its tail: these are the signs, the half-finished, the moribund, the half-forgotten, the endless restrictions, the sporadic bouts of madness. On this path, time collapses into nothing, space contracts and life is a self-evident abdication. Thankfully, great suffering carries within it its own antidote: fatalism – which offers many reasons to die in the shadows, with no regrets, without demanding justice.

How have we managed to live surrounded by so little grandeur, so little clarity? I wonder.

I gave the order to retreat. To stay too long here would finish us off. Under the arch of the monumental gates, Chérifa threw a tantrum that knocked me for six: 'Why did we come here?' 'We're just taking a stroll,' I replied, fingers crossed. 'Just over there is the Museum of Antiquities and Fine Art, you'll see it's educa— ... it's fun.' Seen from without, the building is as chipped and peeling as a leper colony, but to hell with outward appearance, the interior might well be magnificent.

As indeed it was. Though to realise that, you had to have eyes to see, something Chérifa, from the outset, stubbornly refused to do. Four thousand years of beauty, of unfathomable mysteries harmoniously cohabiting beneath dizzyingly high ceilings. They seemed to eye us scornfully as if to say 'What's *that* doing here?' We felt insignificant, ugly, obtuse, in a word humiliated by the outmoded and inefficient ideas swirling in our heads. I saw Chérifa become rigid. At least she felt intimidated; that was a start. The vast entrance hall of stone and marble in the flamboyant Louis-Philippe style cannot but seem overwhelming to people like us who live in dark, sweltering anthills. Then, suddenly, in her eyes I saw the question that would cut my legs from under me and force me to abandon my tutoring: 'So what did we come in here for?'

The spell was broken.

Heads bowed, we traipsed morosely through centuries and civilisations and nothing jumped out, nothing forced us to ask the crucial question: 'What is that doing here?' The galleries were deserted, they told of superannuated futility, of soullessness, of banishment. The paintings, the statues, the *objets d'art*, the gemstones, the engravings looked like antiquated curios arranged by pen-pushers exhausted by routine. The beautiful is beautiful only when one knows. We walked past without noticing and found ourselves outside in the sunshine, depressed, dazzled, tired, disappointed.

All this is another world to Chérifa, a bizarre, artificial world assembled from the flea market of past centuries, past millennia. She stared at everything wide-eyed as an owl woken by a sudden commotion. I wanted her to understand that we had not magically appeared from an Aladdin's lamp or some sleight-of-hand in a laboratory, that we were the product of these things that surrounded us, but no words can pierce a mental block. Chérifa has much to see if she is to make headway and I cannot do it for her. It is for her to decide.

A hasty change of plan – we weave our way through the streets according to the code, prevaricating with the imponderable. Everything else – the Bardo Museum, the great mosques, the Ketchaoua mosque and the Jewish one, the Cathédrale du Sacré-Coeur, the basilica of Notre Dame d'Afrique, the citadel, the Palace of the Raïs, the Villa du Centenaire, the Cemetery of the Two Princesses, the Tomb of the Christian, the Roman ruins of Tipaza and the rest – will have to wait for another time, if one day the wind should change.

We wolfed down pizza in a ramshackle hovel no worse than the next, swigged lemonade from the bottle and headed home by bus having abandoned Mourad – who thought he spotted some old comrades in arms – in a bar that seemed somewhat mysterious through the thick pall of smoke.

I felt Chérifa draw away. She looked at me as though I were a stranger or a relative in whom she'd just discovered some bizarre vice. It was at that moment that I truly understood the meaning of despair.

Education may well be salvation, but it is also the thing that most clearly divides people.

Had it happened, this thing that was inevitable? This is what I asked myself as I turned the key in the door. Was this merely foreboding? No, there was a clear sign: a thick, heavy silence. That was unlike Chérifa, who surrounds herself with noise, all day long she has the TV, the radio, the record player or the CD player turned up so loud the walls are queasy and my poor ears are assailed. Ever since she showed up, I've forgotten the meaning of silence. The silence that greeted me now was heavy and impenetrable, but it was also unusual, deafening, glacial. I ran inside, I shouted, I screamed. I stopped and then I ran again, I ran faster, screaming fit to burst my lungs: 'Chérifaaaaa ... Chérifaaaa ... Chérifaa ... Chérifa ... Chéri ...!' Then I fell to my knees ... I don't remember where. I don't know how, but I found myself on the sofa, head in my hands, trembling and feverish. I felt a terrible pain as, on the horizon, I saw a whole tsunami of pain bearing down on me.

Papa, Maman and Yacine are long gone, God called them to Himself, then that idiot Sofiane let himself be caught up in his own delusions, now it is Chérifa's turn. She is nothing to me, just a stray chick who turned up uninvited, but the love I feel for her has made her my little sister, my daughter, my baby. What have I done to deserve this?

Then suddenly I noticed that her clothes were still strewn about the place, under my feet, draped over the TV, the table, the dresser, the chairs. Where our clothes are, we are. Or not far off. I'm impulsive by nature, I always over-react, I'm my own worst enemy, I act first and think later.

It was a terrible week, twice the little hussy ran away — brief flits of a few hours, but so nerve-racking they have left me wiped out. These are obviously portents.

Like the fledgling that flaps its wings on a branch, is she preparing to take flight?

Day by day I am discovering that our lives only partly belong to us. And there is no guarantee that the part we can control is more crucial than that part we cannot.

She is utterly astounding, that girl. I would never have imagined that the dusty old *douars* of Algeria were capable of producing such a character. In the godforsaken places stuck out in the back of beyond, you come to expect anything — lunatics, neurotics, egotists, runaways, snobs — anything but this. These are city problems, for crying out loud.

What's worse is that I've got used to her little disap-pearing acts. The time will come when I don't even notice her disappear and reappear, it's like having a cat, you only notice it's missing when you try to feed it: 'Here, puss-puss-puss, where are you, you little pest?', and when it finally shows up wanting food, it plants itself in front of the fridge like a carrion eater and yowls, 'Miaow, miaow, open this thing for me!' You end up wondering who is dependent on whom. It's blackmail and I won't stand for it.

The way Chérifa talks about her comings and goings drives me mad. You'd think she was going to the bakery or coming back from the dairy: 'Hello, a pitcher of milk, please, thanks, bye.' I'm the one who is polite and apologetic, she is the one who gets angry, jabs her finger. Besides, there is no dairy around here any more, no milk churns, no cows, no goats, nothing, we buy our milk from the local shop like everything else, it comes in plastic cartons full of botulism. And the bread they sell tastes like soap.

Getting information out of Chérifa is like pulling teeth.

The comparison to a cat suits her, she disappeared last night just because she saw some guy tom-catting under the balcony – the same guy I saw slipping between the poplar trees after midnight the day after she first showed up. It's reassuring to know we weren't under surveillance, we were just being stalked! Phew! Well, that's one mystery solved. This tom-cat lives in a nameless shantytown near Bab el-Oued between Rampe Valée and Climat-de-France, the neighbouring ghetto. He'd been hanging around when he spotted Chérifa looking for my place. I don't know whether he suddenly fell head over heels in love or whether he took a moment to think about things, but one way or another, he clearly decided he had a good reason for hanging around the neighbourhood and loitering under my window. Ever since, this guy has been tracking us, slipping in the shadows, waiting for *mektoub* to tell him when to go for broke. Last night, he finally did.

'So what happened?' I asked.

'Nothing. We talked for a bit outside.'

'What else?'

'We went for a walk around the block, not that it's any of your business! He wanted to show me some of the damage from the flooding in Bab el-Oued last year.'

'I suppose it was exciting. A thousand people drowned, as many more disappeared and God knows how many houses were swept away. So, what else?'

'The poor guy, he lost his father and his brothers and most of his friends in the flood.'

'That's very sad . . . and?'

'We went down as far as Sostara to look at the little restaurant where he threw himself on a home-made bomb. He used to work as a labourer down on the docks and he was on his lunch break. He lost one arm, one leg, one ear, one eye, his nose, a . . .'

'The poor guy, unemployed and disabled, he's really not had much luck, but there are worse things, believe me . . . what else?'

'Around his way, people call him "Missing Parts".'

'Charming. But he didn't drag you into some tramp's hovel to watch television, that's the main thing.'

'We did go to his place in Climat-de-France, he wanted to introduce me to his mother.'

'He's got some ulterior motive.'

'What?'

'Never mind. So how is she, his mother?'

'She was hit in the head by a stray bullet during the attack at the Marché de la Lyre where she sells pancakes. She doesn't get out any more, poor thing.'

'So, after all that, did he tell you what it was he wanted?'

'Just to talk. The poor guy is lonely, he lost half his friends in disasters and the other half in terrorist attacks. He says girls make better friends because they're more likely to survive.'

'If he comes prowling around here again, tell him that girl friends eventually end up getting married at which point "just talking" is almost as dangerous as sticking your nose in a grinder.'

Chérifa wasn't listening, and then stupidly she said, 'I prefer guys, girls can be really bitchy, they steal your stuff and they're always jealous.'

'I agree, but that's not the point. So where exactly were you all day today?'

'Dunno.'

'Don't come the innocent with me, young lady, I want you to tell me right now. If you're going to get yourself killed or kidnapped, I need to know how and by whom.'

'I swear, you're crazy. People go for a walk all the time.'

'True, but you don't know what else people get up to!'

Dear God, why is everything so difficult with some people? This crazy girl is calling *me* crazy, what is this country coming to? Eventually I got it out of her, but by then I was beside myself.

'I just wandered around the neighbourhood,' she said.

'Did you indeed? And what's new since the last century?'

'I had a chat with Tante Zohra.'

'Did you tell her the truth? I hope you didn't, because she'll use it against you, she's never happier than when she's meddling in my business.'

'We just talked.'

'And then?'

'I went into the old house.'

'You did what? Say that again!'

'Over there ... the house across the road.'

'What?? Say that again!'

'The old house. The man waved at me from his window. . . so I went upstairs . . .'

'Bluebeard?!'

'He's a sweet little old man.'

'What?? Say that again!'

'The old guy across the road! Are you deaf or what??'

'Has he got a beard? Is it blue?'

'No, he's got a head of white hair and thick glasses perched on his nose.'

'But he's a human being? A real live person?'

'He speaks some language I don't understand . . . D'you think it might be French?'

'How should I know?'

'He talks the way you talk when you're angry with me.'

'Well then, it's French, I only speak it when I'm angry.'

'He speaks Algerian too, but with an accent.'

'That's the *pied-noir* accent, you'd never mistake it for an English accent. So what did he say, this man?'

'He told me that I was pretty and charming,' she simpers.

'Well, well, Bluebeard was trying to chat you up! I've always known how things were going to turn out, I've known since I was a little girl.'

'He asked me if you had news from Sofiane, he said he hopes to see him again soon.'

'It's a good chat-up line, I'll give him that. What else? I want to know everything.'

'Nothing. He made us some hot chocolate. He's got loads of stuff in his house, it's lovely, he's got furniture and things, paintings, souvenirs, he's got cats ...'

'So, apart from the chocolate and the cats, did he give you a tour of the rest of the museum? Or have you forgotten? And how is it that I've never seen this old friend of yours?'

'His door doesn't open on to our street, it opens on to the hill on the other side. Anyway, he never goes out.'

'Oh, so there's a secret passageway. That's another mystery solved. It's amazing how many mysteries get cleared up when you're around. Before long, we'll know too much, and that's dangerous. So, what happened next?'

'He gave me this necklace – look ... It belonged to his daughter, she died a long time ago.'

'That's what he said, he could just as easily have cut her throat like he did his six wives.'

'What are you on about? She was an only child, she was ten years old.'

'I know what I'm talking about.'

'...'

This snot-nosed little girl has made herself at home in the neighbourhood a lot faster than I did; after thirty-five years of exhausting comings and goings, I still haven't really settled. It's intolerable, she's going to ruin my retirement. She'll turn my house into the Cotton Club, people will come and unravel my secrets, torment my ghosts, annoy my aliens.

No, no, no — I won't stand for it.

While I was about it, I bawled her out good and proper: don't go out, don't talk to strangers, look after yourself, be suspicious of everything and everyone, it's not rocket science, for crying out loud! Then I calmly explained the situation, the strange things that go on in other people's heads, the deaths by the dozen, by the hundreds, the thousands, the tens of thousands, the hundreds of . . .

'You're completely off your head!'

'And you're a gullible little fool! The people who died, they weren't suspicious either. Don't you know where you live? There's a war on and it didn't start this morning! People here have all but forgotten that it's possible to die a natural death, but *mademoiselle* here goes out for a little walk, she chats to people . . . she drinks hot chocolate!'

Thinking about it, I didn't use her pregnancy against her, that might have made her toe the line. I could have scared her with talk of complications, acute septicaemia, ovarian cancer, the foetus turning into a crocodile and I don't know what else. With three months to go before you're due, you don't take risks, you put on the brakes, you look after your health, you get ready for when the baby arrives. You talk, you plan, you prepare, you organise. And mostly you worry; for a child, the future is a big deal.

But all Chérifa thinks about is herself, about living in the moment. The girl is so self-centred.

I don't know what I said to her, I wasn't thinking straight, I carried on yelling at her, repeating myself, probably. That's me — a sour-faced, cantankerous bitch; when I get angry, I don't know when to stop . . . I . . . *Was it something I said?* I think . . . I'm sure . . . I don't know, at some point she froze, her eyes almost popped out of her head, then she turned her back on me and disappeared into the labyrinth. It haunts me still – what was it that I said? What was it that I called her? Knowing me, whatever it was, I probably laced it with my bitterest venom.

The following day, coming home from the Hôpital Parnet after an arduous shift, I knew the house was empty before I even heard the booming silence. I didn't try to talk myself out of it, I couldn't bring myself to, I was petrified. *Chérifa is gone.* A dead voice whispered the words into my ear, whispered them over and over. I didn't understand, I stared into space, I couldn't make sense of anything. Then something inside my head exploded, a terrible howl that chilled my blood, and I threw down my bag and I ran. Her bedroom was neat and tidy, but this was no miracle, it was proof: her clothes had disappeared and the baby's clothes too. And of that scent of troubled little girl, all that remained was the vaguest whiff of inert gas. It was then I truly felt that death was busy digging my grave.

I curled up in a corner and I waited. What else could I do? Like the film *The Langoliers*, with its plot about how 'time rips' affect humans, I watched, dazed and helpless, as piece by piece the world disappeared before my eyes in an apocalyptic silence. Then I reacted. I have this thing I do, something I made up for Louiza when, as girls, we were faced by the unfathomable violence of the world: whenever you're afraid of something, you squeeze your eyes tight shut and think of the opposite and everything balances out. Chérifa will come back, I know she will. She'll come back soon. I could cling to life.

I'm fickle, that's just how I am!

Act II

Memory or Death

Reminiscence is another way
To live one's life
To the full
To its best
Least painfully.
And loneliness is the way
To safely store in memory
What the clamour of things
Sweeps towards oblivion.
You have to let go one side
To hang on to the other.
From what is reborn from day to day
We fashion a new life
And time drifts by and dreams drift by
We journey only in ourselves.

A warning:
Let not sorrows distract you.
Let not emptiness dazzle you.
It is always by some oversight
That we lose life.

Days, weeks, months have passed and still I expect Ché-rifa to turn up at any minute. I leave the door unlocked, she has only to push. I have stopped looking for her, I'm too tired, I have turned the city upside down, I've searched every place where a few paper lanterns might dazzle a silly little goose, I've waded through the vast expanses of poverty where, in the dark dampness of slack days, the hopeless seek out shelter.

I set Mourad to work. He can't refuse me anything. At heart, the man is like a St Bernard — he knows a thing or two about barrels — and besides he has a car, so he can work more quickly. The poor man has given up his job, he spends his days brooding, phoning, chasing down leads, drinking and paying people for any information they are prepared to give; he wears himself out rushing hither and thither then comes back here, half drunk and wholly sickened by the indifference of people, and cries on my shoulder. We review the situation and we sigh, we squabble, I tell him a few home truths and every time he comes out with the same terrible question: 'Why the hell are you still looking for her?' The blockhead reeks of cheap wine, why should I listen to him?

Is it wise to carry on when all is said and done? When the point of no return is passed, we brace ourselves and forge ahead. Chérifa will not come home of her own accord, I know that, I can feel it, and Mourad is too stupid to admit defeat.

But he's right – why am I still searching for her? What can I say? That's just the way it is.

I went back to the Association.

I found the building still standing, which might be a good sign or a bad sign, I don't know, seismic shifts are so common here and the gap between immediate and delayed effect is not always important. Only when your back is to the wall do you find out. But there is a golden rule: hope for the best, prepare for the worst – that way you are ready for anything.

'Well, well, would you look who it is!'

The way she said it, the spiteful government lackey! Like a sentry who spots a figure on the horizon and trumpets it from the rooftops. If she so much as mentions the word 'databasc', I'll burn her alive, I thought as I said, 'Hello, my dear!' and added, 'I'm afraid I have another little problem.' She gave me a savage smile and I played the innocent and let the spiteful bitch walk all over me.

And then we chatted. Nothing new, the young people of Algeria are still draining away, the country is like a bathtub that's sprung a leak. Where there's life, there's death and disappearances. According to the statistics, girls present a different, though no less serious, case to boys. Girls disappear inland while boys head out to sea.

'Who would have thought sexism extended so far?'

'Girls don't have the same reasons for disappearing. They tend to run away from the parental home, they are looking to find freedom, to hide some mistake, to follow some forbidden love; boys are dreamers in search of some great adventure, they don't believe that the country will give them the means to satisfy their dreams.'

'Why do girls run away from the parental home when it is so open, so loving . . . do you know?'

'It's not simple.'

'Tell me anyway.'

'Love is never unconditional, it is underpinned by values . . . by princ— . . . um . . .'

'You mean tradition, the whole Arabo-Islamic thing, the *hijab*, the whole kit and caboodle, family codes and racial laws?'

'I wouldn't . . . um . . . I wouldn't put it like that exactly.'

'But when the home is open, loving, accepting?'

'Even then, it can still impose draconian restrictions that some girls simply can't deal with . . .'

'Then surely you talk, you find a compromise, that's what mothers are for.'

'Maybe, but there are brothers and uncles and cousins and neighbours. Talking involves . . . um . . . exposing oneself, young girls have been brought up to feel shame . . . while boys have been brought up with the most pernicious beliefs. Imagine a young man who suffers from a preference . . . um . . . how can I put this . . . um . . .'

'Homosexual? You mean a queer?'

'Well . . . if you like. Can you imagine him talking to his parents? Our society is . . . well, you know . . . um . . .'

'Hypocritical and backward-thinking?'

'Not at all, I would say that, I'd say ... um ...'

'Tolerant and forward-thinking? I don't think there's a third option, except maybe embryonic and shambolic.'

'No, I would say traditionalist ... faced with the modern world in an ... well, an unwholesome international context ... yes, that's it, unwholesome.'

'If that's the case, I would just have said: moronic.'

'So, anyway, the boy runs away to Europe so he can live his life ...'

'Let's focus on the girls.'

'It's the same thing. Contrary to popular opinion, they are less able than the boys to deal with authoritarian parents and society. The pressures on them are enormous. A girl could have her throat cut, while the worst that happens to the boys is they get a stern talking-to and then they're flattered.'

'Though it might not seem like it from my manner, I'm not authoritarian if that's what you're trying to say.'

'Far be it from me ... I'm just saying that talking is difficult for everyone, even parents find it difficult to broach certain subjects with their children ...'

'Let's get back to Chérifa. She's six months pregnant, she's here in Algiers, ever since she was a little girl that was her dream. Where do girls in her situation go? Are there hostels, homes where they can go?'

'I'm afraid not. They improvise, some move in with the first man they meet, some marry a rich man, some resort to begging, and then there are those who ...'

'Stop! Chérifa is not like that, she's too proud.'

'That's the problem, it's often the ones who are too proud who go down that road. The others go home eventually, regardless of what punishment awaits them.'

'Chérifa will come back! I know it, I can feel it.'

'...'

I wasn't listening any more, I was watching her thick lips solemnly spouting her claptrap, her piggy little eyes rolling with dignified indignation. I pictured myself like this woman, my face contorted with po-faced piety looking scornfully at Chérifa, alone, struggling with her urges, trapped in her infantile world, it was horrible.

What was the terrible name I called her?

What was it?

'Does that help?'

Who said that? Oh, the sad case from the Association.

Then suddenly I understood: the page has been turned. It is pointless to carry on looking. Algiers was designed to engulf people, and those lost within it never return, too many twists and turns, too many blind alleys, too many bottlenecks and closed doors and more complications than any soul could cope with, crowds tramping all over and everywhere, in the shadows and the sunlight, a tropical violence that shrieks and prowls and mauls, that stings and suffocates, intoxicates and leads astray. Chérifa is lost and I have cut off her retreat. I am a cruel, bitter, stupid old spinster. And a silly bitch besides.

We call off the search. Chérifa is out there somewhere, she is in some other place, some other life, some other plight, but none of the places where my legs blindly lead me. And

165

my heartache comes not from the difficulties I meet along the way, but from within.

Maybe Chérifa was dead.

Or maybe I was. I was pale, my eyes ringed with blue, my lips black, I smelled like a sewer rat. Worry had been the death of me, pain had put me six feet under, yet here I was still pitifully shambling along. Passers-by stopped to stare at me with the solemn expression they reserve for the dead. The fact that they are still alive can only be because they are virtuous — that's what the look means. 'What are you looking at? Why don't you just take a photo!' I yelled at someone who clearly thought he was smarter than everyone else. Feeling sorry for others saves them from having to take a hard look at themselves. The pathetic fools can go hang, priggishness will be no consolation.

I shook myself and headed home.

Walking back through my neighbourhood, I stopped with the women who watch and wait so we could compare our sufferings. It is pitiful to see them, forever planted in their doorways, forever nailed into their slippers. They bide their time, neither frantic nor angry, just a little short of breath and a little misty-eyed. And probably a vicious twinge in the bowels, that's something no one is spared. No, I don't know a woman who doesn't complain about her bowels. It'll be my turn before long. Maybe like them I'll park myself on my doorstep in an old pair of slippers, sit ramrod straight in my chair, plagued by an irritable bowel. The wind will bring me news of the world and I will listen and wait to discover my fate. And one day — why not? — I will see some miracle appear at the far end of the street. Is this the forlorn hope that gives these women such patience? What else could it be?

I shuffled from one woman to the next, hands clasped beneath my chin. From each I took a little of her suffering and to each I gave a little of my own. We suffer less when exposed to universal heartache, we see our misfortunes for what they are, mere commas in the immensity of human suffering. We have a duty to forget ourselves.

No, I'll have no truck with their cut-price, off-the-shelf psychobabble. I don't need to confuse myself any further, it's impossible to be both honest and opportunistic. Only yesterday, I looked down on them or considered myself lower still, now here I am today putting myself on their level out of some sense of solidarity. Compassion bothers me, it's not clear-cut. Taking on the misfortune of others and bearing it as some sort of cure amounts to drugging yourself while dosing others. Sorrow, like joy, is something that cannot be shared, I know that, certainly not through the magic of words.

Hold on, I need to sort myself out, to pick up my life from the moment when Chérifa first marched in to colonise me.

The Triple Function of Linear Time

I was
I am
I will be
Three stories to make you laugh, cry and blow your nose

167

I was
I am
I will be
Three times to sleep, wake and wash
I was
I am
I will be
Three words to say, to greet and disappear
A day
A year
A century
Three silent bars and four times three: zero

This is all I have managed to write in two weeks, and it's rubbish.

It is impossible to return to old habits after leaving them behind. We don't know how. Here I was, playing a role I knew by heart and botching it, faltering, overacting or underacting. I found myself stopping in mid-scene, repeating myself, flailing around for help. To be condemned to watch yourself live is a terrible thing, I found myself criticising every move, every word. I found myself ugly, I hated my voice, loathed the way I look, was sickened by my wounded-animal expression. I felt ill, I was stammering, I was thinking in black and white. Yes, that's it, I was a robot, hypnotised by its reflection in the mirror.

In reality it was different, I was afraid, terribly afraid, I plunged back down into the solitude thirty-six floors below. It was too much, God Himself would have been unable to resist. I curled up in a corner, turned my back on the world. Then, suddenly, I leapt to my feet, threw open the windows and sucked in lungfuls of air. I was not about to bury myself alive. No, no, absolutely no way!

I needed a new life, I needed to extemporise, to bounce back, I needed a plan.

The first idea that occurred to me was to leave, to go abroad. I wouldn't be the first or the last to go, and certainly not the only one to think about it. I toyed with the thought and then rejected it. Too complicated, it's an obstacle course, a sea of paperwork, it's humiliation at every turn. Passport, visa, black-market currency, residence permit or political refugee, finding accommodation, applying for social security, registering for this and that. Furtive meetings in corridors with bright sparks who've managed to pass the test. The endless waits, the rigorous screening process, the countless questionnaires, the suspicion you could cut with a knife, the smart-arse computers at every fingertip and in the end, when you finally think you might have reason to hope, the guillotine, the trap door, the categorical *niet*. And my heart stops. Or I end up killing the woman behind the counter, get branded a terrorist only to have the authorities go easy on me for fear of reprisals by some terrorist cell lurking in the suburbs while the newspapers rally to my cause for as long as I can hold their interest. Dear God, the things people think of. Here in Algeria, people would see me as a coward, a traitor, a girl looking for a good time; over there, they would see me as an interloper, a liar, a benefit scrounger and I don't know what else, they would glare at me with my bundles and my hangdog expression. They would refuse to believe I was persecuted by the State and its religion. They would laugh in my face. No Muslim has the right to complain about religion, about petty tyrants; we are seen as collaborators, accomplices or willing victims, or worse, we are unassimilated Muslims who require close surveillance. I would go insane before I could work out what they thought of me.

Move to another neighbourhood, another town? Hah! On short journeys, your troubles and your griefs end up being packed into the removal van with you.

And besides, who said I'm prepared to leave my house? It would kill me: my house and I are bound by blood ties.

Silence was the only solution. No ideas, no noise.

Get yourself married and take each day as it comes! What? Who said that? Husband, hardship – any other bright ideas? A Zorro in my house, Muhammad and his whole family breathing down my neck and the imam keeping an eye on me from the minaret, no fear! Can you imagine me waiting around for a husband to cut my throat instead of shaving? Can you imagine me taking him by the hand and teaching him everything? The men of this country never really recover from their childhood, as you well know. I some-times wonder if they've got all their teeth. I don't understand their fixation with touching everything, with putting things in their mouths. And I'm telling you, I feel like grabbing a knife when I see them scratching their balls, picking their noses at the steering wheel, scratching their arses as they walk, spitting as often as breathing. Even Mourad, cultured as he is, is a good for nothing, he's the last man I'd think of marrying. He can't even find Chérifa for me.

I'm reminded of the film *Not Without My Daughter*. The satellite channels play it on a permanent loop. Will an Algerian TV station ever broadcast it? Not this century, certainly. It tells the story of an American woman married to an Iranian who, finding herself trapped in Teheran when her husband abducts their child, is forced to challenge the Islamic Republic of Iran, its men, its women, its Revolutionary Guards, its preposterous laws, if she is to be free. I've seen the movie ten times and I can't understand how something so absurd could happen to an American.

It begins in the States. Our couple are cuddling in a dream house on the shores of a beautiful lake. A little girl, all dimples and giggles, is chasing after a ball of fur that yaps delightedly. The man – the Iranian – is trying to persuade his beloved to go with him to his home country for a two-week vacation with his family. He talks about it as a pilgrimage which will make their love stronger: 'You'll see, they're charming, they'll make you very welcome,' and so on and so forth. The woman refuses point blank. The man insists, like any good son who longs to see his parents and to introduce them to his wonderful family. At the end of Act I, the miscreant has succeeded in his fiendish plan and we find ourselves in Teheran, in a Third World city in a profoundly deprived neighbourhood in a gloomy house. It's like a descent into hell. The *chador*, the doors of the harem closing one by one, the increasing surveillance, the warnings, the glowering patriarch, his harpy of a wife constantly finding fault, the uncles criticising, the cousins gesticulating, the wives whispering and rolling their eyes in joyful submissiveness while outside the streets are teeming with Revolutionary Guards. What can she do now that the trap has been sprung? Will she lie down and die as we do? Will she weep and wail? Accept her subservience? No, she is a daughter of America and hence a woman of action. In the second part, we watch as the American woman plays a long game, she wears the *chador*, bows and scrapes to the men, huddles in dark corners with the women, washes the feet of her husband and of the patriarch, breathes discreetly, blindly obeys the harpy, smiles happily at her daughter who is also beginning to wither away (God, how beautiful she is in her little black shroud). She plays the happy Muslim wife in chains, uses oceans of purifying water, but whenever she can, she slips out of the house, she runs, she ferrets around, she phones people and, after almost superhuman effort, finds a route by which she and her daughter can leave Iran. And then, one sweltering afternoon, she snatches her daughter and flees. There is a chase sequence that takes us all the way to northern Iran, to the Turkish border at the foot of Mount Ararat. Her (by now ex-) husband and his clan stumble after them. Oh, the blind fury as they shriek at each other, tear at their *djellabas*, splutter with rage; they feel deeply humiliated. We are convinced that . . . and then suddenly we realise: they don't want to kill her, THEY WANT TO BRING HER BACK TO THE HOUSE ALIVE! *Oh no, dear God, anything but that!* With a mixture of dread and relief we watch as our heroines trek the last few miles and, when they see the star-spangled banner fluttering above the American consulate in Turkey, I wept as only happiness can make us weep.

Oh, the terror and the pain of the hour I spent thinking that the way things are these days, it is insane to marry a Muslim and even more insane to follow him to his home country. I was angry at myself for thinking that, it's nonsense, it's shameful, but how can we ignore the reality stifling us, how can I forget my poor Louiza who has spent the past twenty years slowly dying in some godforsaken *douar* and all the women who, one fine morning, watched the sun go out? It's awful to have to live in fear that some bout of depression might suddenly transform your loving Muslim husband into a slavering Salafist. Please God, let our husbands, our brothers, our sons be temperate in their faith.

So, perhaps I should forget about Chérifa? Perhaps, but it would be more accurate to say 'cut myself off', since forgetting is not always possible, you become accustomed to absence, conjure a desert island, a cocoon like Robinson Crusoe, you build a kingdom of odds and ends and commune with the wind, the sun, the rain, the pretty crabs, the shrieking gulls, with nights heart-wrenching in their poetry.

Ultimately, life offers few choices: leave, stay, forget, brood. It's not a cheering thought. We prefer to think we can imagine, attempt the impossible, wipe the slate clean, bring the house down, move heaven and earth, found a new religion, liberate the masses, transform into a butterfly, play among the stars and I don't know what else.

But the days are long and dreams are not easy. In the course of a life, you lose so much. You find yourself alone with tattered memories, dusty habits, worthless treasures, outmoded words, with dates that hang mindlessly on the pegs of time, with ghosts that merge with shadows, landmarks that have blurred, remote stories. You replace what you can, surround yourself with new bits and pieces, but your heart is no longer in it and that colours what little life remains.

What's got into you, you old bat, are you senile, are you going gaga, do you want to die? No, I'm young, I'm a fighter, I'm in control, I'm going to pull myself together!

I took a bath, I got dressed and I made a pot of tea.

Tomorrow is another day, life will smile on me.

> *What is it that moves without moving?*
> *That leaves without going or returning?*
> *And covers its tracks?*
> *What is it that flows without flowing?*
> *That fills without emptying or filling?*
> *And skews the results?*
> *What is it that improves without improving?*
> *That propels without accelerating or braking?*
> *And cuts the ground beneath our feet?*
> *What is it that says without saying?*
> *That dictates without repeating or inventing?*
> *And drives us mad?*
> *What is it that heals without healing?*

That guides without leading or forsaking?
And breaks our heart?
What is it that enriches without enriching?
That gives without adding or subtracting?
And fails us utterly?

What is all this, some flight of fancy? Time is time, it is anything and everything, I don't care about that, all I want is to find Chérifa as soon as possible.

Everything is falling apart, I'm running a temperature, my head is splitting. And my bowels are giving me gyp. I don't know what to do. We start to miss someone and everything tumbles into darkness. I've taken to wandering around the house, I talk to the walls, I question the objects, I find them ugly, I have to stop myself from smashing them. I function like a robot whose batteries have run down, I cook half-heartedly but the results are either mushy, chalky and disgusting, or glutinous, floury, horrible, I can't tell, I throw everything to the ants and the cockroaches and watch as they feast, it keeps me entertained. A creepy crawlies' banquet is something to behold. The house is gloomy, filthy, strange, worm-eaten and ... my God, this can't be happening! I think it's falling down around me! Or maybe it's me, I feel dizzy and faint, I have to hold on to the walls. I try to breathe but I can't seem to, I feel panic welling inside me. I walk, I hum, I try to calm myself. I come upon the ghosts that haunt this house; like me, they are pacing the corridors. I hardly recognise them, shrouded as they are in a cloud of dust. The storm did not spare them. Come on, you need to keep your mind occupied, let's have a little chat with these gentlemen from the past.

Here comes Mustafa, appearing from a dark alcove in baggy breeches, wearing a *saraoul* and a fez, his features mottled, one claw-like hand clutching an Aladdin's lamp, the other a scimitar for decapitating elephants. This is how I see him, this is how he appears, that's fine by me.

As-salam alaykum, Mustafa! What's new since Algiers was captured by the Infidels?

'. . .'

'Well, yes, it's had its low points.'

'. . .'

'Well, if you'd wanted to, you could have gone back to Turkey with the Dey. You might be haunting some palace on the Bosphorus instead of being bored stiff here in Rampe Valée, this place is the pits.'

'. . .'

'A disaster? Who are you telling? There's no question I'd go home if Kabylia were a free and independent country – and if it had nuclear warheads to guarantee its safety from the Arab League.'

'. . .?'

'Sort of a cannonball that makes holes the size of the Mediterranean.'

'. . .! . . .'

'Hmm, yeah, it would take about two or three thousand mules to haul the bombard, but mules aren't the only thing we're short of.'

'. . . . .'

'Oh, no, no, my friend, you've got that all wrong! The Ottoman Empire isn't part of the Arab League or the European Union, it floats between heaven and earth, between the Mediterranean and the Black Sea! I should probably mention that there's not much left of the empire, a couple of acres around the Bosphorus, your brothers have all left to go and work in Prussia just as ours went to France.'

'...'

'As you say, interesting times.'

'...'

'It's true, exiles have an understanding, but don't forget you died so my grandfather and I could live, I can't tell you the trouble it caused. Bye then.'

I can't believe the Turks! Here's Mustafa, the ghost of a nineteenth-century colonial officer, trying to give me advice! 'As long as the Sultan lives, be patient and pay all tributes on time,' he told me. Actually, like any good *Mussulman* tickled by his moustaches, he can't imagine a common woman getting involved in politics and military science.

Even so, we have fond memories of the Turks. We owe them the recipes for *chorba*, for dolmas, for shish kebabs and Turkish delight, thanks to which we acquit ourselves honourably during Ramadan, our month of widespread famine. We bear them no grudge for colonising us, oppressing us, fleecing us and leaving us the legacy of their barbarous customs: scheming, freebooting and a taste for extermination. Muslims have a deeply-held tradition of letting bygones be bygones, the principle being that faith inspires the same convictions and the same abnegations in everyone. Which is probably why their countries spend most of their time justifying themselves. In religion, time does not matter, only fervour counts.

Mustafa was clearly not hidebound by his faith. We have his travel diaries, we didn't need to read them, he travelled all over the place, the swine. It doesn't matter, he left us this confounded house, where he obviously did more than sleep. I don't know why, but he designed it to be gloomy and byzantine, an immense whole that is the sum of minuscule parts, tortuous in layout, extravagant in ornamentation, absurd in appearance. It's a pity we cannot fathom the mysteries that drive people. They're devious, the Turks.

It goes without saying that no piece of modern furniture has any place in this house. It would be impossible to get it inside – the doorways and casements let in a gentle breeze, a ray of sunlight, but nothing more. We had a terrible time furnishing the place. Papa nailed up planks and shelves which Maman variously named wardrobe, sideboard, dresser, and two shelves in my room on which I set my small collection of books and my alarm clock. Later, it was Tonton Hocine's turn to nail up timbers while I took over the naming of the planks. Everywhere in this vast house feels cramped.

As children, we loved it. Playing hide and seek and 'you're getting warmer!' in such an intricate warren was heaven. You can easily end up lost. Louiza and I left the best of ourselves in its mazes and its alcoves. Those things we hid, our choicest secrets, are there to this day, shrivelled, irretrievably lost. Poor, dear Louiza, she was incapable of hiding anything, of finding anything, she trotted after every breeze, panting a little foolishly. 'Can I put it here, lift me up so I can hide it here,' she would say with a sigh, '. . . but don't look!' We made the most of this house. God, how I miss my beloved little Carrot Cake! How have I lived without her?

I spent the day in the attic, *el groni*, Papa called it – in his Kabyle accent, he spoke Arabic as if it were French and vice versa. This twofold solecism is the dialect we call *pataouète*. Here in the attic, two centuries of life lie piled beneath a shroud of thousand-year-old dust. I don't remember whether we fought wars of attrition, or whether it was simple neglect, but the space has long since been overrun by the pitter-patter of mice. I always intend to go through everything, but I never find the time. Sometimes I come up and rummage through a trunk, a basket, a crate, I ferret around upsetting the mice, panicking the cockroaches, exasperating the spiders who hate to have their gymnastics disturbed. A mantle of fur and hair and glowing eyes suddenly skedaddles. Over there is an old daub, a full-length portrait depicting the master of the house in ceremonial regalia, I have summoned Colonel Louis-Joseph de la Buissière, alias Youssef the Moor, the Christian convert. His gaze speaks volumes about the dignity of imperial wars. I have to admit he's a handsome man, tall, thin, with reddish hair and bushy sideburns one can guess are dear to his heart, a gold-rimmed monocle magnifies his right eye and a richly engraved sabre hangs by his side. A helmet adorned with feathers and a cockade. The pose is intended to be distinguished, the shoulders are thrown back, one hand is balled into a fist at the hip, the other grips the pommel of the sword. I have to confess this is the sort of escort with whom I would gladly have galloped through forests or boated on a lake under the watchful gaze of my chaperone. I can just see my red hair fluttering in the breeze making the crystal waters of the lake iridescent. In the background of the scene, dark forest that looks wet with dew and, hence, the silence, the scent of mildew, the play of shadows, the military bearing of the subject, you can picture a castle filled with State secrets nestled in a misty valley just beyond the horizon. In the canvas you can almost hear the whispered conversations, see the long marches far from safety where heroism is the concern of soldiers and property that of the men in tailcoats and opera hats. All at once I hear a revolutionary air and feel an urge to take on the hero. Let's have it out, Viscount!

'Tell me, Sire . . .'

'. . .'

'Oh, you know, I say Sire, but I could just as easily have said "you there", "monsieur" or "Toto".'

'. . .?'

'No, it's not that I object to people correcting me, but never mind. So tell me, my dear neighbour, was it such a good idea to enlist in the army?'

'. . .'

'Really?'

'. . .'

'Just like here . . . imam or soldier, there's no other choice.'

'. . .'

'You did both, did you not, colonel, you served in the 8th Dragoons and the 6th infantry regiment if my records

– I mean your files – are accurate, only to become some-thing of a holy man after your bizarre conversion?'

'. . .?'

'The way I see it, anything that can't be explained is bizarre. In your shoes, I would have taken up music, it soothes the savage breast. No prophets, no preachers, no holy wars and hence no worries for the children.'

'. . .'

'Me, anti-Islam? Don't be ridiculous! I am just weary of the Truth!'

'. . .'

'Sometimes you find yourself on the other side.'

'. . .'

'I'm nervous, Chérifa has left.'

'. . .'

'Uh-huh.'

'. . .'

'I gave her everything, I love her, I need her, I feel so alone . . .'

'. . .'

'Really? And why exactly would Allah will such a thing?'

'. . . . .'

'Well if he carries on being mysterious and we deter-minedly carry on being patient and humble, where does it end, you tell me that?! Actually, you can explain it to me some other time, there's no hurry. If you'll excuse me, I have to go.'

I didn't need a fatalistic philosopher, I needed someone prepared to weep courageously with me. At least Mustafa was good enough to suggest I mutiny. It's not the answer I was looking for, but at least he was on my side. I'm hardly likely to spill my guts to a former Catholic – or Protestant – who converted to Turkish voodoo. I'm perfectly happy to be serious, but not when I'm suffering.

Next!

Daoud the Sephardi, whom I bumped into in a secret hiding place, listened to me at length, his face lined with grave concern, then, out of the blue, he suggests an amazing business deal: sell the house for ten times what it's worth and buy it back a week later for next to nothing. I'm on board.

'Interest. Quick, tell me how to go about swindling the sucker, I could do with some money!'

'. . . . ., ... ! . . .?'

'Well, how do you like that!'

'. . . . .'

'It gets better and better.'

'. . . . . . !'

'Let me see if I've got this straight: I spread a rumour that King Solomon's treasure is hidden in the house, then, after I sell it, you haunt the new owner, terrify him so much he comes back and begs me to take it off his hands for peanuts?'

'. . . . .!'

'Yes, yes, a lot of gold. And diamonds, too, we could say it was loot belonging to Mustafa's cousin Barbarossa.'

'. . .'

★

Carpatus, who was standing by the wall listening, understood the colonel's pain. It was no accident that the real-estate market was bullish on the day he first set foot in Algiers. This was going to be a bumpy night. Let's say no more about him.

In what once was the doctor's surgery, I ran into the ghost of Doctor Montaldo busy treating an invisible patient. Still working his fingers to the bone, the good doctor, clearly his vocation did not end with death. Hardly had he spotted me than he said:

'You're clearly not a well woman! Just look at the bags under your eyes.'

These were the magic words, immediately I felt weak, exhausted, shattered. I tried to downplay things.

'No, I'm fine . . . Just a little low . . .'

'. . . ?'

'Sleep? Well I manage to get some sleep but . . .'

'. . . ?'

'Actually, my tongue is a little furred.'

'. . . ?'

'I brood, I blame myself . . . Chérifa . . .'

'. . .'

'I don't think I could stomach any more herbal tea.'

'. . .'

'And where exactly am I supposed to find fresh air?'

'. . .'

'Really? That far?'

'. . .'

'Thank you, doctor. How much do I owe you?'

'. . .'

'That doesn't matter, treatment is treatment even if it's virtual.'

What can you expect of the dead? Vague advice, antiquated observations, a new hash of old broken dreams, pointless suggestions, out-of-date medications. I can't help but be sceptical of such spirits.

I'm very fond of my ghosts, but only when everything's fine. Right now, I find them tiresome. And upsetting. Not one of them asked about Chérifa, or barely. She is a stranger to this house, she has no roots within these walls, they cannot feel her presence and so on and so forth. Forty-two days she spent here, that's two days more than the official period of mourning. One of these days I'll call in the undertakers and good riddance to them all – bone idle, the lot of them. And chauvinist to boot! Where are their wives, their children, their sisters, their mistresses, the maids? Don't they have the right to come back and haunt me too?

I rushed to Papa, to Maman, to Yacine. I opened up to them. Were they sympathetic? No, they blamed me for letting Sofiane leave and for taking in some girl off the streets. Papa doesn't like the way I look at things, he's a true Kabyle, meaning he's obtuse. All Maman ever does is sigh, Papa speaks for both of them. And Yacine doesn't give a damn, just like when he was alive. I reminded them how Maman used to take in stray cats, and always the ones with mange or consumption, how Papa was constantly searching for the comrades he'd lost during the war and afterwards, poring

185

tearfully over the newspaper, how Yacine's only love was a clapped-out old banger . . . It was a waste of breath, a streetwalker is a streetwalker.

I am alone; truly, horribly alone.

Dear God, what has become of Chérifa's father? I suppose his witch of a wife has finally got him under her thumb, or turned him into a filthy Islamist. He probably doesn't think any more. Poor man, he has lost his daughter, lost his dignity.

What was it that I said, what terrible name did I call her? I'm sorry, Chérifa . . . I love you . . . where are you?

I kept wondering whether our lives truly belong to us or whether they belong to others, to those who gave us life and those who have taken it from us. I don't know, but I have a sort of answer: when we alone are truly masters of our lives, then we are truly alone. Or we are dead.

Three months passed like this in a kind of madness. I didn't see it coming. Because I'm level-headed, or at least I was, I took on the world, I emancipated myself. It was as I thought I was exalted by suffering that I sank into delirium. Is solitude playing tricks on me? Perhaps nothing is happening but for the days passing and me muttering to the empty air.

You quickly fall apart when you lose the thread of time. Living is such a dangerous occupation.

Let not sorrow distract you.
Let not emptiness dazzle you.
It is always by some oversight
That we lose life.

186

To think that I wrote those lines!

I'm not a believer but I can't help wondering what God is waiting for before coming to my aid.

> *The day was not like any other*
> *The ground gaped*
> *Or the sky blazed*
> *The world turned upside down*
> *The Hominids fled to improbable shelters*
> *Followed by animals consumed by the flames.*
> *And someone said:*
> *'God, what is all this?'*
> *Thirty million years later,*
> *We echo that mysterious cry*
> *Each time the sky falls on us*
> *Each time the ground gapes beneath our feet.*
> *The only piece of news: God finally exists.*
> *He has colonised the earth*
> *The heavens have long since been his demesne.*
> *And every day, he rips open our houses*
> *Or has roofs collapse on our heads*
> *For the pleasure of watching us beseech*
> *As we flee for the shelters*
> *And so, God: I BESEECH THEE!*

Serendipity has now arrived, come to twist the knife in the wound. It appeared via *Arte*, a humanitarian television channel if ever there was one. Ever since Chérifa's disappearance, I'd forgotten about my faithful friend the television which had become shrouded in dust, but on that particular evening our friendship was accidentally rekindled. A gust of wind and the television suddenly came on by itself, or as though it had something to tell me. From the very first image, I could see that the programme was about us, the landless, the *harragas*, the path-burners. As part of a series about Great World Suffering, *Arte* took us from an African village somewhere in the deserts of the Ténéré, across the sweeping plains of the Sahel all the way to Tamanrasset where the camera allowed itself a brief pause to flick through the criminal record of the Algerian government, a crucial link in the people-smuggling networks of Saharan and sub-Saharan Africa; from Tamanrasset, it zigzagged through the no-man's-land of Algeria and Morocco, travelling by night, far from paved roads, heading steadily north-west until it arrived, scorched and weary, in Tarifa, Spain, a few kilometres from Gibraltar – which once was 'Jabal Tāriq' in another story –

where the epilogue to this odyssey was played out. In Gibraltar we watched the policemen with their funny helmets fishing bodies out of the sea while, high up on the cliffs, a priest who supported the rights of the *harragas*, surrounded by tearful militants, prays with all his might to a God who refuses to listen to the poor. It is a magnificent scene. It reminded me of Roland Joffé's film *The Mission*, with Robert De Niro as mercenary Rodrigo Mendoza who, after some terrible event, becomes a Jesuit. But rather than honouring God and conforming to the strict discipline of the order, Mendoza rebels and fights for the indigenous Guaraní doomed to annihilation because of some distant, nebulous issue between the Roman Catholic Church and the kings of Spain and Portugal. In the end, he is shot and killed and with him every last Guaraní tribesman while a sanctimonious new order is established all across South America. A harrowing tale filmed in majestic locations. And I thought of *The Name of the Rose* which depicts grim, boorish monks who go to insane lengths to orchestrate bizarre crimes in a monastery constructed like a pagan labyrinth. Do we really kill people simply because they have discovered that laughter exists? It's appalling.

So, we were in Tarifa. Yes, among the corpses is a survivor, a young black woman several months pregnant, beautiful as the sun, no older than Chérifa but twice as tall. Her great eyes roll in her head like lottery balls in their glass cage. She doesn't understand, she raves, she babbles, she trembles, she thrashes about, she tries to run but she barely has the strength to cling to the brigadier. A fat slob in military uniform acting on behalf of the *gobernador* says to the camera that the miraculous survivor will be sent back to her *país* as soon as she gives birth. *Moron, do you even know if she has a país?*

This is the end of the drama for the viewer, who can turn off the television and go to bed. But for the rest of us, for those with no country, the questions are only beginning.

I have never been so moved by a documentary, not just because it directly concerned me but because it managed to show the terrible ordeals that poverty inflicts on those who have the temerity to try to escape it. It's never-ending: at every turn, they are hit hard enough to floor a rhinoceros. It's rather like quicksand, once you step into it, you're sucked down. You can struggle, scream for help or cross your fingers, but the end result is the same. The path-burners know this, they try to deny it, but gradually, as the going gets tougher, they are forced to accept it; they find they become sparing in their words, their gestures, probably even their thoughts. They trudge on like the living dead but still they keep the faith, still they head to where life is waiting: the promised land.

The dream is so beautiful, what can we do but follow it?

It begins in a tiny Ténéré village. The sun is high in the sky; in such hellish places it never sets. The camera does a quick tour of the village: a dozen shacks arranged according to some ancient order, a couple of grain silos that look like abandoned termite nests, a ramshackle paddock where a few skeletal beasts with horns chew the cud and a central building made of logs and adobe whose purpose is never mentioned (a place of worship, a village hall, an *agora*, a school?). Relaxed and noble in their nakedness, the women are grinding millet. Around them, feet in the sand, moping kids stick fingers in their belly buttons or into little pug noses crawling with flies as flea-ridden dogs stagger around or paw through the rubbish and on the outskirts of the village, lying beneath a scrawny tree, two wizened old men chat quietly while they wait to die. There is some desultory conversation between the camera and the women.

– *Where are the men?*

– *Gone.*

– *Where?*

– *We don't know.*

– *Why did they leave?*

– *They are looking for work.*

– *Where?*

– *We don't know, in Africa, somewhere else.*

– *Why is the village so far from everywhere?*

– *We don't know.*

– *Is that millet you're grinding?*

– *Yes.*

– *Is it hard?*

– *No.*

– *Are you happy?*

Silence. The camera pauses, then zooms insistently on the face of a woman of indeterminate age. Finally the answer comes: *We don't know.*

The camera moves on, sweeping around to give an establishing shot of the village, an insidious way of showing the expanse of ignorance in a desert with no connection to the outside world.

The camera pans towards two young men, a rare sight in this village as old as the earth itself. Their only possessions are their white teeth, their threadbare jeans and a pair of espadrilles. And a few stray hairs on their chins, but it's well known that black men are not very hirsute. The camera leads them away to a lean-to where they can spill their secrets. They stand in the silent stare of the lens. They feel strange, helpless, useless. The camera is unrelenting and they both speak simultaneously. They are ready for the great journey, for years they have saved, cent by cent, the smuggler is demanding a thousand dollars a head. The camera flinches. 'A thousand dollars? Where on earth did you come up with that?' it asks. They confess to poaching on the English reserve, but otherwise they have lived from hand to mouth. '*But we have good grigris*,' they add, proud as punch of their own cunning. The trafficker is waiting on the Algerian border at Bordj Badji Mokhtar where they will be joined by illegal immigrants from other countries, other villages, other miseries; three thousand kilometres' trekking, two thousand through Algeria where government bullets and Islamist groups lie in wait and a thousand more through Morocco where the *chaouchs* sleep with one eye open. You have to allow for *baksheesh* to bribe officials and for the slave traders who keep a close eye on the crossing points which they know as well as the smugglers. Then they have to cross the straits, the crossing is made on unseaworthy *feluccas* that cost five hundred dollars – as many as thirty people have to club together to come up with the fare. The

192

Algerian trafficker hands over to a Moroccan trafficker who takes his cut as they embark and sends the signal to the Spanish trafficker waiting on the far coast.

– *You know all this but you're still going?*
– *Yes, we want to live* (laughter).
– *Are you scared?*
– *A bit* (laughter).
– *Can we follow you and film your odyssey?*
– *If you like* (laughter).

I know all this, yet still I feel moved; images reinforce words. African society is pitifully fragmented and it has the memory of an elephant; it was ever thus. There is the world of women, one of confinement and of infinite patience, and the world of men which is focused on survival; there is the world of the young who sit around dreaming of the promised land and that of the authorities intent on plunder. These worlds never collide. To talk about democracy in our countries is to invoke the stuff of myth and legend, our witchdoctors are not likely to devise such a machine.

The camera was less than brilliant on this subject. Africa does not fall within the gravitational field of democracy, full stop. It is simply implied that a gulf spanning a thousand light-years cannot be forded like a drainage ditch. The ordinary viewer might easily come away thinking that things are as they are because that is how we want them, because we love famine and war. There are other factors: government, religion, traditions, the climate and more besides. All these things are oppressive. In Algeria, the camera was more blunt, it surveyed the terrain and it named some of the cruellest and most ridiculous overlords on the planet together with one of their henchmen, a certain *hajj* Saïd, aka Bouzahroun, aka 'Le Chanceux' – 'Lucky'.

And so our two heroes – whose names are Ahmadou and Abu-Bakr – begin their journey for Tarifa, the gateway to the promised land. It is dawn, the desolate plains are still shivering from the nightmares of the waning darkness. Pale shadows gather in the lean-to shack. There is a whispered conversation. Suddenly, a spotlight rips the darkness. The camera captures the fateful moment. What is gripping about all great adventures is that at some point, whether anticipated or unexpected, everything topples into the unknown. The women pause as they pound millet, the children shake their heads to ward off sleep, the dogs stop in their tracks, the old men choke back their nostalgia, and everyone listens. We watch the shadows as they move off and disappear beyond the blinding dazzle of the horizon. There is not a word, not a gesture, not a sigh, but from the distance, from the far distance comes the otherworldly rumble of the African continent.

The first few kilometres move quickly. The Sahel, which spans several million square kilometres beneath the sun, remains unruffled. Further along, the group clambers aboard an antediluvian boneshaker that weaves its way between the gnus and the antelopes. It is filled to bursting and falling apart.

There is a stop for something to eat in a *boui-boui* in the middle of nowhere. They wolf down bucketsful of dust, they talk to lubricate their throats, they do their reckoning: a hundred kilometres lie behind them, ahead, in the blazing heat there are 3,900 kilometres, maybe more since it's impossible to know in advance how often they will lose their way. They laugh because what they are attempting is insane, because failure is unthinkable. The barman spits and goes back to his calabashes. The group sets off again. The camera pans across the horizon. In the distance, near a herd of buffalo, a sandstorm blows up. The temperature rises to melting point. People cover their faces, they avoid breathing. It is a senseless futile precaution since the sand in the Sahel is wily, it gets everywhere. In an old issue of *Science et Vie*, I read that it can travel as far as the Amazon, which gives you some idea. They stop to rest in the shade of a rocky outcrop bizarrely sculpted by millennia of scorching sandstorms. Here they spend the night, they have nightmares, the whole savannah is a distant cry that comes from the bowels of the earth to be taken up by millions of hungry throats. Several days later, at daybreak, a caravanserai appears on the horizon. It is beautiful! Guided only by ancient mysteries, it is heading north. Our group joins the caravan. They chat with the *cheikh* over glasses of mint tea. He is a *Kel Ghella*, a nobleman who can trace his lineage back to ancient upheavals. His face is covered by his *alasho*, all that is visible are his glassy eyes which look as though they are inhabited by a large sandworm.

— *Are you heading north?*

— *Yes, to Tamanrasset, the Assihar begins there at the next moon.*

— *Can we travel with you?*

— This is our route, but the Sahara belongs to those who know it.

— So we can come?

— If that is the will of Allah.

— What is Assihar? asks the camera.

— It is a festival that takes place once a year for all the Tuareg peoples, the Azdjer, the Ahaggar, the Aouellimiden, the Mourines, the Imohaghs, from the seven corners of the earth they come, from Mauritania and Sudan, from Algeria and Senegal, from Libya, Niger, Mali, Côte d'Ivoire, Burkina-Faso, from as far away as the distant empire of Tibesti!

— It must be magnificent!

— It is tradition, we barter, we talk, we celebrate our ancestors. We come from el djanoub, from the south, from Timbuktu, and you?

— From Mali.

— And you?

— From Paris.

— What do you have to barter?

— Nothing, a little hope, a little friendship whenever possible, we are going to Bordj Badji Mokhtar to visit a dear friend.

— Are your papers in order?

— Eh . . . why?

— The Algerians are wary of foreigners, they do not like us, they kill us whenever they can or else they demand twenty bales of rare documents and a king's ransom.

— So what do you do, how do you manage?

— The Sahara is our home for as far as it extends beneath the sun, we need no papers, they are the ones who should have to tell us who they are, where they are from.

★

The caravan is making steady progress. The camels bray just for the pleasure of hearing their voices, the Sahara has long since ceased to amaze them. Travelling alongside them, our heroes become more confident, Ahmadou and Abu-Bakr regain their strength. They make friends with young lanky Tuareg men born on the move and hence unfamiliar with the changing world. They talk to them about Europe, about the pleasures of life, the joy of love and of things that an eternal nomad can scarcely imagine: about the métro, social security, sports cars, snow, cinemas, Christmas holidays, microchips. But they are talking simply for the pleasure of talking, no one needs to understand. Question: *What do they barter over there, in Europe?* Curious, the camera has drawn nearer. Answer: *There, there is everything, you don't want for anything.*

At the Algerian border, our friends go their separate ways.

— *You have arrived, my brothers, we must travel on to Taman-rasset.*

— *But we are going to Bordj Badji Mokhtar. Where is it? We can't see anything.*

— *It is right before your eyes.*

— *But there is nothing here.*

— *It is a mere two days' walk towards the west.*

— *Thank you, noble* cheikh.

— *If the soldiers challenge you, tell them you are going to meet* hajj *Saïd le Chanceux, they will escort you and give you food and drink.*

Bordj Badji Mokhtar — or BBM as we northerners call it — is a large town which grew from nothing and grew too quickly. It is rampant chaos: houses half-finished or half-demolished, streets little better than rutted dirt tracks, ramshackle trucks, camels on their last legs, roving goats, rabid dogs, corrupt cops, all covered over with thick dust imported from the north.

The meeting point is a depot belonging to the aforementioned *hajj* Saïd, aka Bouzahroun, aka 'Lucky', a man who is never seen without his night-vision goggles and his state-of-the-art mobile phone. He reminds me of *sidi* Saïd Bouteflika – also nicknamed 'Lucky' – the brother and special adviser to the president of the People's Democratic Republic of Algeria, a man who is never seen without his ski goggles and his walkie-talkie, but I suppose it's not a crime to look like someone else. The camera, which has been roving around the town, quickly finds out that the mega-rich tycoon is a former terrorist who plotted with the high command and, for his exceptional services, was awarded a monopoly on human trafficking from BBM as far as Bamako and Niamey. *Sidi* Saïd has a fleet of a hundred trucks, a private militia numbering a thousand *pistoleros*, and, in case of war, has the right to mobilise the army and the customs service. When he is planning a particularly big coup, he calls one of a list of numbers in Algiers until he reaches the top. The camera did not hesitate, it was determined to discover what was really going on. It got its answer from an old man sitting lazily at the foot of a half-built wall playing an *imzad* – a violin with a single string stretched across a turtle shell. The camera pulled no punches.

    – *Have you any idea what's going on here?*

– *Go to Laoni and you will understand.*

– *Where is that?*

– *Three days' walk, south-west of here.*

– *Laoni?*

– *Yes, Laoni, the gold mine.*

– *What about it?*

– *The gold extracted from the mine is transported to Taman-rasset and from there it's sent on to Algiers.*

– *I don't see the problem.*

– *The gold never arrives in Tamanrasset; your friend Saïd com-mandeers it for his friends in high places.*

– *Is this true?*

– *And that's not the whole story: Algiers denies that there is a secret American military base in the area and so Saïd is told to supply it on the quiet. He has dollars coming out of his arse.*

– *How do you know all this? No one in Paris has heard any-thing about it.*

– *Why wouldn't I know? I occasionally work as a guide for Saïd and the Americans.*

Over the days that followed, other *harragas* arrived at Saïd's place, and eventually there were a dozen of them. Ahmadou and Abu-Bakr lost their starring roles in the documentary. The camera fell upon the newcomers, beardless boys with big eyes, a Malian, a Nigerian, a Ghanaian, two kids from Togo, one a pregnant girl, a Sudanese boy, an Ivoirian, a Senegalese, a Congolese and a Guinean, the last three having travelled the same route via Gao, the second largest trafficking hub in the Sahel after Tamanrasset. They all told the same story, they were all looking for the promised land.

The tragedy – though they did not yet know this – was that they have come too far to get there in this life.

While they waited for the people smuggler to arrive, Saïd set them to work for the customs inspector. They repaired his roof in exchange for some bread and a little water. 'A man must earn his keep,' Saïd says to the camera, a smiling Good Samaritan. The camera takes the opportunity to rile him a little.

– *How much do you make on the transfers to Tarifa? They say you bleed these people dry and very few make it there alive.*

– *That's just malicious gossip, I do this out of Muslim charity. They want to have a little fun, the little black* bamboulas, *so I help them out.*

As he says this, the people smuggler jumps down from his Land Rover. He takes off his *keffiyeh* and drinks down mint tea. Oh, he looks evil! He is just back from an expedition he is reluctant to discuss. The camera insists. 'I was on holiday with friends in Tamanrasset,' he swears, looking greedily at his new clients. In the camp, there is much talk about a group of Ugandan mercenaries who have been turned over to Gaddafi who, bored as a dead rat, dreams of opening up a new route. It's crazy how much goes on in the middle of the desert.

Dawn the next morning, the immigrants are woken with a boot, loaded on to the back of the truck, covered with a tarpaulin, then they're off. The camera has rented an air-conditioned 4x4, a driver and a guide. The voiceover does not mention the fact, but it clearly belongs to Saïd. The Toyota drives behind or in front of the truck, as filming dictates. The little convoy raises clouds of dust. They take no precautions, they drive at top speed, they have no need to worry since everywhere within a five-hundred-kilo-metre radius is controlled by Saïd. At military checkpoints, they are greeted with honours. Further north, as they enter another private fiefdom the truck pulls off the road before it reaches the checkpoints. Regardless of the faction they're allied to, truckers stick together and so oncoming trucks flash their headlights to warn of an upcoming roadblock. Once means danger is 1km ahead, twice means 2km ahead and so on. Sometimes they stop, regroup and draw up a plan of battle. After the first few deaths, they negotiate over a pot of mint tea. It is perfectly timed and the Toyota, pre-tending to be a tourist who has broken down, manages to film the magnificent jamboree that takes place around the fire in the shadow of a cave.

Every time the truck slows and leaves the road, the *har-ragas* huddle together. The government does not take kindly to foreign intruders. They are beaten and then killed after a period working as slave labour for an officer. This is one of the perks offered to ranking officers, all of whom have palm groves that need tending or roofs that need mending.

The convoy arrives at the oasis town of El Oued, the 'City of a Thousand Domes'. In the desert, it stops to visit a famous *marabout*, a bizarre old man, a dwarf in rags named *sidi* Abdelaziz who stands on solid-gold stilts and calls him-self 'El Mahdi' – the Guided One. The little bastard has considerable influence, he hawks his bullshit prophecies from *douar* to *douar* and the people lap it up. His fame has spread far and wide, all the way to New York where people wonder what it's all about. To some, he is a great prodigy, to others a vulgar charlatan. He looks to me like a lunatic, I thought, the first time I saw him shimmying around his *kubba* jabbering bits of *marabout* gibberish. Time is short. A confab takes place between the people smuggler and the master of the house. They high five, El Mahdi clicks his fingers and from a deep well hidden among the cacti, soaked to the skin, frantic and half-blind, twelve puny little runts appear. These are boys from the area around the fields who protested against poverty and found themselves being hunted down by the police and the Americans. They were looking for work, waving banners outside the Hassi Messaoud oil base. They have endured terrible dangers in order to get here to the meeting point, they have nothing but the clothes on their backs. 'We will continue on foot, steering clear of the main roads,' announces the smuggler. Northern Algeria is tightly controlled, there are roadblocks everywhere, and everywhere there are spies, barons, emirs, armed factions, dishonest officials, brazen bounty hunters. Dear God, what a journey, what terrors they must face; it's enough to break your heart.

They trudge on for two weeks – a century and a half in any normal country. Long funeral marches between two alerts, two watches. The straggling group looks barely human now, a ragman would reject them. I felt wretched and ashamed as I watched them founder, unable to do anything to help.

★

Finally, just beyond the horizon, the border looms. On the far side is Morocco – the Kingdom of the Alaouites as they say in high places here in Algeria to imply God knows what. It is the same land, the same sun, the same peoples practising the same religion, the same food; but there the air is different, there a man can breathe. The group feels a sense of relief, this is like stepping into a picture postcard, one of the hand-tinted photos of long ago so charmingly idyllic that tourists felt a sudden need to siesta in the shade of a palm tree, or saddle the nearest donkey. All along this uncertain line established in endless treaties, everyone is in the business of contraband and smuggling; under the watchful gaze of both armies, oil is exchanged for *kif*. The soldiers keep a friendly eye on each other, a state of war with no war; it is a godsend, everyone gets to line their pockets and no one gets hurt.

The *harragas* are making good progress. Like them, the viewers are eager to cross the finish line. Another hairpin bend or two and we find ourselves in a withered pine forest on the outskirts of the Spanish exclave Ceuta, which in a former life was the walled city of Abyla. Hundreds of *harragas* live here, some have been here for several years. They have clearly put down roots: tents and shacks have sprung up everywhere, pots and pans hanging from the branches tinkle among the pine trees. The camera does a sweep of the location. A quick interview with one person, then on to another. Endless tales of *harragas*. The camp is segregated according to skin colour, nationality, religion, dialect and tribe. This is old-fashioned racism; peoples live cheek by jowl without acknowledging each other. As the camera prowls the Algerian quarter, I keep my eyes peeled. Every boy there looks

just like Sofiane, same age, same pathetic affected air, but of
Sofiane himself, there is no sign. I felt both disappointed and
relieved. Each group has its own territory, its own survival
strategy, its plans for freedom. Some have their sights set on
Ceuta itself, others are merely passing through, heading for
Tangiers, the gateway to Tarifa. This was what Ahmadou and
Abu-Bakr were planning. They have come too far to spend
all eternity picnicking in a pine forest. The film's epilogue
was devoted to them. Having survived the sandstorms and
the vastness of the desert, they died in the arms of the sea
within swimming distance of the Spanish coast. Only a
young Togolese girl, beautiful as the sun at noon, set foot
upon the promised land. Death must have realised that taking
two wretched lives for the price of one was too unfair.

> *They come from afar*
> *Seeking the impossible*
> *Bellies empty, bodies taut with truth.*

> *As they advance*
> *Time flees before them*
> *And behind them the corpses pile higher.*

> *The sun wheels in the sky*
> *Not a soul must escape*
> *All must die before nightfall.*

> *And so they die in their shadows*
> *The wind gathers their bones*
> *And with the earth, so turns the millstone.*

The film ends with a long pull-back shot of the Ténéré while a haunting threnody comes from the heavens, from the oppressive, boundless, ochre sky. A funeral lament. Eyes close and we hear a final prayer as the ad break arrives with tips on how to make money in the capital which reminds me of Jean Yanne's film *Tout le monde il est beau, tout le monde il est gentil*, prophets come and go, but advertising is for ever.

I was exhausted, I felt dirty, tattered, lost in thoughts of Sofiane, of Ahmadou and Abu-Bakr, of the young Togolese girl with the pretty face, and all those flailing in the background. My mind was in turmoil, lightning flashes, waves of sand as high as the Himalayas, the stench of sweat and shit, the chattering of TV commercials, the screams of the insane. It is terrible how painful noise can be in a universe of silence. One must love life to suffer so much. One must love death to court it so assiduously. Where does evil come from? What goes on in our heads?

I spent the whole night fretting.

Sofiane had everything, he had a house, he had my affection, he had friends, he had a routine. *What about the rest? You can't live on love alone when you're imprisoned.* Try as I might, I can't work it out, but it is not always possible to name the thing that kills. *The daily hardship? The all-idiocy?* Yes, these play a part, but there are more powerful reasons: corruption, religion, bureaucracy, the culture of crime, of violence, of clannishness, the veneration of death, the glorification of the tyrant, the love of ostentation, the passion for strident sermons. *Is that all?* There are those who set a bad example. It comes from the top, from a government that mistakes ignorance for a priceless diamond; barbarism for sophistication; shoddy policies for brilliant statesmanship misappropriation of funds for legitimate disbursements. *Oh, the bastards; oh, the stink of corruption! What about the intelligentsia, what do they have to say? They're not all dead.* What do you want them to say? They're in prison, begging for a blanket and a piece of bread like everyone else. *What about the heroes, the veterans, the hard nuts who revelled in the war?* Oh, you poor deluded fool – they're fossils now, their memories belong to others who rake in lots of cash. *So is that all?* No, there are the walls collapsing, the disasters the government has signed us up for, and the fear, the dreadful fears of a static life. *What is left when all routes are cut off?*

> *Dying is no big deal*
> *When living is possible.*
> *One elsewhere is worth a thousand heres.*
> *Misery for misery*
> *Considering the effort of the journey*
> *The pain of being wrenched away*
> *And the fear of losing one's way.*
> *The pleasure of finally believing in tomorrow*
> *Is well worth sacrificing one's life.*
> *Like the bird*
> *Like the prophet*
> *Let us spread our wings, shake dust from our sandals*
> *And walk into the wind*
> *Burn a path*
> *Somewhere in the world is the promised land.*

Suddenly, in my heart, I feel like a *harraga*.

My door did not go *bang bang*, it went knock knock. That sound our doors no longer know how to make came to me like a divine breath. No one visits me except the local moralisers, the gorgon from the rue Marengo, and mad Moussa. I listen to them carefully, but they don't understand, they just talk all the more. Then there are the officials who arrive on fixed dates hoping to take me by surprise, the meter readers for the gas, the water, the electricity, but they don't count, they silently take their readings looking at us as though we're invalids. I never dare to ask them about the charges for services never provided. Sometimes, trudging from afar, shuffling pitifully, the local tom–cat Missing Parts comes round to see if Minnie Mouse has returned home. He never says anything, he simply sighs as his one remaining eye stares down at his orphaned leg. It's pitiful to watch as he contorts himself like a man on a high wire, vainly trying to scratch his missing ear with the stump of an arm. I fear for his safety, one ill-timed sneeze and he's ready for the scrapheap. I've tried explaining to him that it's pointless, that it's all virtual, that Phantom Limb Syndrome means that though a limb is gone, the feeling continues for a time, it is persistence of sensation, a recognised phenomenon, it's nothing new. I try to explain that there are better ways of expressing his shyness than scratching his earlobe or the tip of his missing nose. But I know it's not easy to change one's habits. I thought about bringing him to the hospital and fitting him with prostheses but I gave up on the idea; he would have to be completely rebuilt at which point he'd be even more at a loss. With a hook attached to his stump, persistence of feeling could kill him. I remembered the corny old joke: Tramp goes up to a tourist. 'Hey, monsieur, I would bet a hundred francs I can kiss my right eye.' 'You're on!' says the tourist and stands back to watch. The tramp takes out his glass eye and brings it to his lips. 'And now I bet you a thousand that I can kiss my left eye.' 'Impossible,' says the tourist, setting down the stake and stepping closer. At which point the tramp takes out his false teeth and brings them to his left eye. Missing Parts could earn a living making bets now that he can't work as a porter any more.

Then there's 235, who shows up once a week with his bus. He comes to ask if there's any news, with a bus full of pilgrims in tow, furious to find themselves in the back of beyond. He's really sweet, but he tends to forget himself and his passengers end up hanging around in the midday sun while he's sipping lemonade and telling me for the umpteenth time about his saintly mother. He's a good boy.

My dear friends phone about once a year, always with the same cutting remark: 'So, what are you up to these days?' I always retort: 'What about yourself?' firmly believing 'least said, soonest offended'. It's always the women who don't give a damn who come nosing around. '*Hi, how are*

you?' and they're off badmouthing everyone in the neighbourhood. God, but the women in this country have got
sharp tongues, I don't know where they get it from. You
could cut their throats and they'd still be gossiping.

Knock knock! Knock knock!

My heart was racing. I yanked the door open so fast I
nearly dislocated my arm. It wasn't Chérifa.

A young woman. Twenty-two, twenty-three maybe.
Dark hair, a slightly 'so what' air, jeans that fit her like a
glove, her chest sags a little, she needs to rethink her bra.
Dark eyes, lots of eyeliner, eyebrows like circumflexes. She's
clearly a worrier, she overthinks before she speaks. *Sniff
sniff.* She smells good. Like me, she has her perfume sent
from Paris in the diplomatic bag.

'If you're looking for Lamia, you've found her. And you
are?'

'Um . . . Scheherazade.'

'Please don't tell me you've come from Oran or Tangiers
on the advice of my idiot brother Sofiane because, I swear,
I'll kill myself.'

'Um . . . I'm from Algiers.'

A beautiful voice, warm, a little husky. The name suits
her to a T. She is the Orient that exists only in fairytales.

'So?'

'Um . . . I was looking for Chérifa . . .'

'What? Chérifa? My Chérifa?'

'Um . . . yes.'

'Get in here right now and explain yourself.'

★

From the moment my little runaway from Oran showed up, I was destined to meet people. Missing Parts and 235 were at the top of the list. It was because of Chérifa that Bluebeard lost his sense of mystery; these days I just think of him as one more neighbour to distrust. Now here is the beautiful Scheherazade come to tell me extraordinary tales. I'm up to my eyes in myths and legends. Scheherazade is practically a colleague, she's a fourth-year biology student. She hails from Constantine, a town that died with the Jewish exodus in 1962, all that remains is a pile of stones and a few old men who lean against the crumbling walls pretending to dream of the beauties of the Mesozoic era and to know all there is to know about the charms of Andalucía in their grandfathers' day. An earthquake measuring 9 on the Richter scale could not have done a better job. The few remaining women wear black feathers, she tells me, people call them crows. While Scheherazade describes her curious hometown, in my mind I am flicking through Yasmina Khadra's novel *The Swallows of Kabul*. Her grandfather works in the rag trade, he imports fabric from the Sentier district in Paris.

'Would you credit it? And why not buy from Medina or from Islamabad, after all they are our brothers?'

'They're old boyhood friends.'

'I understand.'

A wise man is a wise man, what can you say? Scheherazade lives in the halls of residence at Ben-Aknoun University, she has a tiny room on the top floor, building 12, stairwell B, which, over time, she has managed to make cosy. This is against regulations but the elderly janitor doesn't know her or has forgotten her. She cooks, stays at home, listens to modern music and invites her girlfriends – some of whom even dare to smoke!

'I know all about caretakers, my dear, I've hoodwinked my fair share in my time. The janitors at the Hôpital Parnet are ruthless, but they've never caught me out. I turn up on time, I leave on time, my white coat is clean and I always give them a cheery *salaam alaykum*.'

'At university we have to bribe the porters, they insist on a tip at the end of the month ...'

'That's new. In my day, it was more about the sensual. They'd beg us to show them our knickers. If you hiked your dress up to your thigh, they'd lick your hand, you could send them off to run errands, they would even lie on your behalf if need be. It sounds like they've aged. So, where is Chérifa?'

'Well, that's the thing – I'm looking for her.'

'You mean she ran away?'

'That's the least of it ...'

'Tell me everything.'

'...'

We talked. For hours. Everything I feared had happened and more besides. I blame myself: by imagining the worst, I brought it about. And that idiot Mourad played on my fears at every opportunity: 'Women are all the same!' he'd say every time I got discouraged and gave in to despair. In this beautiful city, there will never be a shortage of men willing to speak ill of women.

On the fateful day when she left here, Chérifa went into the town centre. This is where waifs and strays converge, the illegal immigrants, the unemployed, the tramps and all the little creatures that the economic reforms have forced to turn tricks for 300 dinars an hour on the byroads off the straight and narrow. Here in the heart of the city, abject poverty meets garish luxury beneath the all-seeing eye of God and his representatives. There's nothing to be done about it, even Hercules would wear himself down trying to understand the topography. In fact the place reminds me of Rachid Boudjedra's novel *Ideal Topography for an Aggravated Assault*, the story of a Kabyle who arrives in Paris from a rocky peak in the Djurdjura and goes round and round and round on the métro, astonished by everything he sees in this never-ending tunnel only to finally succeed in getting himself murdered. He never manages to see the sun shine in Paris or enjoy the peace of its streets. Which in turn reminds me of Camus's *L'Étranger*, which has Meursault going round and round and round in the luminous meanders of Algiers until he finally meets an Arab by a sand dune, can't understand him, and kills him stone dead. The same tragedy, the same unfathomable humanity.

A hundred metres uphill is the seat of government, though that's not really what has people flocking here. A hundred metres downhill is the harbour, with its tubby boats and an army of freight agents afflicted by facial tics. A hundred metres to the left is the Commissariat of Police with its army of informants. A hundred metres to the right is the Kasbah with its inscrutable mysteries. In the shadow of La Grande Poste, in the middle of the square, is the one and only entrance to the famous Algiers métro which has

212

been a boon and a nightmare for five successive presidents, twenty governments and two thousand utterly insignificant *deputés*. Ten times it has been inaugurated, and each time we believed this was the one. The entrance is a fantasia of pink marble and anodised bronze used to great effect. It is possible to go down into the station but the tunnel leads nowhere, it simply trails off into the muddy depths and the prehistoric magma. It sometimes seems as though from the bottomless ventilation shaft, you can hear people whispering in Chinese. As it waits for its trains and its satisfied commuters who, we are assured, will arrive within six months, the passageways serve as a shopping arcade for the local fauna. One person's loss is another person's gain. Here, luxury items are sold, dope, guns, forged identity papers, counterfeit money, merchandise which arrives via the port, the Commissariat, the Government Annexe, the Kasbah, the post office.

There's no need to look, everything is within reach. The place is teeming. Here the little people do their shopping far from laws and from harassment. From an aerial viewpoint, you'd swear they were free electrons, but no, they are controlled by gravitational force. The area attracts teenage runaways the way nectar attracts bees. They've been told that this is the gateway to a new life and that, as with any travel agency, there are endless choices of destination. Two hundred metres away, abutting the harbour walls in glorious confusion, stand the bus and train stations and between them, on a patch of waste ground, are the gypsy cabs, a riot of clapped-out rustbuckets, every one in perfect working order. 'Direct from producer to consumer' is a slogan from the socialist era, but it applies perfectly to the black market.

The elegant women of Algiers also frequent the square; it is the only place where they can find perfume from Paris imported from Taiwan via Dubai. People say that at customs the sniffer dogs are trained not to smell perfumes but that's just a joke the kids tell; in fact in Algiers there are no sniffer dogs in customs – if there were all hell would break loose. The elegant ladies turn up here dressed like paupers hoping to pass unnoticed but their pale complexions and their strange lisping accent give them away and prices are hiked up.

'She came up to me outside La Grande Poste. I . . . I buy imported perfume there . . . you can't find anything in the shops.'

'I get what I need from Tata Zahia who used to work at the Union. She runs a little shop from home. It's all good stuff, and direct from Paris, too, if you please! She's a genuine trafficker, honest, friendly, she'll even have a little chat over a glass of mint tea. Sometimes there are fifty people there and we have a party. She has a cousin who's a minister and he supplies her on the quiet. I'll recommend you. So, what happened next?'

'I brought her back to my rooms in the halls of residence . . . I felt sorry for her . . .'

'Did she have her holdall?'

'What?'

'Her clothes, her gear.'

'Um . . . yeah.'

'So how is she? I mean the pregnancy ... is she eating properly?'

'Um ... yes. I couldn't let her move in with me, my room is tiny ... besides I need peace and quiet to study ... and anyway, it's against the rules ...'

'So where does she sleep?'

'Sometimes my room, sometimes one of the other girls ... we organised a rota ... whenever she needs to move, we distract the caretaker. During the day, she goes for a walk in the city, and ...'

'And?'

'...'

Chérifa is slippery as an eel. After a week of doing nothing, of strolling in the sunshine, she hooked up with a homeless man who smelled of damp straw, he was succeeded by some useless cop, then an incompetent journalist and now, apparently, she's run off with an airline pilot we don't know the first thing about beyond the fact that he dresses too well to be honest.

'We're worried. She's been gone a week now. The girls are really fond of her, she's so happy-go-lucky but she ... um ... well she's due any day now so she shouldn't be ...'

They've clearly been charmed by the siren song of my Lolita.

'I know, I know.'

'So what do we do?'

'Track down the pilot, it can't be that difficult, there's only one airline in this country last time I checked. It's called Air Algérie, right? We'll just wait until he ejects from his glider.'

'I ... um ... I don't want any trouble ...'

'I'll deal with everything. I'll pop in and see him unexpectedly, the same way you came to see me. Did Chérifa give you my address?'

'Not exactly ... I had to search. She talked about you all the time, about Rampe Valée, the Turk's palace, the Frenchman's castle, the Jew's shack, the Kabyle's cave ... I ... um ... I couldn't understand why the house had so many names.'

'It's history, it's complicated. So, what then?'

'She mentioned the Hôpital Parnet, she talked about your friends, about Mourad, Sofiane, Monsieur 236.'

'*235!* I'm not intimate with every driver who works for GAUTA!'

'Sorry, Monsieur 235 ... Missing Parts and Bluebeard, the gorgon from the rue Marengo ... and ... well ... your ghosts ... the ones in the house, I mean.'

'Well how do you like that? A veritable menagerie!'

'She's very fond of you, and she really is very sorry. One day she actually went to see you at the hospital and she came back so upset ... You were in a terrible mood and she didn't dare talk to you.'

'Let's dispense with sentimentality for the moment, just give me the facts. So what happened next?'

'...'

I choked back my tears, I would have to hear this drama out to the bitter end if I was to understand.

So, she had met some peasant in the woods next to the university campus. It's the sort of place that attracts lovers

216

trying to get away from prying eyes and radical preachers. Our two country bumpkins meet and realise they are kindred souls and before you know it they're embroiled in some vegetarian discussion. They pretend they're living in a commune, they draw up a list, life is beautiful. Their little game lasts a week before things turn sour. '*He's as much fun as a lizard,*' she said. That's Chérifa all over, the minute she's bored, she's off.

The next day, some other freak was trailing her back to the halls of residence. No need for binoculars to spot this one, the other girls knew immediately where this nasty piece of work came from. The dark glasses, the walkie-talkie glued to the ear, that swagger like a boat putting out to sea, that arrogance that says you have the world at your feet and a Colt 45 swinging by your side, these are the hallmarks of an institution, the most important institution in this country: the police.

Her new companion offered Chérifa a season ticket to the seediest parts of Algiers which, if Mourad is to be believed, are among the most stomach-turning in the solar system. Things move at a break-neck pace, Chérifa learns to smoke, to drink, to fight, to strike a pose and she also learns a new vocabulary. The other girls stop their ears and listen, the little fool dropped words like bombs. She would go out at ridiculous hours, come back at all hours without so much as a by-your-leave. The girls at the halls of residence couldn't handle it, one by one they closed their doors to her. Young women from good families are more terrified by a whiff of scandal than they are by terrorism.

The caretakers started to grumble openly, the rumours spread. Attracted by the scent, dubious cars began showing up on the campus. Before long the sticklers came out of the woodwork claiming that stranglers were operating in the area. I suspect this means the sermonisers and the Defenders of Truth. It's high time we standardised the vocabulary, we can't go on using different words for the same things. The problem is people stammer and shift and shilly-shally about anything to do with Islam. It's like the Tower of Babel, people say stickler, strangler, cut-throat, Islamist, lunatic, fanatic, fundamentalist, terrorist, suicide bomber, jihadist, Wahhabi, Salafist, Djazarist, Taliban, Tango, Zarqaouist, Afghani, born in the *banlieue*, member of al-Qaeda and I don't know what else – it's like these people had nothing to do with Islam. But they're all basically the same person with different clothes and different beliefs. The specialists should at least agree on their terms, that way we would be able to have a frank discussion about the problem, but let's be honest, if Islam is responsible for any-thing, it's producing Muslims, there's no way of knowing how they will turn out later, and there's no after-sales ser-vice. For crying out loud, if people have children, they should keep them under control.

Chérifa imposed herself on Scheherazade, a seven-month swollen belly commands respect. But Chérifa did not change her ways. A few days later, she showed up with a clueless journalist who had a pen tucked behind his ear and a newspaper tucked under his arm. Scheherazade, who has a mouthful of peculiar expressions from her part of the country, dispatched him quickly: 'A skinny little runt who wouldn't need to catch a sheep to play knucklebones.' The handover between policeman and journalist did not go well, there was a punch-up and the newshound found himself in hospital with cuts and contusions. The following day, the front-page story in his newspaper read: *Our star reporter K.M. suffered a savage beating from police officers as a result of his hard-hitting investigation into the misconduct of Inspector H.B., who has been implicated in a major arms-dealing racket with the Islamist maquis.* Scheherazade showed me a press clipping. What a story!

The authorities' response came the following day via the pages of the government daily *El Moudjahid* (The Holy Warrior), from which Truth spills out over the country. Under the banner headline THERE IS JOURNALISM AND THEN THERE IS JOURNALISM, it reads: *It has been discovered that Monsieur K.M., a disgrace to a profession that has done so much for democracy, is involved in drug trafficking on a vast scale in collaboration with a certain sister country whose hatred for our homeland is matched only by its vicious oppression of the heroic Saharan people engaged in a legitimate struggle for independence recognised by the international community, and with certain groups in Algiers known for their pathological greed and their contempt for the extraordinarily progressive policy initiated by the President of the Republic. When challenged by the heroic Inspector H.B., the suspect attempted to corrupt the officer, offering him the services of a prostitute known to the police, a certain C.D., however the gallant officer, a man of irreproachable morals, flatly refused. Concerned by the seriousness of the facts alleged, and alarmed at the effects on law and order, the Public Prosecutor immediately issued a warrant for the arrest of Monsieur K.M. and ordered a search of the news-paper's offices. The case continues.*

What has Morocco got to do with any of this? And what, precisely, has the President's policy achieved? God, how these people love things to be complicated!

The university campus witnessed a brief war of attrition between the press and the police, and then everything went back to normal, the journalist vanished without trace, the newspaper was shut down, the offices auctioned off and the editor got two years' hard labour. While they were about it, the police interrogated and tortured a few other journalists as a precaution. The inspector was not forgotten in all this chaos: he received a promotion.

Chérifa, having brought disgrace on the university halls of residence, was formally requested to leave the premises. There was nothing else the girls could do, their exams were looming, their parents were panicking and visiting more often. This was no time for jokes.

Chérifa wandered the city for a while before hooking up with the pilot in a café next door to the offices of Air Algérie. Scheherazade caught a glimpse of him behind the wheel of his magnificent car when the runaway returned to campus to collect her belongings. Forty-something and with a little paunch, the pilot looked quite dapper and seemed to be a cheerful character. Scheherazade thought she heard the shameless hussy refer to him as 'Rachid'.

Their goodbyes were minimal, since the little madam is incapable of saying good morning or goodnight.

Since then, there had been no news. Had she taken the train? Had she gone back to Oran? Is she somewhere else and, if so, where?

Curtain. End of drama. Now, I could let myself weep.

Who would have believed that I, Lamia, a paediatrician, a strong-minded, intelligent woman, oblivious to everyday contingencies and immune to sentimentality, would be turning my life upside down for the sake of a little country girl who's become a scarlet woman! I was filled with a curious feeling. *Guilt?* That's certainly part of it, I smothered her and she ran away. Telling her she needed to be educated was another mistake, it made her feel a fool, cut off from the world. *Anger, the resentment that comes from failure, from . . .?* Not just that, rage, a desire to . . . *It's envy, pure mother-daughter envy!* Yes, I suppose. Chérifa is happy to give her all to the first man who comes along, and yet I love her, I offered her my life, my home, and she refuses even to grace me with her presence. Not a single visit, not a phone call, not even a message. It's stupid, it's pathetic to get involved in such idiotic relationships.

What was it that I called her, what was the word I spat in her face when all she wanted was a smile, a glance, a hug?

I give up. I've already given her everything I had to give!

Louiza and Sofiane left me with deep scars, Chérifa ripped my heart out. It's not fair. I'm done with it, I need to move on. I am not going to let this haunt me to my dying day.

'So, tell me, my dear Scheherazade, do you really miss that lunatic so much that you've come all the way to Rampe Valée? Isn't that a little like something out of a fairytale?'

'We're very fond of her ... um ... we ...'

'Go on.'

'Well, um ...'

'I get it.'

We're all in the same boat; like me, the girls at the university are filling an emptiness in their lives. Apart from their textbooks and their notebooks, they have nothing that makes them feel human. Their lives at the university felt hollow, formless, a prelude to their lives as women, a shadowgraph, a mere outline; they were hardworking, diligent, dutiful, submissive, slaves to timetables and rituals, and Chérifa, naive and happy-go-lucky, came along and challenged everything. In discovering our innermost dreams, we do not emerge unscathed. And, being women, we have too many dreams.

Scheherazade abruptly got to her feet. The night porter was about to begin his shift and would discover she was absent at roll-call. After six pm, the price of his silence is exorbitant.

She promised to come back and see me.

Algiers airport is unlike any in the world. All the dangerous contraptions the commercial aviation industry has devised ever since Icarus first flew too close to the sun are to be found there. With all its junk and all its gaping wounds I can't understand how it's still standing. The building is all splints and plasters. It's a miracle the planes still remember how to fly. I had a knot in my stomach as I stepped inside this beleaguered world that looks like a national disaster and where a sizeable subset of humanity rushes, shrieks, weeps, jostles and gesticulates. After several collisions and copious sweating, I found myself standing in front of a breeze-block barrier next to the public lavatories, a mouldering area where the ambient temperature was several hundred degrees. Above the low wall a cardboard sign suspended from the ceiling was emblazoned in red with the words *Bienvenu, Information* in twelve different languages (or simply repeated twelve times). I stepped forward. Behind the counter, a phalanx of bungling idiots were playing a game a little like 'Battleships'. The aim is to destroy the maximum number of planes with the minimum number of bombs in the shortest possible time. Brazenly, I addressed them, but they spoke a language I could not quite place, something gruff, halting, punctuated by sprays of black spittle and accompanied by threatening gestures. Nearby, sitting cross-legged on blocks of wood, girls wearing *pagnes* and bonnets were shelling peas, grinding millet or knitting mittens. They were not happy, something is bothering them so they adopt the pose of scorned lovers. I often prefer to view things and people through a distorting prism, I find it makes them easier to understand, they prove to be different to how they appear. The leader of this tribe, easily identifiable by her headdress, her sceptre and a fine collection of pendants dangling from her neck, her ears, even her navel, looked daggers at me, but when I explained that I had not come to disturb their glorious rituals but to see my cousin Rachid, a pilot, about a family matter of the utmost importance, she flashed me a lewd smile. I was treated to a volley of crude sniggers and a barrage of innuendo. Rachid clearly has something of a reputation among his fellow pilots who envy him and covet his many 'cousins'. I squeezed my eyes closed and imagined them all being strangled by King Kong and, emerging from this therapy, I found myself face to face with a man in his priestly garb, a sort of evangelical minister with a firm but gentle voice. He had appeared from a hut behind the stockade. Beneath his penetrating gaze, I felt childish and naive.

'What do you want, woman?'

I was safe, this fellow spoke my dialect of Latin. I explained myself again, employing broken Arabic the better to flatter his eloquence and get the information I needed at a bargain price. The minister gazed at me for a long time, peered searchingly into my eyes until he could see the colour of my knickers, then he nodded, shrugged, bustled about behind his pulpit, scribed a few hieroglyphics with the aid of a golden flint, mumbled some incantations into a handset and in the time it takes to roast a lizard over a slow flame, a knight from an operetta appeared in full regalia whom I immediately recognised: fortysomething, pot-bellied, a cheery fellow, he went by the name of Rachid. When he saw me, impeccably dressed in my immaculate chasuble, he unsheathed the smile reserved for fine ladies, a solemn, sophisticated, nonchalant rictus that twitched at the corners of his mouth. Scheherazade was right, the handsome hunk was a miserable loser.

I needed to quickly befriend him if I was to achieve my goal: to find Chérifa safe and sound.

True to the dictates of his shallow, callous nature, he immediately attempted to seduce me. Usually, I am brutal with self-styled Lotharios who try to chat me up, but in this case I decided to be tactful:

'I'm in a relationship with a sort of Bluebeard who's planning to cut my throat, but if you want to try your luck in twenty or thirty years' time, and assuming I'm still up to it, I'll willingly give myself to you for free.'

The man's a chancer. He said, 'You're on.'

Via a rickety metal fire escape, we headed down to the terrace café like a couple of travellers each with his own map. Panoramic views of the hinterland, lifeless suburbs sporting a shock of state-of-the-art satellite dishes, abandoned building sites with girders soaring into empty space and cranes slowly rusting, the motorway sweeping impetuously away with its miscellaneous cars and vehicles and, in the distant mountains, a raging forest fire. This is the ravaged, windswept landscape of Dinotopia, where bellowing pterodactyls take wing and tyrannosaurs breathe fire. The magic of the IMF has done its work here and we have been sent back to the Middle Ages filled with fearsome *djinns* and comical mendicants. Below us sprawled the airport, the hangars, the ramshackle planes lined up with their noses to the wind, the runway with its puddles, its potholes, its air-stairs, its windsocks; the ballet of baggage handlers. I can't begin to describe the strange things that were happening on the ground, light-fingers were fluttering and filching and in broad daylight. Oh, yes, and there were policemen, dozens of them everywhere.

'I'm listening,' I said, before he forgot himself.

Though I know it all too well, as I listened to him regale me with tales of his conquests, I was reminded how intelligent imbecility needs to sound if it is to prosper. I've never heard the like. He'd met Chérifa in the café next to Air Algérie downtown. His heart had skipped a beat, the sight of a Lolita in distress moved our gallant hero. He had qualms, but he did what he felt was his duty. He is prepared to try anything once, and he likes to show off his trophies. He felt particularly proud of this catch: a pregnant, abandoned girl – what better? Good lord, he paraded her around the Great South, flying her in his rusty crate to Tamanrasset, Djanet, Timimoun, Illizi, tourist destinations for those of us from the Great North, sand upon sand in millions of tonnes, heat capable of melting stones, clumps of palm trees here

226

and there to indicate areas of human habitation surrounded by the vast immensity and by silver-tongued men with sombreros and Toyotas who pretend that they have a time-table to respect. That little wretch Chérifa manages to commandeer bus drivers, pilots and army officers, while I'm having trouble making ends meet! Chérifa, of course, was delighted; she laughed at everything, marvelled at everything, was thrilled to see the white-hot sky floating above the boundless, white-hot sands and, between the two, the Blue Men, those magnificent nomads, trailed by gentle, gallant dromedaries across the rolling dunes. Dear God, I picture her there and I feel distraught, how could she have thought life in the desert would be fun? Then, of course, she started having pains, vomiting, thrashing about.

'I can guess what comes next! You tossed her aside in a region so vast that people get lost inside their own homes.'

'How dare you suggest such a thing! She left of her own accord . . . I . . .'

'She's not even seventeen years old, she knows nothing about life, she still believes in fairies, she'll swallow any nonsense, but even she realised that you were the biggest cretin of all time. I'm just dumbfounded that it took her a couple of days to tell it to you straight.'

'I . . . I . . .'

'Go to hell!'

Going to court is out of the question, Chérifa is known to the police as a prostitute and she would probably be blamed for the battle between press and police at the university halls of residence. As a woman, she has no rights, as a prostitute she has a lot of explaining to do, as an unmarried teenage mother, she deserves the death penalty. Godforsaken ignorant fucking *bled*! Besides, what judge would listen to me? I'm a woman, I'm a spinster, a troublemaker, I don't wear the veil, I don't own a burka, I walk with my head held high, I give as good as I get, and in the eyes of their infernal laws Chérifa is nothing to me. And I have no one to sign for me.

I crawled home. Emptiness, which after all is my universe, exploded inside my head; I couldn't see, I couldn't hear, I couldn't breathe. I ceased to exist. Everything I loved, everything I had dreamed about with all my heart, everything I missed to the point that I turned myself into a nunlike automaton had miraculously come to life in the form of that uneducated, ungrateful, emotionally unstable girl. Life tore through me like a tornado through a cave. I gave her everything, she rejected everything and the breath of life that her presence inspired in me has leaked away like air from a burst tyre. I was angry with myself. I was angry with her, but I also saw a kind of fulfilment in that fundamental imbalance, I felt both uplifted and reduced to nothing, a nebulous middle ground between the happiness I had finally glimpsed and the perpetual, unending sadness of our life.

Where are you Chérifa? How far can your life take you when there is nothing to hold you back? Wherever you are, if you can read my thoughts, you should know that Rampe Valée, the haunted house and the heart of Lamia will always be open to you.

It's time to go home and get ready to wait; eternity is a long time.

A bird is a thing of beauty
But, alas, a bird has wings
Which, just as they serve to alight
So too they serve to take flight.
That is the tragedy of birds.

I was inspired when I wrote those words.

Act III

To Live or to Die

All that is begun must end
This we have known since the dawn of time.
Already to speak is to be silent
And to be born is already to die.
What matters that God wills
And the Devil laughs?
Our reason for being
Our incessant lunacy
Is doggedly to believe
In the impossible.
That which is finished is invited
To begin again
And thus
Living is possible.

In my stupor I see everything in shades of grey, a shabby, squalid grey. The world seems a thousand leagues away, or somewhere off to one side, I'm not sure. I pass my days without seeing it. I remember that the world existed once, that as the result of some accident, some curse, some wasting disease, I have been exiled from it. I allow myself to drift, it is futile to cling to anything in a world that is crumbling. I lash out between the falls, I rant and rave between convulsions, I pull myself together but it doesn't last and the pain after the calm is more intense.

I watch television the way you might leaf through a book in the dark, I listen to the radio, but all it does is buzz in my ear and when I retreat into silence a terrible roaring fills my head and turmoil crushes my heart. At the hospital, I manhandle the kids as though they were my own brats and their mothers tear them from my arms. They are suspicious of me, there are rumours of children being stolen, clapped in irons and sold at auction, rented out to beggar women, shipped off to war zones. Some are found alive, others dead, but most of them are never seen again. And once more I am faced with the Dantesque vision of a starless sky, a planet with no children, and – on the small scale that is my world in the arse-end of Rampe Valée – a house with no Lolita.

How did I ever manage to live without my Louiza, my sister, when the absence of Chérifa is killing me? In me, the same causes do not produce the same effects, each time the result is worse. Either I'm starting to show my age or I'm sick and tired of watching my life draining away in torrents, Papa, Maman, Yacine, Sofiane, Chérifa and everything else that's ebbed and gone: people, little pleasures, daydreams in the moonlight, even the kittens that purred on the sofa have grown into fat alley cats that keep us awake at night. Dear God, how painful this life is!

I hate what I've become, I'm emotional, hysterical, quick to confuse things, too unbalanced to keep on an even keel, I've tipped into catatonia. I tell myself that reason is the antidote to these bouts of madness but even as I think this, it occurs to me that healing simply clears the ground for new contagion. God forbid I should have come to the point of finding my pleasure in pain, my freedom in captivity, my clarity in chaos, my tranquillity in turmoil. It's a terrifying thought.

I began to search again, I'm not one to sit around doing nothing. Scheherazade visited less and less so I went and surprised her at the university at Ben–Aknoun. After all she might have heard something. Monsieur 235 went with me at a moment's notice, his rustbucket of a bus spitting fumes and flames. I thought it might be a good idea for him to visit the halls of residence so he could keep his mother supplied with lady's companions and – who

234

knows? – might even find a lady for himself – or two, or three, or why not four, after all he is a Muslim, a religion that favours one-sided polygamy. Scheherazade's rabbit hutch was minuscule, but absolutely charming; it would make a lovely cupboard in someone's mansion. She was wearing slippers and a night cap, her eyes were red and her eyelids twitched. I was worried I had tired her out with all my questions, but no, she had been cramming, burning the candle at both ends, exams were looming and rumours were rife that quotas had been imposed by people in high places. She was a nervous wreck. I tried to reassure her: there have been all sorts of rumours since the programme of reform proposed by the *marabouts* that would spell triumph for cretinism, militant fundamentalism and galloping racism. I know all about these reforms, I was a nervous wreck myself. The ministry wants no more nurses, no more doctors, and certainly no more lab assistants and absolutely no ... what else ... oh, that's right, no more people who can read and write! Apparently there are so many we don't know what to do with them, but then suddenly we find out that actually we don't have nearly enough and have to start churning them out again. Still the ministry ploughs ahead, slashing funding, turning a blind eye to negative results, opening new hospitals wherever it can find four walls, operating on the basis that hiring thirteen numskulls to the dozen is the perfect solution to rampant unemployment. Development has become a co-ordinated series of imbalances, or at least that's what I heard on some deathly dull TV talk show. This makes sense if you already know how to walk, otherwise it might be best to stay sitting down – something armchair pundits are experts at. The real problem is that the restricted intake into the medical profession is based on the size of the population and not, as it should be, on the number of people who are actually ill; while the former is dwindling dangerously, the latter is growing exponentially. In such circumstances, it seems obvious that the way to calculate is not simply by adding zeroes, but the ministry refuses to acknowledge this, preferring to cling to the old methods that worked well back when the dead did not talk.

To distract myself from my woes and Scheherazade from her fears, we had some mint tea and sang old songs which, given our mood, were deeply depressing. The girls in Block 12, who had either been dozing and fretting or swotting and daydreaming, joined in and our *sotto voce* blues became a raucous racket that echoed down the corridors, leaving nothing to the imagination of Satan himself. When women get together, they quickly become shameless. The girls dug out scarves and tambourines and started to play and suddenly it was pandemonium, there was winking and belly rolls and more besides. It's a glorious sight watching people revert to the wild state, and rediscover their vices. It was so loud we wouldn't have heard God Himself raging against the infidels. Finding himself the centre of attention, 235 took the opportunity to hard-sell the virtues of his saintly mother. He was exultant, everything suddenly seemed possible. Every single girl there promised to come and sit with his Maman once their exams were over. And when a girl is perfect for a mother, how much more perfect is she for the son? All 235 had to do now was trust to the skills of these girls to capture him dead or alive.

The fires of love having been kindled, I could slip away and carry on my lonely quest. From time to time, it's good to stave off the tears, but mostly, the best thing to do is cry your eyes out. Just then, I felt torn.

I did the rounds of the maternity wards, there must be about twenty in Algiers and the suburbs, I sowed some seeds by which I mean I appealed to colleagues, to those who still remember their oaths, to friends I knew from university, to friends of friends, and to their pals too.

'You couldn't miss her,' I told my conscripts, emphasising the importance of doing a good job when you're lucky enough to have one, 'the second she walks into a room all eyes turn. She's eight months gone, a Lolita dragging around a beach ball, if you keep your eyes peeled, you'll spot her.'

As a *quid pro quo*, I offered to get each of them some piece of medical equipment in return, the poor things have only their fingernails to work with and only their eyes to weep. They drew up a wish list that would have brought tears to the eye of a medical supplier. One of them asked for an electric generator. There's no shortage of equipment at the Hôpital Parnet, the hospital manager is well connected, being the minister's cousin and the Pasha's nephew, but even so, this was some list! I needed to work out how to smuggle the things out of the hospital without being spotted. The security guards sleep all day, but if I trusted to that I was bound to get caught.

★

I went back to waiting. I was tense, I spent my time agonising, surmising, supposing, going round in circles, never straying far from the phone. I thought about buying a mobile phone but they cost an arm and a leg, I don't have the money and I don't have the energy to traipse round the shops, it's all too exhausting and I'm sick to the back teeth of sales patter. I trusted in my own alert system, Chérifa's not the kind to sleep in the streets, she'd show up at some hospital demanding bed, board and blanket – something the King of Spain would be hard pressed to find if he took it into his head to seek treatment here. Life has given Chérifa a rough ride, yet somehow she's managed to develop the personality of a spoiled brat; she could bring the sternest hospital porter to his knees.

Minute by minute, I counted off the remaining weeks, the last days, the final hours before the end. By my calculations, on May 22, under the sign of Gemini, the nine months of Chérifa's pregnancy elapsed and she was delivered. Wait ... wait a minute, say that again, old woman! De ... delivered! So ... so soon, so early? Wh ... where ...? When ...? How ...? Is it a girl ... a boy? Sh ... she's a mother ... That makes me ... makes me ... um ... I was babbling. Shock, delight, sorrow, worry, anger, disappointment, I felt all these things seething inside me.

I know a thing or two about giving birth. Time was the maternity ward at Parnet exercised an irresistible fascination for me. I was obsessive. I would come and go, pretend to be dawdling like everyone else. The truth was I never tired of the joy of seeing those little amphibious monsters, flushed with fury, struggling like the devil to emerge from their

238

mothers and greedily latching on to the breast. Hardly born and already starving. I was awed by the beauty of these wrinkled, blind, bawling, blood-streaked creatures that smelled of sour milk and yellow diarrhoea. And I also watched, distraught, as angels arrived dead, their bodies limp, their skin blue, watched their mothers gazing fondly at them clinging to the belief that Allah knows what He is doing. I call that murder, but deaths in hospitals are not counted that way and we have been taught to accept whatever Allah wills. I have watched wonderful midwives clucking contentedly as they worked and poisonous witches who acted as though they were in the pay of rich landowners anxious to enhance their health, their youth, their social standing; I have seen doctors who were the epitome of kindness and many more who are repulsive shits. And the problems of underdevelopment, the idiocies of religion, the dodgy deals of the cliques lining each other's pockets as they preside over the neglect.

One day, I'd had enough, I don't remember whether I was chased out of the maternity unit or whether I simply got tired of remonstrating with self-important idiots.

The idea that Chérifa is somewhere in that grotesque system is unbearable.

I phoned again and again and again. My heart was filled with such rage . . . and yet with such hope.

'Sorry, she's not here.'

'Nothing to report.'

'Are you sure about your dates? She's definitely nine months?'

'Try calling Beni-Messous Hospital, it's like a battery farm, she's bound to be there.'

239

'She's not here with us, I just hope she's not in the maternity unit at Belfort – remember what happened there six months ago?'

'There was a little Lolita here, but she was completely crazy, she acted like my ex-husband's grandmother.'

'Call the police, we could do with them investigating this place!'

'Get in touch with the association for missing babies, you've heard the rumours . . .'

'Sorry, I completely forgot that you asked me, I've got my own problems, my husband is . . . hello? Hellooo?'

I hung up on her, I wasn't going to get stuck listening to her problems, I had more than enough of my own!

'Maybe she gave birth in a taxi . . . you know yourself that traffic jams are the biggest maternity unit in the country.'

'Why don't you put an ad in the paper?'

'I've been off work the past few days. Give me a call tomorrow.'

'. . .'

You wouldn't believe the things I had to listen to. Useless, the lot of them, looking for any excuse to give up. Some of them I'd happily kill with my bare hands. I'll have to check for myself. Where the hell is Mourad? He's never around when you need him! For pity's sake, a man can have a hangover and still show up for work. I called 235 and he zoomed here in his bulletproof bus. He'll get himself fired if he keeps doing me favours. We did the rounds of the hospitals, it was tedious, tortuous and disappointing.

You can refuse to accept them, throw a tantrum, but facts are facts: Chérifa really had disappeared.

I suppose that I might say: everything has come to pass. It was at this point that I truly gave up hope.

★

One after another the days slipped past, stealthily, invisibly. Hardly had Monday passed than Friday drew to a close in shame and disgust. The noise of the city came to me as though from some distant planet, I don't know whether it was this that I heard or the wind whipping up. My mind was on other things, I was connected to the ineffable pulse of time itself, that steady drip that echoes from one end of the universe to the other and deep within our every thought. Something had happened, far from me, beyond my control, beyond my means. Fate – I have no truck with it, but *mektoub* was clearly to blame – had proved more powerful, more cunning, more bitter and more swift than my love. I had been naive, I had been stupid, I had believed that love conquered all, that you only had to open your heart, your arms, your home to clinch the deal. I did everything I could – God is my witness – everything but what mattered: selflessness, doing something without expecting something in return. It's too late, I know it all too well, I have ceased to weep, to complain, to fear, I have ceased to suffer.

The days lose their dread the moment you cease to count them.

What else is there to say? Nothing. Nothing happens here in Rampe Valée. And nothing happens here in Algiers. Like a cemetery on an autumn day in a dying year in a deserted village in a godforsaken region of a country lost in a misbegotten world. I think about it, but then I realise that thinking changes nothing, something either happens or it does not happen. In the desert, it hardly matters, in fact it is probably more futile to do than not to do. How dull is life, how insipid misery and death when they are stripped of meaning. What I mean is that without love and its torments, living is a waste of time. Of course people seek out what is best for them, and so they may delude themselves and even feel pleased with themselves. Me, I've ceased to believe and I cannot understand how I continue to exist. From time to time, between bouts of spring-cleaning, there comes a little shudder, I surrender to it, still in control, I find myself hallucinating. I imagine myself fulfilled, having given all the love, the truth I have to give. I picture myself in a better world, not one where I can take it easy, but one where I can get rid of the deadwood, weed out the rabble-rousers. I would have done a thousand things because I knew they were possible, because I knew I had the strength to do them. I would have brought charges against the loathsome minister: statutory rape, child abandonment, breach of trust and, of course, misappropriation of public funds. I would have prosecuted the Association and its Ladies Bountiful, Parnet and its Pasha, the State and its imams, the police and the judges, the army and the President, *El Moudjahid* and its henchmen, and every Saïd, whether from north or south, whether *hajj* or *sidi*. I would have moved heaven and earth to make the world better still. And I would ask for nothing but the chance to watch people come and go in peace. Dear God, I would have made the most of such a life to visit every restaurant, every dancehall, every cinema, to fall head over heels fifty times a day! Yet in a country where nothing happens but for the sand shifting beneath our feet, the wind whistling above our heads, what can I do?

★

Since we are all masters in our own homes, I have decided to change everything in this house. As I said before, I'm not one to sit around with my arms folded and I can't bear people feeling sorry for themselves before they're dead and buried. I set about it with a vengeance, my ghosts were completely flummoxed! A sort of madness came over me, I went overboard, I emptied my piggybank, scraped together every *santeem* I could find, rushed into town and bought everything in sight. It was all just as shoddy and illicit as ever, but I didn't care, I paid them with the money I was paid and rather than feeling cheated, I felt as though I was cheating them at their own game. I set a few past masters to work, those with golden fingers and modest appetites like Tonton Hocine and conman-cum-bus driver Monsieur 235, to clear out the warehouses then, shut away in my cosy house, I sewed and knitted, embroidered and ironed and I don't know what else. Late into the night I was on a war footing. Following the example of Fantine, I got ready to breathe my last, crippled with pain, eaten away by tuberculosis. I got very emotional as I thought about it, mothers are extraordinary when it comes to laying down their lives for their children. Would Chérifa have the same chance as Cosette?

And then, one day, feeling my work was finished, I slowed my pace. It was time to survey my magnum opus. Hmm ... not bad, not bad at all. I had created the most magical nursery in the world. If Chérifa and our little baby could see what I had fashioned, they would rush home at the double.

There is no message
And certainly no moral.
There is no joy
And certainly no bliss.
There is no truth
And certainly no clarity.
There is no hope
And certainly no faith.
There is nothing
But what exists inside our heads
This clot of madness.
It is from here we must set out
And the path is steep.
La la li la laa!
La la li la laaaaa!

Act IV

Life is a fairytale
By dint of suffering, we forget.
We do not only grow through pain
Joy is a more powerful fertiliser.
It is enough that God should will it
And spring should come.

A nd God had willed it.
And spring had long since come.

And still I would have to drain this bitter cup to the dregs.

On the seventh day after what I had calculated to be Chérifa's due date, the message came by telephone. It was early in the morning on 29 May and I was getting ready to go to the hospital. I still work there sometimes as a doctor, but more and more often I go as a patient eaten away by some deep-rooted disease. When the phone rang – though I had probably already been warned, in a dream or by some other means – I realised that the end of my long ordeal was on the other end of the line. When flustered, I find it difficult to control my actions, foolishly I smoothed my hair, rubbed my hands on my thighs and even more foolishly I glanced around, searching for some help, some pretext, before nervously lifting the receiver as though angry at myself for behaving like a cornered animal.

To my dying day I will remember that conversation: every word, every inflection and every ache in my head, in my body, in every fibre of my being. A few brief, banal phrases, a few simple words, a few unexpected, awkward pauses that succeeded in conveying extraordinary things. True, the turmoil of the past few weeks had heightened my senses to the point where the slightest thing seemed a sign of tragedy, farce and madness waiting to explode.

'Hello?'

'Mademoiselle Lamia?'

'Um . . . maybe . . . yes.'

'Hello, my name is Anne . . .'

'Sorry . . . Hanna?'

'No, Anne, but it doesn't matter. I'm calling you about . . .'

No! Dear God no, not that! I can guess . . . she . . . she's going to tell me . . . It . . . it will kill me . . . I'll scream until the end of my days.

'Please, madame, not that . . . For pity's sake, please.'

'I'm sorry . . . I truly am sorry. We need to meet.'

'Why? What's the point?'

'It was Chérifa's wish . . .'

'What? . . . Dear God.'

'I can't tell you anything over the phone. Please come and see me.'

'Where?'

'Blida, the convent of Notre Dame des Pauvres. It's on the outskirts of the village, on the road to Chréa. Ask anyone, they'll know the way. I'll be waiting.'

I had considered every scenario, the impossible and the improbable − a commonplace in a country at war with itself − fate standing on a street corner and something that happens once in a thousand years, only once, a miracle so to speak, but this was something I had not considered, an intercession by the Church. I thought that this country was completely controlled from the mosque.

I jumped into a taxi, a rusty old heap painted New York yellow driven by an elderly man as fat and hairy as a walrus who for some reason was trawling round the neighbourhood. The people here in Rampe Valée never go anywhere, or if we do, we walk down the hill to catch the bus, praying to heaven that the GAUTA is running today. Was it *mektoub* that brought him to me? I refuse to believe it. Both man and machine were old and clapped out, which meant they would know every lane and byroad within a thousand-kilometre radius and since Blida's only fifty klicks from here, they could get there with their eyes closed. Sobbing into a hankie, I sat wringing my hands and trembling. The driver was sympathetic, he chatted away mostly to himself, a lone windmill turning in a gale. I offered monosyllabic answers as grist to his mill. It took my mind off things, I couldn't bear to stare out at careening carts and old nags fit only for the knacker's yard. Panic pounded in my temples and my heart was fit to burst.

'Did your husband beat you?'

'Snff … snff … yes.'

'So where are you headed now … to your parents?'

'Snff … snff … yes.'

'Did you defy him?'

'Snff … snff … I think so.'

'You have the look of a good woman about you. I suppose it was the devil led you astray?'

'Snff . . . snff . . . yes.'

'And this man who claims to be a Muslim is letting you travel all on your own without a veil?'

'Snff . . . snff . . . yes.'

'Back in my day, it would have been a disgrace!'

'Snff . . . snff . . . yes.'

' . . .'

I felt tempted to upbraid him, we had inherited 'his day' a hundredfold, but given his age and the state of his car, I worried that his heart might burst or the fan belt of his jalopy might snap. I would be to blame for their deaths, for the martyrdom of a devout Muslim and the demise of an ancient rustbucket hallowed by the hundreds of pilgrims and who knew how many imams who had parked their posteriors on these seats. And besides, I wasn't really listening to him, I had no wish to add to my sorrows the ravings of some oddball about how the female of the species likes to cavort with the devil.

On the second leg of the journey, he broached the subject of the punishments to be inflicted on wives according to the faults committed by them, their sisters, their daughters and their confidantes. A personal and a collective scale underpinned by an absolutist rhetoric. Guilty or not, they deserved to be punished, that was the gist of it. He talked about the *talaq*, but he seemed to think repudiation was a convoluted process suitable only as a last resort. *What, did I hear right?* I was about to demand that he explain what, exactly, was convoluted about a man throwing his wife out into the street or breaking her neck, and what precisely qualified as a 'last resort', but he didn't wait, he had already launched into a comparative analysis of flogging and stoning before moving on to his favourite method of chastisement: having the woman clapped in irons and tossed into the bottom of a well for seven days and seven nights after which, with feverish devotion, the well is filled in. He talked at length about this authentically corrective ritual, largely forgotten these days probably because most wells are dry. He went on to discuss cremation, throat-cutting, quartering, the boiling of all or parts of the body, pouring molten lead into the ears or the nostrils and who knows what all – the Muslim world being as broad as it is rich in such *pièces de résistance*, he cast a wide net. It all sounded rather old-fashioned and ignorant of state-of-the-art techniques. Good God, they could simply put women in factories, gas them, electrocute them by the dozen, by the thousand, dissolve them in acid – what else? turn them into candles, into polish. Better yet, melt them down and turn them into some revolutionary alloy, use them as fertiliser, or maybe for road resurfacing – they would provide a much more flexible surface. But I wasn't really listening, I wasn't really looking; we would soon be arriving at the convent and my heart was hammering. I decided I would send him away and tell him to come back in about an hour. I would give him some money and suggest he unwind in a nearby *café maure* – that mysterious space where never within the memory of man has woman set foot. He rolled his eyes, he could not understand what a creature who had defied Qur'anic law was doing at a Christian refuge.

The convent of Notre Dame des Pauvres is a squat building covered with wild vines set well back from the road that connects Blida to Chréa next to an overgrown path that smells sweetly of the Mediterranean. Everything about the place seems to smile, but it would be unwise to trust to appearances; there is a microclimate that exists in the mountains that look out towards the sea, it is a whimsical place where grass yellows before turning green and the blue of the sky can veer unexpectedly from white to red. No barometer on earth can comprehend its neuroses, it changes its mantle of cloud the way a person changes their shirt. Clouds scud past, heedless to the prayers of empty rain barrels, they linger for a moment in the heavens before heading for the sea there to surrender to the splendours of the water-cycle. How remote the sordid streets of Algiers seem, how strange the sky! The taxi slipped into first gear and climbed slowly between hedgerows of whispering spikes and thorns. It valiantly juddered along, strewing bolts and washers and, at every hairpin bend, another cog fell off the chassis. Under my breath, I recited a pious rosary of heave-hos. There is no shortage of cicadas, they are all one can hear. After a few scant minutes it feels as though, but for cicadas on earth and God in His heaven, nothing else exists. Blazing sunshine is guaranteed year round, but for the turning of the season when there is one whole week of actual snow, something skiing buffs in the days before the troubles spoke of as though it lasted twelve months of the year. Once more I thought of Camus, a son of the soil; he had spent time here among the crickets and the olive groves before exiling himself to the north pole, to the grim absurdities that dog us from birth to death. I think about Rachid Mimouni, another son of the soil who people say spent time here before becoming a *harraga* and leaving to die over there, in Tangiers the magnificent, gateway to every destination. It is piteous to be so impoverished. From our native soil we expect abundance and joy, not exile and death. *Who tumbles into darkness lapses into violence* is a saying that well expresses the descent into hell, but up in these mountains, ringed by radiant light and serenaded by homoptera, how could anyone be malicious or miserable without feeling ashamed? Absurdity again, madness again.

The door is sturdy, carved from solid wood and set on ancient iron hinges. Beyond it, well protected, silence reigns. It conjures a world of timeless mysteries, of lives lived plagued by worries and thorny questions, crippled or exalted by doubts and surely denied happiness – the elixir we poor wretched, helpless creatures do our utmost to filch where we can to avoid annihilation – or quite the reverse, spared the terrible misery that keeps the rest of us clinging to life like a buoy in spite of everything. I don't know what to think about it, personally, I live in utter solitude in a ramshackle mansion surrounded by a vast prison that is falling down about our ears and taking us all with it.

On the façade, the name of the institution was carved in relief above the lintel, a single slab of pink marble: *Convent of the Sisters of Our Lady of the Poor.* The faint air of neglect hinted that the members of the order could probably be counted on the fingers of half a hand. Where are the beggars, Lord of the poor? Where are the nuns, the churchwardens and the donors rubbing their hands with glee to see their money so wisely used? Where are the processions, the saint's-day celebrations, where is the smell of warm bread broken in the spirit of fraternity? Everything is in ruins, all our possessions and those of our friends, all our good wishes for happiness have been swept away.

The door made no sound and I had only my fists to make myself heard. What could I do?

An old woman sitting on a hillock, a basket at her feet, a bundle of firewood on her head, was struggling to catch her breath before continuing her journey into the unknown. Her wrinkled face suddenly came to life, she stared at me as though I were a freak of nature and spoke to me: 'Where'd you spring from, you? The great door is for religion, if it's healing you want, it's round the other side – a white door with a green cross, you'll see.'

She said the words as though speaking some great, evident truth, the care of the body is not that of the soul. Was she right or wrong? I thanked her with a blink, it was the best I could do, I had a lump in my throat and the rest of my being refused to respond. I needed only to hear Sister Anne say the last word to fall silent for ever. I knew, I could feel it, when I left the convent my life would be over.

Everything happened very fast although my nerves crackled with unbearably slow suspense. I was ushered inside by a vague young woman, a local peasant girl who had taken up medicine. Though her white coat was genuine, she wore it like a costume at a village fête. I remember my first white coat, I was so proud, I wore it like a wedding dress, sunlight shimmered on it and the air moved deliciously over its curves. Later I cut it up to make dusters. The girl's unduly careful movements clearly signalled a fresh graduate. It probably takes her two hours to plunge a needle in, a slow death for her patients, but given time she will learn to look the part, to jab a patient faster than her shadow. She spoke the way she moved, groping for words, taking time to weigh up their solidity and only reluctantly pronouncing them. I pictured her as a tortoise afraid of tumbling into the void. She probably believes that the modern world is all prudence and precision whereas actually it's quite the opposite, we make do and mend as fast as we can without troubling ourselves about old-fashioned considerations. She knew who I was, someone had told her I was a *toubib*, a doctor, she gave me a deferential smile and greeted me with a *salaam*. What more can a pilgrim wish for than to be expected? It's pleasant. At Parnet, visitors are never welcome, the matrons and the porters ignore them until they pathetically turn tail and leave. The girl rubbed her hands together, then, shuffling away in her harem clogs, I mean her wooden-soled flip-flops, she led me to the Mother Superior whom she referred to as *Lalla* – mistress – via a vaulted maze that sprawled and coiled endlessly. It seemed to me only reasonable that it should require some effort to reach the saint of the sanctuary. I busied myself with such pointless thoughts to keep my mind occupied, I knew what was coming next. In front of us, a door opened and . . . yes, there could be no doubt, this was Sister Anne. The moment had arrived, my heart was fluttering. She was expecting me. Slim and scarcely taller than her white, starched wimple, utterly radiant and dressed in harsh grey. She was ageless, in the way that nuns so often seem to be, but she had certainly seen forty Lenten fasts. She smiled warmly at me and, in a sudden surge of heathen feeling, hugged me hard and kissed me. It was nice, she smelled of lavender, of soap and incense and the fine rich loam of the kitchen garden.

'Come, my child, enter ... You are exactly as I foresaw. Come, Lamia, sit by me ... Here is a glass of cool water; take, drink ...'

She spoke just like the Bible: *take, eat; for this is my body; drink, for this is my blood.*

She exuded an extraordinary sense of strength and gentleness which immediately calmed me. It is precisely the attitude I would like to adopt in my dealings with people though I realise I am merely a would-be virago trying to hold her own against the harshness of her Muslim brothers rather than a true saint capable of soothing lions with a luminous glance. For me, force of circumstance has always worked in the negative, I am contaminated, embittered, intolerant, spiteful, quarrelsome, impulsive and I don't know what. I hate myself. I have been spared plague and cholera, which I suppose is a good thing, though for how much longer remains to be seen! And yet, I'm also a romantic, I write poetry, I believe in simple things and above all I cherish truth over sentiment. I was spellbound by Sister Anne, prepared to accept whatever she had to offer, whether grace or *coup de grâce*. She went on speaking in a distant, barely audible voice.

'Chérifa came to us three weeks ago. She was in a piteous state. She had been wandering the streets of Algiers when a charitable soul, a friend of the order, noticed her. She brought Chérifa here, thinking it was the best thing to

256

do. And in all conscience, I believe it was, though ordinarily our standing and our means make us ill-equipped to deal with such requests. We are tolerated here, no more than that. We offer some small service to the local people, they are so poor they dare not go into the city. I thought long and hard, it is a great responsibility, but given her circumstances, I took her in. I don't know whether a hospital would have admitted her, she is . . . she was a minor, unmarried, pregnant and . . . bizarrely attired, hee! hee! Blida is an extremely conservative town, ruled by the Islamists. I was frightened for her, they can be so . . . so . . .'

'If they were just evil, spiteful, vile and satanic, I wouldn't mind, but they're narrow-minded and stupid too,' I said, to help her out.

'You should not say such things, they are very dangerous. If they should hear you . . .'

'There's no fear of that, they're deaf to all things human.'

'I called upon a doctor who is a friend of the convent, Doctor Salem, it has been a long time since he practised, but he still has his wits. He took care of her and she quickly recuperated somewhat. I have a number of useful skills myself. We therefore felt she would be able to give birth here in the convent . . . She was so endearing, with her belly button almost touching her chin and that fearless air of hers!'

'Did she have her holdall?'

'Pardon?'

'Her clothes, her belongings, the baby clothes.'

'Her bag? Oh yes, she dragged it behind her by the strap, it looked like a puppy refusing to walk, hee! hee! hee!'

★

The slightest thing made the Mother Superior giggle. But she quickly became grave and abstracted. She sat for a moment, silent, thoughtful, staring into the distance, glancing here and there, at the ceiling, at her pale, slender hands clasped in her lap, at the crucifix hanging on the wall or a particular book on the shelves. This, to me, is what religion should mean: to silently contemplate the world, alert to its every murmur, its every tremor. There should be no need for troops and cannons. Words, sighs, glances, they are sufficient. Sister Anne's eyes radiated the sort of awed apprehensiveness that clearly came from constant prayer. And from penitence, I imagine. Though they live isolated from the world of men, and in close proximity to the Lord, every day the Sisters here must find some minor sin to be erased. I would not be at all surprised to discover she experiences ecstatic visions. There are places such as this, austere, modest, where dream and reality become one as prayers are said. My old house is a little like that; ringing as it is with myth and mysteries and with the echo of unanswered prayers, I don't know whether I am more enthralled by image or by shadow, nor why I spend my time talking to the dead, or rather to their ghosts. I thought about Maman who had the same habit of searching around whenever she began recounting one of our old family stories. It was as though, rummaging through a cluttered past, she chanced upon it by accident. At some point in this ritual, her eyes would suddenly light up. Something that had baffled her a little she could now see clearly, see the thread of the story amid the confusion of sundry images, she could draw it towards her and reveal its warp and weft, its magical design.

In fits and starts of 'Um ... Oh, that's right ... ah yes, I remember now ... let me just think,' she would beat this carpet, dust off the cobwebs then, not quite herself, she would gently tease it out, as though fearful that, if she brought it too quickly from her memory, it might break or that our family secrets might come into contact with the poisoned air of the present, might wither before they could be known. We would wait with bated breath, ready to draw near the better to take in the apparition. I still have her words in my ear; one by one I took them in, treasured them, stored them in the hollow of my memory, more to reassure her than to hear them. She told us these wondrous stories so many times that we scarcely thought about them. I am obsessed by the tale of Tata Houria which is fascinating and terrible. I often think about Tata Houria, one of Maman's cousins, about what part love played in her odyssey and what part madness. Because to do what she did, for as long as she did, there had to be something going on in her head. In those unfathomable and uncertain days back in the *douar*, where there was no thought of deliverance, people lived and died as Adam had done. Firstly, Tata Houria refused to mourn her husband and allow herself to be remarried. Then, she died far from the *douar*, something no woman had ever done before her – indeed so far from the *douar* that no one knows quite where – in India, Guatemala, America, Poland or elsewhere. Maman could not remember the name of the country, the poor thing had no notion of geography, she knew the village where she had grown up and Rampe Valée and nothing beyond. She vaguely knew the Kasbah, where she would go once a month with her old friend Zineb to drink mint tea and discuss all the misfortunes in the world since Adam and Eve, talk a little about magic to steel themselves, then, all keyed up, they would rush around visiting the shrines and the mausoleums. Beyond these frontiers, all the world was darkness. Houria's odyssey began during the Second World War and ended thirty years later in obscurity and legend. Scarcely had Tata Houria been wed than her young husband was called up and sent to war. She waited for his return as women have long learned to wait, praying and weeping in secret. Then one day came the marvellous, unexpected news: all over the planet, people were celebrating the end of the war. One by one survivors trudged home, scrawny, haggard, crippled, but not her husband. 'Missing, presumed dead,' according to the government letter read out to the villagers gathered around the local schoolteacher. 'Wait and see,' was the unanimous conclusion as everyone returned to their own preoccupations. The post-war years brought famine and unleashed great anger.

For several years Tata Houria waited in her tumbledown hovel as the days trickled past; she moved to Algiers where she waited a few years more then left for France where in this town or that she continued her wait. When nothing came, she moved to Germany – a country where disappearing was commonplace in the years after the Apocalypse. There, in one city or another, she waited a few years more in the company of others who had come from far-flung places in order to wait. As the circle rippled out, she waited all over the world. One day, a scrawled letter arrived in the *douar* announcing her death. The schoolteacher – a different one, a young man freshly graduated from university – was unable to read it and asked around until finally one day he appeared in the tiny village square, brandishing the letter to announce the results of his research: the letter, dated 22 June 1966 and written in pidgin French, had come from the far side of the world and was signed simply Rosita. This good soul said that it was she who had closed the eyes of Tata Houria, having taken her in and cared for her. She had found her by the roadside waiting to die. But by then the *douar* was no longer as it had been; the children had left never to return and the old people no longer remembered anything. The story was forgotten by everyone but Maman, who would tell it to us every time it rained on the city and every time it rained in her head. Poor, wonderful Houria, she died without ever giving up hope that she might find the man she had loved as a girl. Like Maman I would like to believe that in the next world, her husband had been waiting for her just as lovingly from the very moment he lost his way and his life. It's true, this story haunts me.

The Mother Superior spoke to me at length after her fashion, using few words and long silences. Chérifa made herself at home in the convent precisely as she had in my house and at the university halls of residence. I'd describe it as an invasion followed by a systematic obliteration of the inhabitants' frame of reference at the cost of great sacrifice. Her blood pressure was dangerously low, she was nine months pregnant, all skin and bone, yet in a few short days she managed to turn a tranquil convent into a railway station at rush hour. Her laundry fluttered from every window,

every arrow-slit, her radioactive perfume drowned out the
scents of incense and soot which had good reason to linger.
The nuns rushed around trying to keep up with her, they
could not possibly catch her. They're all ancient and they
have no flair for competition. Eventually, she came to a stop
in mid-dash, overcome by an inexplicable spasm. And then
her waters broke. She was running a high temperature, she
visibly paled. Everything happened quickly, the contrac-
tions, a last gleam shone in her eyes, a last word trembled on
her lips. 'We were confused, we were helpless, we prayed
harder than we had ever done in our lives. This calmed her,
the pain subsided or she found it easier to bear.' Sister Anne's
voice was heavy with remorse. I know the feeling: at Parnet,
we are constantly dealing with emergencies and, not having
the resources, we suddenly panic and we appeal to God,
implore any name that comes to our lips, and then, abruptly,
comes the silence and the cold that sends us back to our
corners, pale, dazed, clammy, and overcome by guilt once
more.

'She died peacefully . . . she was smiling, her mouth was
open,' the Mother Superior whispered tenderly.

'Yes. That's how she always slept, her mouth open, her
eyes half-closed, her arms crossed . . . and her legs.'

'Yes, she had her peculiar little ways.'

'She had her peculiar little ways in everything she did. I
mean, she decided to die in a convent while giving birth,
which says a lot.'

'It's cruel to say such things.'

'I apologise. Like her, I have my little ways of being
stupid and cruel.'

'She talked about you all the time. Lamia, Lamia, Lamia . . . Just before she passed away, she whispered *Where's Maman Lamia? Please tell her to come.*

'Ma . . . Maman?'

There are words like this, words that express all the happiness in the world. I have spent so many years longing to hear that word. I felt myself melt inside while an electric current trilled through me and every hair on my body stood on end. I could no longer contain my tears, nor could Sister Anne.

'Yes . . . Maman.'

'I suppose I was her mother and I didn't realise it . . . or she didn't realise it. We somehow kept missing each other . . .'

'God willed it so, my child.'

'You believe that He willed it so?'

'I do.'

'I wish some things were in our control, at least that way we'd know why we make each other miserable. But I suppose if I am here it is because God wills it.'

'No doubt, no doubt.'

The ensuing silence seemed the only possible answer to these delicate questions. I did not dare to break it. Realising this, Sister Anne continued in a lighter tone.

'She told stories about you and she mimicked the phrases you use:"*Would you credit it! Did you ever hear the like? And I don't know what else!*" She could be difficult . . . but it was just that she liked to poke fun.'

'Oh, she could be absolutely unbearable.'

'Now she's with God, she'll calm down, depend on it.'

'Hmm . . . maybe . . . maybe you're right.'

'After the birth, she regained consciousness just long enough to see the baby, she smiled down at that little face and explained the great plans she had. It was so funny! She ...'

Something had clicked. Some vast, incredible piece of news had fallen into place.

'Say that again ...' I spluttered.

'It looked like she was going to pull through, but two days later ...'

'No, what you said just before.'

'I'm sorry, I don't ... What's the matter?'

'The baby – it's alive?'

'Of course.'

'Why didn't you tell me that before?'

'I ... I'm sorry ... I wanted to, but I'm in a delicate position, you can't just hand over a baby without some assurances, surely you can understand my misgivings, dear Lamia?'

'Oh my God! Oh my God!'

'Chérifa used to say, "My little baby will drive Tata Lamia mad." I think now I understand why.'

'My dear God, our baby is alive ... my baby is alive!'

'I'm not asking you to take care ...'

'Oh my God! Oh my God!'

'An adorable baby, the spitting image of its mother. She named the little mite Louiza ...'

'Louiza? It's a girl? Oh, my God! Oh, my God!'

'We've grown very fond of her, in fact I don't know how we will manage to live without her.'

'Thank you ... thank you from the bottom of my heart.'

'May God forgive me, but I could not bear to think of that baby being taken into care, Child Services simply don't have the means, this whole wretched country is sinking into . . . into . . .'

'If it was just the poverty, the corruption and the brutality, I wouldn't mind, but when the idiots are in power, what's to be done, you tell me that!'

'She'll be happy with you, I can tell. All I ask is that you bring her to visit from time to time, it would make us so happy.'

'I owe you my life . . . I'll never forget that.'

'But I implore you, be more careful when you speak. You're so forthright, it could land you in trouble.'

'Don't worry, I'll play the hypocrite with the imbeciles.'

'I'll leave it to you to decide what to do about Chérifa's parents. Duty would dictate that they be informed and the child given into their care. That was not what Chérifa wanted. She pleaded with me. "Don't do it, please . . . to them my baby is nothing but a bastard, they'll suffocate her and toss her out with the rubbish."'

'They're simple people. Weighed down by tradition and the pressure of other people, they would do precisely that with a clear conscience.'

'We can't know that . . . we are in no position to judge.'

Oh, please, not that! Anything but that! It was on the tip of my tongue to say that it's precisely because we refused to judge when there was still time that we are in the mess we are in today. We accepted barefaced lies as honest truths, traded fine promises for utter madness and we have ceased to try to find our way. Islam lapsed into Islamism and

265

authority into authoritarianism and still we felt we had no right to judge. I wanted to tell her that it's one thing to stare at the pretty flames through the window of a stove, but to be bound hand and foot and tossed into an incinerator is a very different matter. I was tempted to tell her that we judge not like judges or policemen, but like human beings who do not understand and yet recognise those things that hurt, that kill, that demean. Judging is like breathing, a power bestowed by God that we must not give up, it is the very essence of our humanity, it must not be sub-contracted or scattered to the first wind whipped up who knows how by who knows whom. To hell with tolerance when it goes hand in hand with cowardice!

I responded with an all-purpose platitude, I can't remember what exactly: 'You're absolutely right', 'Maybe, maybe not', or something more heartfelt, something more my style: 'We know all we need to know, they would toss the baby out with the garbage because that's how these things go. There are days when the Algiers rubbish tip is like a nursery crawling with kids, these days they're tossed away alive, no one takes the trouble to suffocate them. Call it tradition, murder, madness, governance, it's all the same.' Thinking about it now, I believe I was silent, I just sighed, we were operating on different levels, she was considering the question from a transcendent viewpoint while I, being caught up in the bedlam of everyday life, relate everything to the abject folly of men.

Epilogue

Sometimes, God listens to us.
Sometimes, life smiles on us.
Sometimes, in the distance, a light glimmers
At long last.
It is deep within the abyss this comes to pass
It is here that we are
Closest to happiness
Perhaps.

When the words have been said, we must fall silent, pray in our hearts and, when calm is restored, carry on our way. Nothing is ever finished.

Chérifa lies in the old cemetery next to the convent. The place looks set to be an archaeological relic; to those who come after us, it will speak of the end of a reign that was cruel and inglorious. No one had been buried there for years since no one lives here any more; the Islamists long since subverted their *maquis*, the army destroyed their villages, made their lives a living hell, so they left to die elsewhere, in the shantytowns on the outskirts of the cities, living cheek by jowl in even greater poverty. One day they, or their grandchildren, will return, as migratory birds unfailingly return, but they will be strangers in their own land; life waits for no one and the land is thankless.

A slab of marble is carved with her first name and the dates that mark out her time on earth.

Chérifa
1986–2002

At the town hall, it was stated that the dead girl had no family, no home and no identity papers. It was further stated that, having lost her way, the girl had asked for refuge at the convent for a few days, which was granted. And then, following the mysterious ways and designs of Heaven, she died in her sleep. Sister Anne did not mention the pregnancy. In certain circumstances, to lie is not to deceive, it is a means of safeguarding life. The secret will never go beyond the four walls of the convent.

Nothing moves the bureaucrats in this country. They would happily send each other to the gallows if it were a matter of sharing out three lean cutlets. Insipid and underpaid, they drift towards crime as naturally as soap suds flow towards a drain. The one who talked to Sister Anne was a hard-headed brute, he paid her no attention but simply chewed his gum and picked his nose, all this with his eyes closed. 'It was like talking to a brick wall the live-long day,' Sister Anne smiled, 'and they say walls have ears!' A lost girl is a lost girl, there are so many of them, they disappear every day, their names are jotted down in the daybook and that's the end of it. In witness whereof, a permit was granted to inter the deceased stipulating that the aforementioned, identity unknown, had died of natural causes at the convent of the Sisters of Our Lady of the Poor located in the commune of Chréa. All that would remain of Chérifa was a pending file in an office which in time would also disappear. A request for information would be circulated to the various regional police stations and one day she would simply melt into air.

★

Far from the city and far from danger, sheltered within its circle of lopsided stones, the cemetery has a tranquil air. Step inside and time seems to stand still. Magnificent trees solidly rooted in the stony ground serene as Buddhist monks. It is deeply reassuring. In summer and autumn and especially in spring, the birds will come to disturb the peace of these leafy branches, but it is always wonderful to see life whip up the wind, anarchic and joyous. So it had been for me back when I trudged through the wilderness. A bird landed on my shoulder. 'Cheep cheep, cheep cheep . . .!' he chirruped in my ear as he fluttered and frolicked. I did not understand since my life was made up of silences, mindless rituals and second-rate ramblings. Since then, I have learned the language of the birds; it is glorious. Wild cats will come and brush against the trunks of these trees and mewl at the moon. Right now, they are pretending to doze on the ramparts. They too have abandoned the cottages and forever forgotten their masters. Blood will drip from the low branches as, breaking the hushed silence, frantic squawking erupts from the higher branches, a terrified chirping that could put a scarecrow to flight. Cats are like that, it is senseless to condemn them, it is in their nature to lie in wait and attack by surprise. Chérifa will have all winter to sleep like an angel; here on the shores of our much-loved Mediterranean, the rains merely soak the grass and the winds scarcely ruffle the owls' feathers. The skies are so deep that everything vanishes into the distance and the nights too short to give melancholy time to fear the worst. The cold is piercing, but this is not the North Pole, it would not kill a homeless tramp. For the dead who have felt the cold when they were alive, it is an evening by the fireside. And besides, three months' sleep is enough for a flighty girl with all eternity ahead of her.

With my black marker, I added a line to the gravestone that the sun will have faded before night falls:

Her Maman who loves her

And then I remembered what I had called her, the cruel taunt I had spat in her face: *harraga*. 'You're a *harraga*, that's what you are, and you'll die as one.'

God, I can be cruel when I don't listen to myself.

Forgive me, ma chérie. *I said those things, I screamed and spluttered not because you couldn't hear, but because I couldn't understand: you were searching for life and in these parts we can only talk about death.*

Sister Anne could read my thoughts. I suddenly turned and we stared at each other through the curtain of tears. In her poor, tormented face I saw strength whereas mine was a mask of defeat, of helplessness, of infinite regret. She blinked her eyes gently, and on her closed lips I could read the entreaty: *Pray, it is the only thing we have to overcome fear and find our way.*

> *Where can it be, the path*
> *Which from the unknown*
> *Will fashion my native soil*
> *My love, my life*
> *And my death?*

272

I had been feeling somewhat melodramatic and a little foolish when, in the depths of despair, I wrote those lines; the reality had proved to be infinitely more heartbreaking. It brought a lump to my throat.

I fell to my knees, I threw my arms around the headstone and I prayed:

God who art in heaven, my daughter Chérifa is with you. She's sixteen, she hasn't got a lot of meat on her bones, and life had left her black and blue. I couldn't protect her. I only had a few short months in which to find her in this misbegotten world and to realise she was my daughter. Please, take care of her, love her as I loved her, but keep a close eye on her, she's quite capable of doing a bunk from heaven and leaving a dreadful mess behind her. I know it doesn't look good, a Lolita among all the sinless souls dressed up in white silk, but give her time, she likes to be eccentric. Intercede on my behalf, tell her I never intended to hurt her when I called her a harraga. *This country is governed by soulless men who have refashioned us in their image, petty, spiteful and greedy, or rebels who curl up in shame and insignificance. Our children are suffering, they dream of goodness, of love and of games and are lured into evil, hatred and despair. They have only one way to survive, become* harragas, *burn a path as once people burned their boats so they could never return. My idiot brother Sofiane is caught up in that chaos, help him find his path. Take care of my sweet, gentle Louiza, my beloved Carrot Cake, her life is a living hell. Thank you for giving me a daughter and a granddaughter when I had long since given up hoping for anything from life. Believe me, I will prove myself worthy. Give my love to my parents, to my brother Yacine and watch over us. Amen.*

I took a deep breath, I could feel life coursing through me. I was like a ship run aground suddenly floating free and setting a new course. I am not the sort to let myself be beaten or to give up along the way, this was something else I could ask of God:

Please, God, recall to Yourself the ghosts that haunt my house, Mustafa and the others. They deserve some rest, life betrayed them and death has forgotten them, I think that they are tired having wandered the earth for so long. They are my friends, they supported me when I too was but a shadow on the walls, but now I have a baby to bring up, I need freshness and light.

I long wondered whether our lives truly belong to us, I despaired of ever finding meaning. All things come with time. Was it foolish of me to doubt it? At the time, I could not have known: I was dead then, my eyes had yet to be opened to life.

I kissed Sister Anne, I cradled little Louiza in my arms and I climbed back into the taxi. Before it disappeared around the first bend, I glanced back to that place, that convent, where I had just been born. The nuns waved us off cheerfully but I knew, I could sense, that in fact they were crying their hearts out.

To Bluebeard at his window, quivering with joy, like a hunchback dancing a jig, I sent the silent thought: *Oh, Bluebeard, Sister Anne was right, Chérifa has come back to us!* I felt inspired, Sister Anne really exists. I should bring Louiza over to visit the old hermit and tell him it's Chérifa, wasted away from all her running around. At his age, he's bound to be half-blind so he'd probably believe it. And when she smiled at him, he'd have a stroke.

On the way back, the gallant and dangerous cab driver didn't say a word, or perhaps he muttered to himself but I heard nothing, not even the sound of his rattletrap leaking oil; I was beyond the reach of the diatribes that he and his kind liked to spout, I was already dreaming of a new world.

> *Louiza, my child*
> *When a new sun rises*
> *Upon your first smile*
> *We will take to the road*
> *We will become* harragas.

> *Louiza, my love*
> *We will leave our misfortunes*
> *And wash away our memories*
> *In the first river we find*
> *As* harragas *do.*

> *Louiza, my darling*
> *We will travel roads unknown*
> *And watch where flowers grow*
> *Where birds go*
> *As* harragas *do.*

> *Louiza, my heart*
> *We will find way enough and time*

We will learn to live
We will learn to laugh
As harragas *dream.*

Louiza, my life
When the sun shall rise
On your first spring
We will be far away
As harragas *go.*

My child
My love
My heart, my life
Like your mother, my daughter
We two will be harragas.

Written in Rampe Valée, in 2002,
in the house of the Good Lord
(for that is now its name).

A Note on the Author

Boualem Sansal (b. 1949) is the author of six novels and various other books. His first novel *Le Serment des barbares* (*The Barbarians' Oath*) won the 1999 Prix du Premier Roman. In 2003 he was dismissed from the civil service for criticising the Algerian government. Since the publication in 2006 of *Poste restante: Alger. Lettre de colère et d'espoir à mes compatriotes* (*Poste restante: Letter of anger and hope to my compatriots*) his books have been banned in his own country. Today he is considered not only one of Algeria's most important writers, but also a literary figure of international stature. *Le Village de l'allemand* (translated into English as *An Unfinished Business*) won France's Grand Prix RTL LIRE 2008 and Belgium's Grand Prix de la Francophonie 2008. In 2011 he was awarded the German Booksellers' Peace Prize and in 2012 the Prix du Roman Arabe, but this prize money was withdrawn, despite protests from the jury, following his visit to Israel to speak at the Jerusalem Writers Festival. He lives in Boumerdès, near Algiers, with his wife.

A Note on the Translator

Frank Wynne has won three major prizes for his transla-
tions from the French, including the 2002 IMPAC for
Atomised by Michel Houellebecq and the 2005 Independent
Foreign Fiction Prize for *Windows on the World* by Frederic
Beigbeder. He is also the translator from the Spanish of
Tomás Eloy Martínez's *Purgatory*, Miguel Figueras's *Kam-
chatka* and Carlos Acosta's *Pig's Foot*. In 2014 he was awarded
the Valle Inclán Prize for his translation of Alonso Cueto's
The Blue Hour.